Over Here

Jane Taylor

TP

ThunderPoint Publishing Limited

First Published in Great Britain in 2014 by
ThunderPoint Publishing Limited
Summit House
4-5 Mitchell Street
Edinburgh
Scotland EH6 7BD

ISBN (Paperback): 978-0-9929768-2-8
ISBN (eBook): 978-0-9929768-3-5

www.thunderpoint.co.uk

Cover Image Front: © angie2028
Cover Image Back © Doug Berndt/Shutterstock.com

Acknowledgements

Above all, I am deeply grateful to my family who have never failed to offer me their loving support and belief in my work. There are friends, too, to thank, especially Barrie Selwyn, Julia Newton, Helen Davis and Martin Conboy, whose ready listening, good humour and encouragement remain a constant beacon.

I remember with gratitude those at UEA whose original guidance helped me to understand and develop my writing, particularly John Cook, my supervisor when I was working towards a doctorate in creative and critical writing. The quality of our discussions back then never failed to ignite in me the excitement of pursuing new ideas and possibilities, contributing surely to the eventual writing of Over Here.

Seonaid at ThunderPoint Publishing has been a most tenacious and sensitive editor, and I would like to thank Huw at ThunderPoint as well for his care in producing Over Here.

'Dangerous Trades' by John Murray, 1902, was a revealing source for laundry practices in the early 20th century. Dr Oates at the Local History Centre in Ealing gave me a flavour of what life was like in Acton and Ealing at the beginning of the 20th century. Important leads were provided by East Kent Archives Centre regarding the First World War. The Canadian War Brides Bureau yielded a mine of information about migrating war brides. The Cunard and Canadian Pacific Lines, amongst others, are well chronicled on the Internet, and some picaresque passenger anecdotes made me think about the vagaries and excitement of ocean going travel in its heyday. The rest, as they say, is history.

For Tiffany and Toby with love

DISEMBARKATION

1

Liverpool, England, December 1921

'RUN!'

Such urgency pierces the boy to the core, alerting him to take off immediately in blind obedience to a command which, for all he knows, might be an echo of his own voice from within or that of a supernatural ally, also internal. In a state of terror, not for one instant does he pause to wonder where it comes from as he darts past a legless beggar scavenging nearby, whose jagged curse follows him across the rubble in that lately strike-riven city, its dying rattle only serving to amplify the trouble he is in.

It's coming up to twenty-four hours since the boy stepped down from the big passenger liner – it must be, he reckons foggily – because morning has come around once more with the awful irrevocability of time destined to lead nowhere in this worrying new situation. His temporary minder on board – last spotted heading for the bar some while before the lumbering process of docking got underway – seems to have vanished for good. Where does that leave him now? All on his own in a new country: that's where it leaves him. He is just nine years old.

Was it only yesterday that groups of disembarking passengers were purposefully eddying past him as he cowered on the quayside? He exhaled hot air from his lungs into the chapped cup of his hands and stamped his feet in an effort to staunch the perishing cold. At first, all he wanted was to blend in – not to be regarded as odd or questionable, which he rather feared he was. To the boy, all those fortunate people speeding onwards seemed to have "destination" stamped on their foreheads which emphasised his own plight all the more and caused him to feel awkward and conspicuous.

In the beginning of it, he was embarrassed about his solitary state. Soon enough it began to trouble him.

Gripping a small bag (his only belonging) that first morning, he squatted down on his heels to prepare for the humdrum business of watching and waiting, wearing the same knee-length short trousers, crumpled woollen jacket, cap and boots he had on at the start of his journey from Canada six days earlier. *Someone will come,* he reminded himself, several times over. He had been given to understand that an aunt would be there to meet him. He had never met her and didn't know what she looked like, all of which persuaded him to keep a discreet watch for anyone who might appear to be looking for *him*.

No-one came.

The coarse bark of a ship's horn soon enough turned into a personal accusation ('what are you doing in this place, then, eh?') and he longed to hide from its blast. So he cast his eyes downward, right down to where the great ship's bowels touched the dirty water and discarded fuel filmed it with a rainbow of multi-coloured wrinkles. It couldn't help but strike him that this was where all the unwanted stuff takes refuge, stale and forgotten. He watched bundles of jetsam stroking the side of the ship each time a passing tug deposited its diminishing energy towards the jetty, sending up a draft of mouldy breath in the form of a deep sigh, seemingly in response to his own, both destined to become indistinguishable from all the other strange airs in this frightful place.

Darkness descended abruptly and with a sense of alternating menace and futility that first night. It was getting on for Christmas and a wintry crispness starched the sour smelling mist settling on the city. From time to time he caught the squeal of a gangplank being retracted, the mourning wail of a ship's siren out in the bay, or the wiry rasp of the last of the day's freight being set down some way off. He hugged himself, as if by doing so he would be able to squeeze some warmth into his body. Despite his worries, he allowed himself to drift into a series of brief, fitful dozes.

He was woken early the following morning by the dark, bulbous shape of a policeman shaking his shoulder. 'Who are you, boy? What are you doing here? There's no more big ships coming in today, if that's what you've come to watch. You'd better clear off home.'

'Yes, mister,' he replied instantaneously, and swiftly hobbled off. He felt sore. A perishing hunger gnawed at his innards. When he spotted some men squatting in the rubble nearby he approached them in the hope of food. That's when he was first attacked.

On the run and in blind haste to avoid coming to the attention of any more policemen who may be out patrolling the docks, as well as sundry potential assailants (it doesn't strike him as a friendly place, not at all), he loses his footing on a stony mound and something sharp pierces his left thigh. He pauses long enough to gather his breath and give the gash a prod, testing it. For a moment or two he is transfixed by the sight of carmine liquid leaking out of his leg – his own blood! – depositing a series of fresh gouts which create instant stains on a broken paving stone. Brushing himself down and readjusting the ripped and by now dusty arm of his jacket, he tries once more to make sense of it, only to find his thoughts diving into a pit of confusion.

Reduced to performing spurts of directionless running and furtive attempts to be invisible during the course of a long, long day – day two of his arrival at this foreign port – he is learning very quickly to keep on the move, rationing his pauses in answer to the degree of pain in his bad leg, and maintaining his bearings by making sure the sea remains always in sight. In due course, when the afternoon starts to turn on its axis, he is surprised to realise that this immediate terrain has become a *known* place to him, in a strange sort of way – being the only one he currently knows.

Hours pass in this way.

Following a day and a half with no food he is so famished that his stomach is gripped by cramps while his mind begins to stray. By now, he is convinced that he must have done a very great wrong to merit being so adrift and that someone must have deemed him unworthy of a lighter sentence this time: a beating, for example. Aw, brother, he would willingly deal with a beating right now if there was food at the end of it. That he would.

Just as the weak light of late afternoon renders most of his landmarks less clearly delineated, a new phase of this miserable existence comes upon him, giving him a strong sense that he is being spied upon. Closing his eyes in a desperate attempt to ward off this next threat ('what you don't see won't harm you' is his rickety reasoning) he turns his attention to what his thoughts configure as a row of sniggering, mischievous wraiths lined up behind him – determined, it seems, to make him the butt of some cruel cosmic joke by jeering at him with icy titters for cutting such a ridiculous figure. How he wishes he knew what sin has been committed to cause such a falling out with them all, *all* of his persecutors – if he could only work out who they might be. It doesn't take too long before *she* floats across his mind, yet he can't bring himself to entertain a suspicion that she may indeed be one of those who mean him ill. He initiates a deliberate scribbling in his brain to take care of *her*, for the time being. In such a powerless state, it's the best he can manage.

At the fading of the light on this, the second day of his arrival – early, because it is getting close to the shortest day of the year now – he watches a few gas lights sparking up in some tenements nearby. Oh, how he would like to put his hands round the glass bowl of one of them, just as he had done – when? At this point, memory simply refuses to supply any coherent answers at all.

He is stirred by the sound of an organ from a nearby church as it layers velvet chords on the murky air of the city. He listens to it intently from his latest temporary refuge – a shop doorway – against which its rumbling sweet sound shudders along wooden shutters, to be transformed into a soft blanket tossed around his shoulders, embracing him with a passing waft of ancient kindness.

Coming across a dilapidated railway arch, he makes out half a dozen men crouching inside. One or two of them are wearing worn out pieces of uniform. This doesn't surprise him at all since he is aware that it is only three years since the Great War ended. He spots the fact that they have built a mean fire out of discarded newspapers and a broken crate.

They have bread.

He asks for a piece. He can't help himself – the words just come out.

He receives a cuff for his impertinence and several of the men make a lunge for him, just as the other lot had done, as though his very existence causes them offence – as though his very being is enough to put them in a horrible temper. One of them grinds out a terrifying '*gurn*!' and comes so close that his spittle lands on the boy's jacket.

Run! It seems there is to be no beginning and no end to it.

TREACHEROUS CURRENTS

2

Acton, west London, 1909

Kate Fitch, one-time laundress, is presently confined to a narrow, scratchy, stale smelling bed in a dormitory catering for forty sick people in the Infirmary for the Poor in west London these days. Here, her fellow inmates are prone to letting out a spontaneous groan from time to time, as if to remind themselves of their own existence.

Visitors to that place are rare.

Losing herself in the gentle breathing of a roughly strung up and none-too-clean curtain by the open window next to her bed, she drifts into an incomplete and increasingly abstract reverie about something which has lately floated out of her life entirely: *family*. As her own beloved family recedes, it's as though the *idea* of it is gaining enough room to surface in its stead. It is soothing, in this respect, for Kate to picture the idea of a perfect family in association with the trawler men's nets in Portsmouth, where she'd once lived, spread out on a wide beach beneath the frenzied applause of the ever-present seagulls. Yes, in her delirium "family" comes to resemble for a moment or two a hardy fishing net spread out to dry above the high water mark, stretched out in readiness for the well-defined job of participating in the day about to bloom, each knotted square connected to its neighbour in such pleasing symmetry. And mine, she can't help thinking, is but an untidy fragment of such a rig, shredded to pieces. This brings on an overwhelming and wholly futile sense of regret which settles heavily across her bed. For Kate Fitch is a mother in name only now, with no way of redeeming her current failure to sustain her three young daughters when they come drifting in and out of the limited orbit of her mind. What is *family* to people like me, she wonders passively? What *can* it be when it has lost the ability to draw itself in clear, straight lines of succession on the sand, like those nets?

Maudlin thoughts never used to trouble her. But they make her wistful nowadays.

After all, what chance is there of her daughters staying together? She begins to compose a message in her mind that she knows will never be conveyed: *My little darlings: you brave Violet, you sharp Lil, you sweet little Mary Ellen ...* for Kate Fitch is not a bad mother. In fact, she possesses qualities that would surely qualify her as one of the better sort, possessing an innate compassion and a generosity of spirit which moves her to put others first as a rule, despite her circumstances, coupled with a sustaining sense of humour and a will to work in order to provide for the four of them, with little in the way of complaining. If only she could shift herself and regain some authority over her life. But since her centre has collapsed, along with her lungs, it is all but impossible to sustain these fruitless meanderings.

A sailor's wife in better times, her thoughts eventually come to rest on other cherished memories of Portsmouth. Nothing of consequence: just pale and rather enticing images of naval frigates slipping anchor on moonless nights until they turn into vague shadows against the opaque blackness of the ocean, with little to distinguish them but the sense of their substance out there as they slowly vanish altogether.

At this late stage of her shortish life Kate knows for certain that she'll never see the sea again. And yet it seems that her memory will not let go of Portsmouth Sound, that inscrutable, muscle-bound expanse of salty water whose sole purpose, as she recalls, is to be the backdrop for a complex and extensive metropolis of rigging associated with the docks. The sea. It is out there. And there, it seems, it must remain – for Kate Fitch, anyway.

It was on several ships based at Portsmouth that her husband, Jack Fitch, served as an ordinary seaman, and when she was 18-years-old there was nothing more thrilling than being pregnant with her first child and standing on a jetty with the other women, a legitimate member of the crowd, banging her gloved hands together to keep the circulation going while they passed the hours observing the achingly slow progress of one of the ships preparing to cast off, heading for somewhere in the Empire – vessels which at their moorings often appeared stunted by the enormous permanence of the jetty itself, that witness to the eternal hope of return. Wives, young and old, turned out whatever the weather when there was a sailing, becoming gradually subdued at the thought of the long separation ahead in their relative ignorance of the trajectory of such voyages. Sometimes, a voice from the crowd was minded to toss out a platitude meant to signal comfort to those nearby ('don't fret, girls, it's only for six months this time') – blunt utterances which were instantly fragmented into shards of sound buffeted by a stiff breeze that was common down by the sea front. These terse remarks were almost always based on conjecture, but it didn't matter since they were hungrily accepted by the listeners as a cheap insurance against the uncertainty harboured by the women left behind, both for themselves and for their men folk.

Then again, navy wives were not without rivalry about whose husband had travelled furthest, or brought back the most exotic trinkets. At which boasting (even now, Kate's lips curl into a wry smile at the memory of it) someone with a long record of marital service would eventually fling out a sardonic comment inviting a murmured chorus of general agreement, going something like: 'You can keep your fripperies, missus. To get my hands on more of the wages would be a fine thing'. How Kate enjoyed those rough asides. In the early days of her marriage she particularly liked knowing that they were including *her* (such a novice) as part of the makeshift audience. She enjoyed belonging.

And so up goes the cheer once more in her sickly imagination, and look, just look how they all wave their handkerchiefs in a flurry of miniature flags in reply to a series of retorts from the innards of a bronchial funnel signalling that the ship in question is at last gathering steam. Kate was always with the hardy little group who stayed on for another while until it slid out of its dock, heading at what always seemed to be a snail's pace towards the horizon.

She had met Jack on her home ground in Holloway, east London, at a church fair where she was serving cakes cooked that very same morning with her friend Jemima, and he had been visiting his sister who had recently married a tin merchant lodging in their parish. Coming from what she would cheerfully (and accurately) describe as the bottom of the pile, she felt elevated at first by being a navy wife, particularly after growing up in Archway, where her father was a costermonger who died young and her mother took in washing after times became hard.

But by the time Kate's first daughter, Violet, was born, the sheer novelty of being a seaman's wife in Portsmouth had quite worn off. So, hankering for the sort of company she felt most at home with, she took her infant daughter off back to London one day, to the place she knew best, where she could await Jack's visits on leave in a more familiar setting. This solution seemed the best of all worlds to her at the time – not that she had much to compare it with. He came – he always came home to her – jolly at first, restless to be off again after a week or so. It was during these leaves that two more daughters were conceived in rooms Kate had rented in Acton, west London. She was able to earn enough to sustain the household while he was absent by working in one of the laundries, and in due course, after Lil then Mary Ellen were born in fairly quick succession, they moved to a terraced house not far off which they shared with three other families.

A retrospective glimpse of her during 1906, in better times, finds her out one rare Sunday afternoon with her three girls and her long time friend Jemima, now a widow, who had been married briefly to an Ealing man and lives only a bus ride away. Jemima's presence in Ealing is the very reason Kate headed west instead of back to east London after she left Portsmouth. Today, the two friends are listening to an assortment of musicians playing in the brand new bandstand in Acton Park, unable to restrain their giggles when distracted by the sight of the well-dressed young folk of the new Photographic Society involved in the fiddle and fuss of setting up their tripods. It is always quite an outing for Kate, to Acton Park. She is more used to walking the children to Baron's Pond on Pope's Lane where they can splash about for an hour or two in the muddy water there, free of charge.

More likely than not on days off which aren't blessed with an "occasion" like this one with her friend Jemima, Kate and her three girls may be spotted wandering along the Uxbridge Road, peering at the trains of the two underground lines that have surfaced to serve this quickly growing suburb. For Acton village, or "Laundry Town" as it is better known, has not yet quite merged into London itself.

On this day, thanks to Jemima winning some money on a church raffle, they are to be treated by her to a ride home on one of the new mechanical buses, and the girls have been looking forward no end to getting an upstairs seat in the open air, despite the mild drizzle setting in. Kate, who is technically illiterate, has a new project in mind which she is keen to discuss with her friend. It is too late for Violet, now aged 12 and already working alongside her mother, but she would dearly like Lil and Mary Ellen, the younger two, to start at the new Rothschild Road School only a few minutes from where they live. She isn't exactly sure where that may lead, but it seems that by getting an education they might avoid ending up like her, which can't but be a good thing.

For Kate is already elderly at the age of 30, struggling to stand up in the park and dust down the grass cuttings and dried leaves that have been pressing into the seat of her long brown woollen skirt since she sat herself down with Jemima and the girls. She has permanent ulcers on her legs from all the standing demanded by laundry work. These, she is in the habit of dressing herself, using whatever scraps of material are available since there is no money to purchase expensive medical treatment. From time to time her lesions turn septic, and although she is eighteen months away from knowing it, her lungs are already seeded with the tuberculosis which is rife amongst the laundry people.

How quickly Kate's stiff body tires nowadays. Jemima has noticed this herself, but does not pass comment in case it is received as intrusive. They are careful with each other's feelings, these two dear friends.

'Let's be off then, duck,' Jemima says at last, responding to the three girls' suppressed impatience for the novelty of the forthcoming bus ride. She takes her friend's arm with confidence after they have packed away their picnic hamper and adjusted their wide-brimmed hats. Jemima is the possessor of a most fortunate gift – the gift of security – thanks to money she has been left by her dead husband.

Kate, on the other hand, has been obliged to put to use the modest skills of a lesser trade, and is making her own contribution to the febrile industry of "Soap Suds Island," (Laundry Town's other alias). Washing and ironing, thanks to her own mother's endeavours, is what Kate happens to know a bit about. The demand for laundry work is growing fast as the better-off people in central London are now shipping their dirty laundry by the ton out to Acton in a daily caravanserai of loaded carts, all grinding westwards and returning later, freighted with clean clothes and bed linen.

Having been laid off recently, Kate surprises herself with the realisation that she misses the company (though nothing else) at the particular establishment which has given her a living for the last seven years, especially the beer man's visits mid-morning and again at half past six in the evening. His popularity is universal: who knows how many laundry people have been saved from fainting from dehydration by the time he turns up, regular as clockwork, every day?

Despite doing many of the jobs at the laundry in her

apprenticeship there – turning the great tubs, hanging heavy wet garments on lines splayed outwards around the stove in the vast drying room (a place both hot as an inferno and suffocating as a tropical rain forest) – it beat her in the end. The daily fatigue, the crushing headaches and raw eyes caused by fumes from the gas jets heating the water proved too much for her, what with looking after three children as well. But she was lucky, because the head laundry man was beginning to out-source much of his ironing by then, due to demand, and to this end he installed at Kate's lodgings in Rothschild Road several pieces of equipment for her to use, in the form of a curling machine for collars, a gophering machine to wave the frills on gentlemen's shirts, and a steam pressing cylinder that was longer than the kitchen range, to accommodate which they had to heave their tin bath out into the small back yard.

She has become an ironer by trade – of shirts and collars, lately, to give her specialism its due. As for griping, there is neither time nor opportunity. But: 'Oh my lord,' she confesses now, half to Jemima and half to herself as they amble towards the bus stop and her chest labours for breath, 'how much longer can a body stand up? They expect sixty or more hours of work every week, you know.' *Sixty?* Jemima tilts her head towards the ground in silent sympathy. How long? This is anyone's guess, and she knows that Kate's question is posed not in order to seek an answer but to un-screw the valve of her resilience – to let out a portion of her *own* steam, so to speak. Violet, the eldest, helps her mother out, Jemima knows, but the poor child had been lucky on more than one occasion not to lose a finger feeding in material to the big machine, hour upon hour. All it takes is a moment's lack of concentration and – pwft! Not to mention the all-pervading steam contributing to a permanent cloud of condensation dripping from their shabby ceiling, only to form an acid fog, blurring this laundress's vision in more way than one.

One thing Kate doesn't miss at all, though, is the pungent acidity issuing from the row of established laundries they are now passing, its intensity compelling Jemima to place a gloved hand as discretely as she can across her nostrils. 'You have to keep the windows closed otherwise the smoke outside clings to the clean clothes hanging up,' Kate mutters, noticing her friend's distaste, trying to distance herself from those laundry houses as they hurry on by. 'Oh, my goodness, the boiler in that place over there – just you look – it makes the washing *sweat*, you know, until the walls run with water. You should see it.' Jemima's tight smile suggests that indeed she would rather not, and Kate's mouth now begins to water pre-nauseously at the memory of it, which she doubts will ever be diluted or expunged.

'No wonder so many laundry workers turn to drink,' Jemima contributes, without thinking – adding quickly: 'No offence, dear.'

And Kate (who neither takes offence nor even notices that it might be due) nods in a distracted way, still absorbed by how it had been in that hellish place, relentlessly driven to turn around ever faster the complicated assembly line of sorting, washing, hanging up to dry, ironing and folding in the feverish commerce of Laundry Town. 'What makes it even worse', she continues, by way of self-justification, 'if you combine *that* with those blimmin' soda particles hanging in the air all the time and the stink of ammonia – oh, that stink, Jem! – well, it doesn't surprise *me* if any of them get a reputation for being short-tempered and rough spoken.'

'How indeed, dear,' Jemima concurs gravely, thinking herself very lucky indeed to live up-wind of all this. 'You know, it's a wonder someone don't complain about it.'

'Mustn't grumble,' murmurs Kate – not a grumbler by nature and the last person in the world to wish to elicit pity from anyone, particularly her friend. Like some of the other laundresses made ill by their working conditions, it would have been the easiest thing in the world for Kate to round on Jemima with something a little more tart at this point, something like: 'It's alright for some'. But they were friends, such good friends. And each, in her own way, had need of the other, appreciating and respecting the special durability of a bond forged in childhood.

At this point, Kate falls silent.

She hadn't the energy to listen to the angry youngsters who were beginning to agitate for a laundry workers' union, any more than she would give time to the nicely spoken young lady who knocked on her door several times, wanting to speak up for laundry folk through a local branch of the National Federation of Women Workers. Kate's experience told her that change wasn't what happened to folk like her: that sort of business was far above and beyond her. Anyway, she always had more pressing things to be getting along with.

The local union man had called on her, too, in due course, but Kate remained sceptical. She told him he'd do better to bring her a jug of beer if he really wished to improve her condition, ha, ha. 'Come, madam,' he replied in all seriousness, 'just you listen to this,' and he read to her from a pamphlet to explain the power of concerted action. But it fell on deaf ears and she swung her iron and pounded a shirt on the board as he read on, as if to let him know how she felt about *that*. He didn't give up on her, though. He called several more times and their conversations began to contain less of politics, lubricated as they were by the beer he duly brought with him. In the end, he looked at her squarely one day and, summing her up, saw how dirty she was, all except for her swollen red hands: twice the size they should have been, he reckoned. No point in any further investment here, he decided.

So on this disappointingly wet afternoon, it seems Kate has unwittingly become lodged in an anonymous place attaching her to an almost forgotten footnote to history, having joined the ranks of those who choose not to exercise their voices, whose enthusiasm is all but used up. People like Kate always far outnumber the change makers. All that work – and for what, she asks herself from time to time? She, and so very many others who share her situation, usually come round to the same conclusion: why should any laundry owner bother, when all was said and done, to spend money on better conditions when bigger profits can be made by leaving things as they are? At least there are jobs to be had. 'That makes sense,' agrees Jemima, who is anyway convinced that protest and agitation – you only have to look at those bare-faced hussies chasing after the vote – is unseemly, and not worth risking your reputation for.

Coming out of Acton Park, a sudden gale of boys in pursuit of a ball caught up in a bush nearby furl past the women, their fractured squeals causing the air to crackle. Being nearest to where it lands, Kate instinctively bends down to retrieve the ball, supporting her back with her other hand. With an underarm movement that lacks much momentum, she grins at the boys and tosses it towards them, rubbing her large, empty hand on the coarse wool of her skirt with a single syllable laugh that suggests she is glad to have been able to join in a bit of their fun, to be of service.

Work – her laundry piece work – otherwise never stops, apart from these occasional Sundays. Still, there is a tin shoved to the back of a shelf in the kitchen that has been slowly filling up with spare pennies and Kate has a dream that one day it might provide for the treat of an excursion to Portsmouth for the purpose of introducing her girls to the sea and watching their delight unfolding on the freedom of the beach. Now *there's* something to hold onto.

Home Kate shuffles some time later, the girls waving towards Jemima (who remains sitting on the omnibus bearing her on her way to a far better place) and yelling at the roadside silt it flings up at them in its wake.

And here, in Rothschild Road, Kate remains for three more long years following this day out with Jemima, until one day in 1909, worn out and debt-ridden, she finds herself quite unable to stand any more, let alone to think or dream or laugh much, and she is taken into the free Infirmary where she lies in a dormitory with all the other coughers and smokers, the hawkers and spitters, the diseased, the rotten in body, the weak, the malnourished and the industrially maimed, each of them with little to look forward to but a mutual desire for what they call a "blessed release". Goodbye Rothschild Road, then, with no one to pay the rent. Jack has quite disappeared; there's been neither sight nor sound of him for two years or more. Where *is* that man, when she needs him so badly?

A door slams at the other end of the dormitory where she lies helpless, and a fellow inmate curses it. All of a sudden her chest, starved of air, heaves in resistance to the searing sensation of her upper body being scored by a knife. This puts paid to further imaginings for the present. In the bright light of her pain, all she can see is the empty wall opposite her bed, pitted with empty holes where the render has fallen off.

3

Ealing, west London, 1909

Once her mother had been taken off to the Infirmary –
and with no parent left to counsel otherwise – Violet
knew she must be the first to leave Rothschild Road
herself, discovering a loft room for rent above a
haberdashery shop in Ealing where there was a job going
downstairs as a shop assistant. That way, she reasoned,
she might be able to see to the needs of the three of them
somehow, though it was a prospect that filled her with
terror. She was fifteen at the time. As for Lil and Mary
Ellen, unburdened by the mechanics of choice (quite
simply, there was none), they waited for a few days as the
last of their food ran out, impotent and fearful about
what might happen next.

It was all about self preservation now – this was the
unequivocal message for the two girls left behind, one
aged thirteen, the other twelve years old – but they were
ill-equipped for it and were reduced to existing in a state
of uncertainty wrought with dread in their new state of
vulnerability.

The laundry man had wasted no time in coming for
his equipment. In the end, Lil and Mary Ellen had no
choice but to place themselves in Jemima's hands since
there were no current prospects and they were painfully
aware that bailiffs were poised to remove their scanty
belongings.

And because Jemima had lately fallen on her feet yet

again and married a Mr Dalton of Oak Street, Ealing, she was, mercifully, in a position to offer them lodging.

So off the young pair walk, each carrying the sum of her possessions in a single carpet bag, stunned raw into a necessary attitude of total submission and heading for a road where the air promises to be much sweeter, being relieved of the sickening miasma of the laundries adorning Soap Suds City like a damp curtain.

And to a rather merrier household, it turns out. It seems that Jemima has chosen well once more. (Some people just *do*, Kate observed to Violet when she visited the Infirmary, pleased for her friend and quite without envy). Mr Dalton – Vic – turns out to be a thoroughly modern man, a man of confidence. He is proud to describe himself as a "car man", with duties which include chauffeuring and light engineering work underneath the bonnet of a bright blue, yellow-wheeled open-top car, built, as he is proud to relate, by one Mr Gottlieb Daimler. This vehicle is sometimes to be seen parked outside on Oak Street, although it belongs to a wealthy merchant who lives in one of the more prosperous households to the north. Vic ferries the owner of this splendid vehicle to his office in the City and back again three days a week, dodging the laundry carts. Sometimes they go to the races at Epsom in the Daimler. From time to time Vic is bold enough to use it independently in order to visit a young lady in Hackney, who is known neither to his new wife, Jemima, nor to his employer. The motor in his charge is maintained to perfection at all times, its horizontally placed external water cooling tubes polished until they gleam like a soldier's boots. In service to the car rather than its owner, Vic Dalton is moved to offer its bonnet the familiarity of a casual tap from his leather driving glove from time to time, an expression of both pride and deference. 'This is the age of the motor car, you mark my words,' he has been known to prophesy when he gives court occasionally at the King William public house nearby, in such a way as to indicate that he is entirely at one with the era in which he finds himself, and confident he will ride its wave. Fortunate Vic Dalton: he will be too old to enlist when the whole world erupts, no more than five years hence.

At first, Kate Fitch's two youngest girls take much gentle cajoling by the Daltons to do anything at all to distinguish themselves as discernible human beings, responding in half whispers when spoken to and sitting with their hands in their laps for the most part. Both are entirely familiar with exhaustion and disappointment and the ceiling of their expectation is so low as to bear down upon them, a heavy sack of troubles. Mary Ellen, the youngest, sits with permanently rounded shoulders, a habit that will result in her walking at a forward tilt by the time she is an adult, like a flag pole that needs shoring up. Even now, children in the street make fun of her for it, which only makes her hunch herself even more. Lil, whose curly blonde hair and forget-me-not blue eyes regularly invite the praise of strangers, appears to be a little less abject than her younger sister at this time, though she is equally silent and watchful. It seems like a very long time indeed since they had occasion to run circles around each other in Acton Park.

'Well, now, this won't do,' announces Vic Dalton one evening a few weeks into their residency, when his efforts at light teasing have been met once again with expressions of startled incomprehension. He is a kind man – if there is a marriage these girls will be referred to on paper as his daughters, he has decided – but he can't abide *gloom*. He mis-reads the girls' demeanour for sulkiness at first whereas, if the truth were known, it is a manifestation of extreme discomfort about their new state of dependency, exacerbated by the innate stigma of being regarded as a burden. (*Where are you, Jack Fitch, when your family needs you so badly? Why don't you come home?*) In later years, not one of Kate's girls would ever say of their youth in Acton (as they'd heard their mother reflect about Portsmouth, with the nostalgia of hindsight in her voice): 'ah, those were the days.'

But here they are. They sit and try to stare politely at their host with blank, animal eyes while he tries in vain to give them reason to smile back at him. 'It's as though they've been cornered at the edge of a field,' he remarks to Mrs Dalton one evening when they have gone to bed.

'Poor things, with no pa, or a ma,' she answers.

But he is right: naked instinct has prompted them to take cover for the present, on the alert for potential predators, as though a safety switch has been turned on causing them to place themselves on alert in a world which seems so very much bigger than they are.

Nonetheless, after some months of ghostly tiptoeing through the Dalton household, a vacancy for a scullery maid comes up at the house in newly fashionable Hanger Lane and 14-year-old Lil, Kate's middle daughter, is ready to accept the opportunity as an appropriate advancement in the state of things, her only experience of work so far being shoring up her ailing mother's ironing in Rothschild Road when Violet was too tired. Lil's news is welcomed by Kate Fitch on a visit by all three of her daughters at the Infirmary – they came on alternate Sunday afternoons throughout that spring and summer, less so during the following two years – and these dutiful visits may well have contributed to her dying in relative peace during a humid August in 1912, some three years after her children were forced to leave Rothschild Road.

One day, towards the end – fully aware of her inability to affect whatever fate awaited her daughters – Kate makes one last feeble grab for Lil's wrist and manages to pull her down low so that she can rasp, with the little breath she has left, and as privately as she is able: 'Just you remember, Lil, keep your hand on your ha'penny.' By that time she is too sick to register the girl's recoil at the crudity of such a remark.

'I'm not Lil anymore, you know,' comes the embarrassed retort of the scullery maid. 'I'm Lilian.'

At sixteen, it is hard to guess how informed Lil/Lilian is about anything at all, after enjoying only three years of intermittent schooling. But it seems that she is preternaturally astute by nature, not unlike a ferret, and this enhanced sensibility of the world around her was at least partially tuned by the time she began at last to settle in with the Daltons in Ealing.

There are certain people who can absorb any slight if they reckon it will lead to better things in the long run, and during this time Lilian is beginning to discover that she may be one of them. A pragmatic humility in the face of setbacks had been built into the very fabric of her being by the time she was in her mid-teens. One night, though, while finding it hard to sleep, an important insight coalesced in her mind which she was able to repeat to herself, particularly during the more challenging phases of her life. 'All right, then,' it went. 'I shall turn necessity into a partner, rather than an obligation.' She was pleased with this, and it kept her going whenever she was exhausted or downcast. As a result, unguided as she was during these formative years, Lilian made a pact with herself to continue her education by making use of the tools that were at hand – what else was there?

In the schoolroom which was also her place of employment, she became an acute observer of those superior folk's manner of speaking and gestures towards each other. No nuance escaped her – no knowing smile, no meaningful inclination of the head, no suppressed yawn. Hovering hawk-like and unnoticed, she took it all in, immersed herself in it, filing away a multitude of impressions until she could recognise what constituted the rhythms of gentle conversation and the degrees of deference expected of everyone according to the minute gradations of rank, mood and atmosphere that were common amongst the better off at the time. Her natural, defensive reticence began to prioritize critical vigilance at all times, even when she made her way back to the Daltons' house down the hill alone at night after a long day, pacing herself with quiet deliberation, her face set in a frown, so that anyone who might notice her – anyone at all – should not be tempted to delay or molest her.

Unimpressed, and a little intimidated by the tenacity of her sister's ethnographic endeavours, Mary Ellen – the youngest of the late Kate Fitch's three daughters – can't help but notice how her sister is changing as the person hitherto known by all as Lil is firmly put to rest, to be replaced thereafter by someone called Lilian.

'Why are you talking like that?' Mary Ellen asks her one day, out of naive curiosity rather than scorn – aware of certain new vowel sounds her sister has begun to experiment with. Lilian offers her younger sister a pert sneer and does not deign to answer. For what does Mary Ellen know of the ferocious concentration that transforming herself into *Lilian* happens to entail? Mary Ellen recognises that look only too well: she has previously spotted it on the faces of the ladies who used to hold their coats close round their mouths in Soap Suds City when they walked past, bracing themselves against the stench of the laundries. Little does she know that that close observance will become her sister's main tool in the art of mimicry, practised for the most part silently but manifesting itself in the odd conversation between them as well. It's early days, but Lilian is promising to be a gifted mimic.

It takes a further two years of skivvying for her unobtrusive and painstaking manner to earn her a promotion, which instantly extends her area of access to the draughty corridors and heavy furnishings of *upstairs*, where she is required to look after the wardrobe and the laundry of the two teenage daughters of the house. She, who finds the clamour of their silly intimacy mawkish, now has the opportunity of gaining real insight into how well-off young people behave. She takes some pleasure in having sole care of their blissfully clean linen when it is returned from the laundry (ugh: let's not dwell on that). In time, she gets to help the girls select which dresses they will wear. She quickly learns how silk is never brushed but rubbed with a piece of merino of a similar colour, that summer dresses require shaking, and that damp decorative feathers after a ball may be held very carefully near a fire for a few minutes then gently brushed, or re-curled with a blunt knife dipped in hot water. But the shoes! What shoes they wore! Shoes like you've never seen before! Satin boots, she learns in her self-taught school of life, must only be dusted or softly wiped. For kid or varnished leather, what you have to do is wipe it with a sponge dipped in milk. Before long, she remarks to Mary Ellen one evening that she could surely write a book on it.

More importantly, she is perfectly confident about being asked to lay a table with silver in the correct order, and telephoning an order through to Barker's of Kensington in a high-pitched, clipped voice. If asked, she would no doubt say she is happy to bide her time in this job, lodging with the Daltons and nurturing a private conviction that it could – *should* – be leading somewhere, if only she can keep her wits about her.

So far, she has made no mistakes.

4

In and around west London the winter of 1912 was particularly chilly, resulting in early morning frosts and a sharp drop in temperature once the sun began to set at the early end of the afternoon. The Dalton family, including the Fitch girls, were used to spending their evenings huddled round the fire in the front room, just like all the other families along the modest grid of terraced streets nearby, Jemima and the girls wrapped in shawls whilst Vic Dalton sported a scarf knitted by his ever resourceful wife. How that coal fire blazed, pinking their cheeks and sending out sharp darts of light across the dark green wallpaper.

On one such an evening in early October they receive a caller. He turns out to be the son of a Fulham tea merchant, this young clerk – who happens to work in an upstairs office of the big house where Lilian is employed. After finishing his ledgers rather later than usual, it transpires that he has been dispatched with a carton of eggs surplus to requirements, thanks to the generosity of the lady of the house, and since he lodges alone nearby he has decided it would make more sense to donate these to a family, after reserving three or four for his own use. Jemima, noticing the poor boy's red nose and eyes glassed over by the cold outside, invites him in for something to warm him up and he readily agrees to stop with them for a short while. Lilian and Mary Ellen put aside their game of solitaire out of politeness while Jemima readily busies herself with looking after him, though she could have done with resting her legs on the *pouffe*. This involves routinely straightening the antimacassar before he sits down as well as preparing him a drink of warm milk with a drop of brandy in it. 'You'll keep the boy company, won't you, dear?' asks Jemima, placing a second glass before Vic. Yes, he will.

'You've been working at the big house, I hear, like our girl?' she continues, turning to the young man in order to ease him into being conversational. 'Go and fetch the biscuits, Lil,' she adds.

('*Lilian*,' mutters the one so bidden with her back to Jemima as she heads for the kitchen, since Jemima is one of those who are proving frustratingly slow to adjust.)

'I have,' replies William Smithyes, for this, as Lilian well knows, is his name. 'Call me Bill, won't you?' he suggests. 'Everyone does.'

Casting his eyes round the little group assembled in the compact Dalton front room (such a room still experienced as luxury by the Fitch girls, since the living area at Rothschild Road had accommodated both the range and all three girls' beds), Bill Smithyes politely averts his eyes from first one then another of the two girls, who don't actually help matters by doing their best to indicate that a young male visitor is something they are quite capable of taking in their stride by making all the appropriate responses (which are, perplexingly, to say nothing at all unless asked, whilst on no account meeting his eyes either, maintaining stiff backs throughout).

After ten minutes or so of this, Bill Smithyes has thawed out enough to allow Jemima to suggest he might be warm enough to remove his coat, which he does, and she leaves the room to hang it up on the hall stand. The process of thawing progresses: he soon finds in his hands a second drink which Vic Dalton himself pours this time (the ratio of milk to brandy having been reversed) passing it to him to rest on the edge of the card table. At a certain point, led by Jemima, the women partially resume their activities (though not without half an ear to the conversation between the two men, dull as it is since it centres on balance sheets, order books, cars (of course) and the proposed design of new packing cases which have something to do with Bill's master's business). There are morsels to be gleaned, though, for those with sharp ears: the fact that this Bill has recently reached the age of 21, announced with a sense of pride that suggests he is *moving on in life*. It transpires that he is looking for a new, independent job as an insurance agent, after attending evening classes to improve himself.

'Bit risky, isn't it, insurance?' ventures Vic Dalton, man to man. 'What do your father think about that?'

'He's not against it,' replies Bill Smithyes.

'Well, you seem a lively sort of chap,' says Vic Dalton, warming to a certain chippiness about their guest.

Bill Smithyes drops by again a few days later, and by his third visit there is no doubt in any of their minds that what draws him there is an interest in Mary Ellen Fitch, who, at 15, is permitted to partake in a certain amount of bantering with him in her childish way, given the presence of Lilian and the Daltons. Mary Ellen still has no job but Vic Dalton, out of respect for his wife's recently deceased friend, Kate Fitch, has indicated that she need not be pressured, not yet a while.

It is soon after Bill's visits become regular that an unexpected reversal of fortune causes a sudden fracture in the limited geography of Lilian's own life since moving to Ealing.

At first, it is only a rumour that she picks up,

suggesting the likelihood that her own job will come to an end before spring time when the girls are due to leave home to be "finished" in France. It has become awkward for her, as she explains it to Jemima, not knowing quite how she is placed. But although this was indeed about to happen, it was some way from the whole truth of the matter, only the version Lilian chose to relay. And she was determined to keep it that way.

It all started when a significant piece of jewellery belonging to one of the young ladies – a pretty *art nouveau* necklace – went missing. The first to be alerted to this, Lilian immediately joined the search, demonstrating her concern and making attempts to reassure the owner that it must surely turn up, eventually. The trouble was, it didn't, though they dug down into every crease and cranny of furniture, shaking out curtains and coverings, bending over the skirtings and fiddling about with all manner of ornaments and items of clothing.

'But it has to be here,' comes Lilian's high, insistent voice, urging further searching. They are taken aback momentarily by the clarity of it – a voice rarely listened to apart from when it is responding to a demand. 'Yes,' she continues, as if to underline the veracity of her statement, 'I believe you were wearing it when the Constances came to supper and you haven't been out since then'. She finds herself embarrassed by the unusual attention being paid her and makes a silent appeal to each of them with her eyebrows raised.

Lilian passed the following days in mounting discomfort, days in which she was left in little doubt that certain whispered conjectures were being formed, suggesting that increasingly outright suspicion was beginning to isolate her. Maybe she even began to wonder herself: after all, she was cleaning the blessed thing herself only a day before it disappeared. No accusation could be made on such flimsy lack of evidence, but Lilian perfectly understood the unspoken rule decreeing that in the end it is the always the subordinate who gets the blame. However unfair it was, there was nothing, absolutely nothing she could to do about that.

The girl who is the owner (or former owner) of the necklace in question now requires someone to directly point an accusing finger at. She is haughty with Lilian over the next few days, then bored, and finally lets it be known how irritated she is by all sorts of imagined mannerisms and shortcomings in the maid. A mental assault on Lilian intensifies, via frequent squibs of ill will consisting mainly of cold looks and small, pointed acts of exclusion. It takes an amount of courage and determination on Lilian's part to pretend to ignore these slights, but she is determined not to lose sight of hope. For if you have no hope – well, just look at her poor mother.

Witnessing the unkindness of her daughters, it is all too easy for the mistress of the house to assume misgivings of her own. From then on, Lilian accurately predicts that it is only a matter of time before she is told she is a "bad influence" – something like that, she supposes, or they'll concoct some way of proving her incompetent – and that the best she can do is to find somewhere else to work as soon as she can. This way, she is finally told during a brief, chilly, one-sided conversation in the drawing room, there will be a written "character" for her at the end of the day.

She knows when her number is up.

But she tries to convince herself that any felt humiliation, any remnant of a desire to justify herself will have to be mitigated by what she will take with her – that internalised manual of knowledge which must surely be useful. In an oblique sort of way, it also prompts her to offer to join in when Bill Smithyes and her sister play their games, instead of getting on with reading the book in her lap. Bill doesn't say no to her inclusion, and Lilian is nothing if not persistent in her attention towards him. Clumsy, juvenile Mary Ellen – well, she doesn't stand a chance after that: this is what a significant look or two between Jemima and Vic signals one evening.

Back on the work front, the last few days of Lilian's employment arrive. Can it be that she is about to find an ally in that household, even at this late stage? How she needs one. So: if a young man sees a young woman he thinks is not half bad being bullied, and if he perceives that she's not in a position to stand up for herself, what is he to do if not at least put some comfort her way?

On a day when the whole family embarks on an expedition to the riding stables in Hyde Park, Bill Smithyes experiences a rather frequent need to leave his desk in the upstairs room that doubles as a home office for his employer (to pour himself a glass of water, to visit the privy, to check for the fourth time whether mail has yet been delivered downstairs). By lunch time, on one of these sorties, it is logistically inevitable that he will find himself squeezing past Lilian on the stairs. 'Cheer up,' he says, taking her hand. 'It may never happen.' Such unfamiliar – such *knowing* – kindness, throws her off balance for a moment. She gazes up at him in order to allow him to witness the full effect he is having on her, then makes a quick decision. He is not a bad young man. So much seems certain, to her way of thinking. She clutches the banister, yet seems reluctant to move away.

Her forget-me-not blue eyes fasten on his. What can he do next? What *should* he do? Her hand is so very near to his and she does not move it. What shall he do, then? He draws her back upstairs with him. He wants to say something, but for the life of him he doesn't know what.

That Christmas, Bill Smithyes sits with the Daltons in church and goes back home with them afterwards for his lunch. 'This is all happening too quick,' murmurs Vic Dalton to Jemima after they have eaten, just before he goes upstairs for his nap and the pair can be heard in the front room, playing a lively game of whist. 'Maybe it's for the best,' suggests Jemima. 'He seems like a nice enough boy.'

'Too young, far too young,' is Vic's last word on the subject that day.

Lilian Fitch married Bill Smithyes the following March and six months later, in June, 1913, their son Thomas was born, a large baby for such a small woman. Despite his misgivings and Mary Ellen's nose remaining out of joint, Vic Dalton, true to his word, played the part of father, footing the bill for the church and such trimmings as were expected. As it turned out, both he and Bill Smithyes appeared to be decent men, for which Lilian was grateful. Violet came over for the occasion and followed them into the sacristy, as a witness.

5

In relation to the warren of squat Victorian houses – some of them ambitiously bearing the name of a famous English writer of the past (Shakespeare, Goldsmith, Milton) Birkbeck Avenue slants at a right angle down towards the drabness of the main Uxbridge Road running through Acton at the point at which it ceases to be a conduit for traffic ceaselessly delivering or collecting laundry to and from London. As such, it forms a boundary to all that, a high water mark beyond which life (and especially the quality of the air) promises to be less stale. Along this modest street, the houses are slightly taller than the literary terraces, and with their street-facing exterior walls washed in a range of pale colours they are incongruously reminiscent of photographs Lilian has seen depicting Italy, of all places, in a copy of the London Illustrated Magazine displayed in the window of a nearby newspaper vendor.

So. Lilian has arrived back in Acton – Laundry Town, Soap Suds City.

But all is not running entirely downhill in this particular spot. At least the infernal heart of the laundries is half a mile to the south of Birkbeck Avenue, although from time to time a baleful blast of its musky smell can't be ignored, even here. It's just that instead of being constant, it now depends upon the direction of the wind. Meanwhile, the young trees growing out of the pavement on one side of the road sometimes give Birkbeck Avenue a deceptively languid aspect, as if it should be sweating in Mediterranean sunlight when not protected by the jigsaw of damp shadows cast by their limp green leaves. All things being equal, it is not a bad place for a young (a very young) couple to be starting their married life.

The sun beams low and late during one early autumn afternoon of 1913. Baby Thomas bawls with harsh energy in his cradle and Lilian stands alone for long hours at a deep china sink veined with the cracked black capillaries of many years of usage, in front of a window through which she can see close at hand the soot blackened rear of a parallel row of houses. That they appear cramped, she surmises, could signify that their occupants might be ashamed enough of such tenements to remain out of sight for the most part, opting to remain humbly huddled indoors. Not unlike herself.

It was a difficult birth for a little person like Lilian, aided by a midwife living nearby who consumed their meagre savings in the process. Thomas was a big baby and now he cries so much she often wonders whether something is wrong with him. The noise he makes rather grates on her. She had never wanted a baby, only to be taken away from the ignominy of living on the Daltons' charity after the double disgrace of losing her job and being pregnant out of wedlock, those two incontrovertible marks of universal shame. Wearily, wearily she shuffles and pounds and squeezes the endless washing produced by this baby. The odour of ammonia rising up from the terry towelling nappy bucket makes her eyes smart. Lilian is galled by the amount of laundry she is obliged to deal with. But at least it is her own.

Ha ha, giggles the gremlin she fancies peering in at a window to catch her off guard, its apparent purpose to tease her from time to time from its perch on one of the trees outside: *look at Lil with her hands in the washing once more. Ha ha.*

Bill is out all day at his new job (he calls himself an insurance agent but as yet he is an insurance *clerk*, let's not exaggerate, as Lilian has pointed out to him more than once). He sports a squat black bowler hat like all the other city workers and takes the nearby underground train each morning to Liverpool Street Station, returning in time for supper at seven o'clock with a fresh layer of smoke oiling the surface of his suit. Lilian is left with plenty of time on her own to think, meanwhile, as she gets on with the daily grind of all that needs to be done to maintain their little two-room dwelling on the first floor. Thoughts, her only companions nowadays, gather in a pallid cumulus above the drudgery of those early married days, knotted through by the shock of an occasional insight to help her make sense of what has come to pass: to begin to compose her own story so far ...

A girl finds herself without father or mother ... a young man appears ... who can blame her for thinking he may be "the answer" – as though her life were a piece of unvalued and unscrutinized merchandise needing the scented drawer of marriage offered by Bill Smithyes to place it in order to keep it fresh? *Aha,* interjects the gremlin. *Such a drawer has no windows: it can only be managed by someone on the outside. Ha!* Very well, she is tempted to retort, perhaps I shall just stay shut up, then. Is she yet fully aware of the attrition to her soul caused by the daily act of folding herself away inside this, this – *union?* Is this the price of too hasty expedience? Is it only what's to be expected? Do other women feel like she does? She'll never know unless she speaks to some of them about it, yet no-one ever seems to talk of such things. Is this *it?* What exactly *is* "it" if not the finality of everything, then, a kind of living death?

Bill laughs affectionately and with a familiarity she finds distasteful at what he refers to as her trumped up ideas about accelerating the process of bettering themselves. He is aware that she believes she got less than she bargained for when she married him. This could be demeaning to him, but it only serves to freeze the ready smile on his face, not to wipe it away entirely. She'll knuckle down eventually, they all do, and he knows it. What other choice has she got?

Perhaps this really *is* it, then, she suspects at least five times a day. As if on cue, up wafts an unpleasant stink from the direction of her son Thomas, infecting "it" in turn with an additionally dank aspect – rubbing it in, so to speak. She begins to form an ominous vision of the future: decades (decades!) rolling out across uniformly grey-shaded nothingness that seems to go on for ever. It's a living desolation: rather like death itself, she supposes. Or a mouldy heap of cold cinders too unyielding to bear the imprint of any script she may have once half believed herself capable of creating.

Today, as on all the days, back to Acton Park she trudges, the same Acton Park her mother once took her to only a few years previously. Each stiff pace seems set to intensify the depth of her thoughts, but they can never penetrate the grey, however hard she tries, because there is too little substance in her attempts at reasoning to provide her with a proper judgement, let alone a plan. Totally sealed within herself, she fails to acknowledge the passing uniformed nanny pushing a commodious pram who might have shared a smile with her, just as she is too withdrawn to even register the women from the bread shop who pause to gather on a bench when the sun is out, and who occasionally lift their eyes as if they might recognise her when she passes by to do her daily bits of shopping. Her mission on these walks, she has decided, is to modestly, aimlessly, with as much patience as she can muster, waste a little time most afternoons with Thomas in his squeaky pram bought from the scrap yard and done up by Bill himself. Yet, if she raises her head and fans her gaze across the spread of grass in the park from time to time, it is not to ponder her Bill's limitations, after striking this necessary bargain with him (this is the point at which the gremlin is prone to let out a single hoot of scorn). No – the whole situation, she reminds herself, must be balanced by the relief of being kept, for the moment. It will have to do. For now, at any rate.

Bill seems to have adjusted with much more ease to his sudden married status, although the baby gets on his nerves at times, too – at which point out slips his watch from his waistcoat pocket (the warm-hearted Daltons' wedding gift to him), and without much preamble, he abruptly takes himself off to the Prince Regent where it is his habit to spend an hour or two with his newspaper, his pouch of tobacco and a pint of ale or two, accompanied by a growing band of youthful accomplices.

Meanwhile, each evening as dusk gradually falls, Lilian may be found alone in her modest home while the hours of his absence tick by, getting on with her mending by the light of the gas lamp from the street outside which sends out a buttery beam that pools in her lap and exaggerates the huddle of peripheral shadows obscuring the cheap barometer and the "Cries of London" prints hanging from the picture rail.

And so the months slip invisibly past Lilian and Bill and their son Thomas and they manage to keep afloat, without being too disturbed by the turbulence which is ruffling the surface of time all around them.

Nevertheless, both of them are obliged to think

beyond themselves towards the middle of the following year. By now, other events are starting to crowd in on all the Lilians in the evening solitude of their dimly lit houses, causing a rising swell in the murmuring queue at the butcher's. Who can ignore the way that the newspapers have become both bombastic and patriotic of late in their tone, providing reports laced with mischievous tendrils of anticipation and speculation which are proving very tempting for ordinary folk like the Smithyes' to absorb at face value. Such newspaper reporting isn't in any way reassuring, though often it feels like it is, wavering between gravity and calls to a reader's carnival sense of occasion. It is from the papers that Lilian and Bill first learn that neither animals, nor first aid supplies nor silk braid are to be sent abroad any more, and in time Bill duly passes to his wife the Daily Mail's tips on housekeeping for wartime. 'Take a look at this, Lil.' *War?* 'A bit premature, isn't it?' queries Lilian. Bill, by now, has given up reading the Daily Herald – his paper of choice – in protest, because it has turned anti-war. A copy of the Daily Express passed around the Prince Regent one night produces a spontaneous roar of approval at a report that there has been 'groaning and hissing' from a crowd of protesters outside the German Embassy.

It is almost a relief when Bill comes bounding indoors on August 4 to tell her that war has been declared.

'Oh, Lord,' is Lilian's response. 'What's to become of us?' At which Bill puts his arm round her and gives her a rough shake and for a few moments it feels like they are in the process of setting out again and he seems once more important to her – although even as he does so he can't resist projecting his imagination beyond her small blonde head to a place which has already merged with a time, making him feel as though the future itself is bowling towards him, gathering him into its oncoming surge in a way that makes him thrill with a sense of his own significance.

Lilian isn't particularly surprised one evening shortly after this when Bill dashes in wide-eyed with excitement to inform her that he's joined the Middlesex regiment. Everyone is doing it, all the young men, he announces by way of an explanation – under the influence of their own limited perceptions and an outbreak of viral impetuosity in equal parts, no doubt – much encouraged by the popular newspapers they read. (*Abroad!* He can barely suppress a grin as the word slips out of his mouth.)

She finds it unnecessary to mourn his leaving home when the time comes – she reckons she is not the sentimental type – though for a while she looks forward to his letters, terse as they are, noting that he is somewhere on Tottenham Marshes for the present, which distinctly lacks a ring of the heroic. Instead, by increments, she begins to experience a prickly sensation of being *left behind*, not just by Bill but also by the rumbling vehicle of this war as it gets into gear.

Thomas heaves himself upright one day that summer and starts to totter. This means he is no longer a baby any more, but a toddler. Very occasionally, Violet visits, but not Mary Ellen, who will never forgive Lilian for stealing her young man from beneath her very eyes. Occasionally, also, Jemima Dalton comes, bringing one of her pies or a few flowers from the garden. It's not the same between them any more, though, because Jemima has indicated that the propriety of the Dalton household was betrayed somewhat by this hastily arranged marriage. They are cool with each other, polite at best, and Lilian makes no attempt to reciprocate. For her part,

Jemima keeps in contact solely out of respect for her late friend, Kate Fitch, who always did her best though it was never enough, the poor creature, and that was the real tragedy, to Jemima's way of thinking. As for the Smithyes of Fulham, Bill's family, there never was a sign of them, either at the impromptu wedding in Ealing or afterwards in Birkbeck Road – they made plain their understanding that Lilian had trapped their son, and more fool him for falling for it.

Perhaps it is unspoken attitudes like these, whose suggestiveness unsettles her with a draught of accusation as she hunkers down alone in her dwelling in Acton, which begin to tempt Lilian to wonder whether now might be the time for her to think about moving on herself.

THE RATTLE OF ANCHORS

6

Canada, around 1865

Nova Scotia is suspended like a large butterfly from the eastern seaboard, perfectly poised to receive and send forth ships. It lies east of New Brunswick and just below the Gulf of the St Lawrence river which gathers momentum as it flows from its source in Lake Ontario, en route for Montreal and onward to Quebec City. Yarmouth, Nova Scotia's most easterly province, was first settled by French Catholics who violently resisted being removed from their homeland there in 1756 by the British who "won" Canada following the European Seven Years' War. After that, the disgruntled French were taken to Louisiana, where they formed the Cajun community ("Cajun" was a local corruption of "Acadian"; Acadia was what they named their original settlement in Nova Scotia). A perfect place.

By the middle of the nineteenth century, pretty much all the men descended from the English settlers on the Acadian Cape of Nova Scotia were working either on or for the sea and establishing a number of well-known local dynasties through fishing, ferrying cargo and passengers across Massachusetts Bay, building and repairing boats, mending nets and tackle, crewing on the great three and four-masted windjammers that set sail for foreign parts from here. Some of those who survived rose to the rank of captain, returning home to build one of the grand gambrel houses there, each with its distinctive lookout facing the sea, as if paying an eternal tribute to it. Such men tended to retire in relative comfort, greatly respected by their fellow-townsmen, and those old captains were held in even higher esteem by the local boys, who were ravenous for sea-going adventures of their own.

Captain Adam Pengarth had been one such boy in his time, and by his maturity he had developed a reputation that would outlast him by a generation or two after his death, which is surely more than most people achieve. Pengarths had been settled for at least two hundred years in Acadia which, by his time, had become a place of considerable pastoral elegance. How ever did they get there in the first place? Perhaps, he sometimes fancied, he was descended from William Pengarthey, a young man who crossed the Atlantic to Massachusetts with the Pilgrim Fathers on the Mayflower – a voyage into utterly unknown territory at the time which, to his way of thinking, had a certain romantic appeal. Or maybe his ancestor was the Reverend Hugh Peter Pengarth of whom he'd also read in a book he owned about Cornish history that had long been in the family. That notable gent left England after Cromwell's fall, bound for the New World, but he made the mistake of later returning to England – a bad move, because poor Hugh Peter's crime was being on the *wrong side*, turning him into a wanted fugitive over there. So, for his pains, he was hanged, drawn and quartered on arrival in London, his head stuck on a pole on Charing Cross Bridge.

Alright, then, pondered Captain Adam from time to time – might a more likely ancestor from the old country have been a Geoffrey Pengard of Place, Cornwall who served under Sir Walter Raleigh at the time of the Armada before emigrating westwards? 'There's no doubt,' he was fond of telling anyone who would hear him out, 'my family has the sea in its blood.' Then, likely as not, he would add: 'Listen to this,' and sing, a little off-key, an old refrain about common prefixes to Cornish names:

'By Tre, Ros, Car, Len, Pol and PEN

You well may know all Cornish men.'

Pengarth, Pengard, Pengarthey ... a name subject to instability, just like some of its subsequent owners. The interfering agents are usually unexpected warps in a family's sense of continuity caused by conflagration or separation, the capriciousness of both oral records and memory itself, and the tendency of old ink to fade and blur and blotch, providing unreliable information for those to come. Most of all, perhaps, by the long reaches of the Atlantic ocean itself – the way to over there (or here, of course, depending on what shore you are standing) – which by its nature most annoyingly refuses to yield any palpable map of the stories enacted upon it by pioneering sailors like Adam Pengarth.

He grew up in Chebogue, a township at the southern tip of Nova Scotia facing south-west to Boston and east out across the Atlantic, as if on permanent alert for passing vessels. He lived in one of the roomy captain's houses that proclaimed the prosperity of their owners, with their dormer widows and double-jointed roofs resembling the joint (the gambrel) of a horse's hind leg, constructed deliberately with upwardly curved ends at the eaves in order to reduce the slippage of heavy snowfall in winter. The early mariners who built these houses were said to have brought back the distinctive design of the gambrel house from voyages to south East

44

Asia. To this day, they say, similar architecture can be spotted in parts of Cambodia.

But it wasn't eastward that the young mariner Adam Pengarth set his eyes on: rather, it was due south.

By all accounts, he was a burly, good-looking young man at the start of his nautical career. Before he reached his teens he'd been out many times with crews of local fishermen. They would tie the boy to a mast when the boat started to roll and pitch due to a rising swell: that way, he wouldn't lose his balance or trip overboard.

At one point during his long nautical career, it came to pass that the Captain was persuaded by his sister Elsie, who plainly adored him – utterly revered him more like, she being the eldest and he the youngest of six – to set down for posterity in his careful, rounded handwriting details of one of his earliest ocean-going journeys in the brig Martha on which, at the age of 19, he was employed as second mate. Perhaps writing it down was his way of reconstituting some of his own vanished nautical footprints, set down like passing ghosts on the Spanish Main, that southern stretch of the Atlantic ocean.

Not then, as he prepared to embark – not ever – did he harbour any fear about what may or may not lie beyond the thin blue line of horizon he kept always in view, whether on land or at sea. On the contrary, he could never wait to get started, spurred on by youthful restlessness and what, to a landlubber, might appear to be a most unwise sense of complicity with the sea itself, as though he were in cahoots with it, on equal terms.

Well, the destination of the Martha on that occasion was Rio de la Hatche, Venezuela, 'a Spanish port on the Indian Coast of the Spanish Main,' he tells us. Here, they were to collect a cargo of "divi divi" ('a kind of dye used by Indians to paint their faces with when on the war path' his devoted sister Elsie usefully explains in one of a number of busily scrawled notes in the margin).

The weather was set fair and he had already learned to identify many things that those accustomed to living on land don't see: certain cloud formations created by the proximity of land masses, as yet out of sight ... vague shadows on distant shores presaging the existence of a colony of natives ...sporadic groups of birds drifting by with their own sense of purpose which, confirmed by the movement of the stars above, informed a mariner that they were sailing along known migratory routes.

One day, as the Martha was approaching the equator, the young merchant sailor came to feel as though the world had indeed begun that very morning, doing him the great honour of carrying him along with it. The sea was flat as a half-set jelly that day, heaving ever so slightly as though a giant bowl was gently tilting it this way and that with particular unconcern, auguring fair weather ahead. Just then, he spotted a single shark's fin that appeared to knife the surface of the water, creating a cuff of pure light for a moment before it descended into the deep.

The ocean, a glistening, empty stage, began to lighten in colour with each day that passed, until its turquoise assumed a neon sheen as the water began to warm up. The further south they travelled, both the air and the sea itself shimmered with an intensity that threatened to burn his eyes.

'We arrived in Rio in the afternoon,' he recalls in this, his one and only sea journal, 'and were ordered to an Indian village about sixty miles to the eastward up the coast. We had on board guns, ammunition and stores, and a quantity of dry goods such as factory cloth and calico thread and needles and scissors, likewise a quantity of fancy coloured beads and a large amount of rum to trade with the Indians.' The sight of them approaching soon attracted an entourage of local Indians who they proceeded to recruit. These Indians would crew three large additional barges which would travel alongside them. The Indians brought along their wives, who remained with them throughout the expedition.

'It had taken us nearly a month to get to our destination as we had to beat to windward against the NE trade winds,' relates Captain Adam. 'Finally, we arrived there all right one fine afternoon and came to anchor near the shore in a large bay. The shores were all a kind of white sand in those parts. With no signs of life to be seen thereabouts, and in order to inform the natives that there was a new arrival, we started a hullabaloo by firing guns and blowing horns and howling till after dark, so as to give them to understand that we were well armed and would stand no fooling.

'Next morning, several canoes came along side and took the news into the interior that we were there for cargo. They soon started to bring all kinds of meats and vegetables to sell, even girls. Our Supercargo' ('this is the officer looking after commercial aspects of the voyage, including sales,' informs Elsie) – 'bought one of the nicest looking Indian girls I ever saw. Let me tell you, the Indians here wear very little clothes. Children of both sexes none, until they are about ten years old. Some of them marry when they are about twelve. They have no marriage ceremony. The parents sell the girls for so much and they just pair off like ducks.

'Well, the girl the Supercargo bought turned out to be our salvation, as I will inform you later on.

'As we could not trust an Indian we took all knives and weapons from them at the gangway and only one boat was allowed alongside at a time. And they were not allowed to go about the ship, forward or aft. Strange, busy little critters they were, like marionettes and rather silly, I would say. They came out with hoots of laughter and were given to making sudden loud, moaning noises for no reason at all as far as we could tell.' Along with one or two of the other sailors, he took the trouble to learn bits of their language which, he remarked, was like nothing else he'd ever encountered.

'But we got by. One night, I had charge of the Dog Watch' ('one of two watches of two hours each, between 4.00 and 8.00pm' – Elsie, again, who might well have been a sailor herself if she hadn't been a girl). 'The Indian boatmen were lying under the awning when all at once one of them jumped up and commenced kicking his wife. I immediately unsheathed my bayonet and stopped him. He cried and took on dreadfully because I wouldn't let him kill her. He took all her clothes from her and put them on himself. And he said he was going to take her next day about ten miles away to where it was customary to take their wives to kill them when they did anything wrong. What this particular wrong was I did not fathom.

'She heard and understood all he told me and she only laughed at him and did not seem the least bit ashamed of her scanty attire. He walked the deck and cried all night with her clothes on. I coaxed him all my watch to forgive her and the next morning he gave her back her clothes and went to work as usual. She was about thirteen or fourteen years old.'

Querulous Indians and suspicious sailors notwithstanding, during the days that followed Second Mate Adam Pengarth found himself out and about alongside his Captain on something of a lateral mission whilst they waited for trade to be completed. Taking with them a grappling hook, they planned to fish for treasure from a nearby wreck set in shallows of about ten feet deep. 'She had seven brass cannon that were worth a lot of money'. On the last of these sorties they were suddenly summoned back to the Martha by guns being fired – only to find out that they were aimed at what he describes as 'an enormous sea serpent about twice as long as the ship. Well, that settled my diving for curios.'

But there was serious trouble ahead. Alerted by the 'whizz splash' of arrows being fired across the Martha's stern, back on board they discovered that the Supercargo had fallen out with a boatful of Indians and he had put poison out of the ship's medicine chest into their rum and many of the Indians had died as a result. 'So they rose up, and as the wind was off shore they (that is, the Supercargo and his party) slipped their anchor and fought the Indians off until they were out of sight of land. The decision communicated by the Indians to the Supercargo was that all of us were to be cut up alive in one inch pieces,' reports Captain Adam.

'Now, our position was two anchors down, all sails unbent and our decks full of rum casks and dry goods and awnings fore and aft and the hold about half full of cargo. So we got busy in a hurry and dumped everything on deck in the hold, took in our awnings, bent our sails and hove up our anchors, all in the night time. At daylight we got underway and moved off from the shore into the middle of the bay and let go anchor again.

'The trade winds always blowed into the bay except about two hours every morning. The second day we lay there we saw close up, on a point of sand at the mouth of the entrance of the bay, about a thousand Indians. Now, in order for us to get to sea we had to go so near to this sand point that they would be able to pick off every one of us that showed his nose above the deck rail, with their bows and arrows.

'That night, our informant (who was the lady I mentioned to you) came again and told us they couldn't attack us in the bay as they hadn't canoes enough, but that they intended to capture us as we passed the point at the entrance of the bay. We were by then able to spy the Indians going down behind the sand banks to hide, and about every hour they would come up on the Point and look to see if we were moving, and when one came to look they would all come, so about every hour this point of sand looked like bushes and trees as it was covered with Indians.

'Well, we were obliged to lay at anchor in that bay for three days. On the morning of the fourth, our Captain arranged to be first to take the wheel, and as soon as he was shot away I was to take his place, and I never was so excited in my life as we drifted within ten feet of the shore.' They were thus obliged to watch and wait, nothing else, holding on for the moment to escape. Young Adam Pengarth felt for a time as though he was hovering above himself as he considered death for the first time, hawk-like, while at the same time pure exhilaration raced through him with unstoppable velocity.

There was an unexpectedly auspicious conclusion to the stand-off. 'The Indians were starved out and they had to go about thirty miles inland to get something to eat,' he goes on to report. 'Wherever one went, they all went. We were about the gladdest crowd to slip out to sea that day as ever I saw, and I have been to sea a good many times since.'

Here, he brings his yarn to a close.

Later, his soul mourned the passing of such moments – and there were a number of them in his twenties and thirties when he was at sea, never to be surpassed over here, on dry land – moments when he found himself to be so close to death he could almost smell it. As ever, a sense of being gripped by suspense only sharpened his sense of being. Was he a reckless man? When he mulled it all over subsequently, he concluded that the dangers he had survived served to lift him out of what he sometimes felt was the mild cowardice of the rest of his life after he stopped sailing in favour of dealing with paperwork, in order to find a wife, sire five children and become a strict father and a rather demanding husband. And be persuaded by an adoring sister to at last write this one bit of it down.

Later still, he resisted colluding with his growing family when they started to turn him into a living legend because it felt kind of ridiculous, to his way of thinking. Nevertheless, the most comfortable way of living with that darned image his family had of him, thanks to Elsie and many other tales – told and re-told orally, over the years – was in the end to half-heartedly go along with the inflated self they lumbered him with in their affection for him. If they insisted upon it. And so it was that any sense of his own heroism, should he succumb to it, would immediately result in a case of indigestion.

But by their stories shall you know them.

Many years later, Elsie completed her notes about her brother with a tender afterthought. Maybe her interference with his scrawling was her own attempt at locating herself within the expanding Pengarth brood, those scribbled interventions a way of participating in all that was prohibited her. How readily would she have tried herself against the trials her brother had undergone, given half a chance. Nevertheless, generous to the last, she never once gave out any sign of envy, choosing only to lavish on him her sisterly approbation.

Their family home was by now in the hills, in a village by the tidal Chebogue River, but every day, after his retirement, Captain Adam came down to the waterfront with his dog, Sport, to run the ferry boat across to an island summer resort, Bay View Park. When this resort burned down, he spent much of his time duck hunting and sailing. 'He would take with him in his little boat his dog Sport – of course – and a box of provisions, and spend a few days on one of the islands,' wrote Elsie. 'He maintained a little shanty, crudely furnished with an old cook stove, a wooden table and a couple of chairs, one made out of an old barrel. In one corner were three bunks, with ropes for springs and mattresses no thicker than your thumb. He was in his glory those days, and so was Sport. He would always come home with a few wild duck and a bucket of soft shell clams.

'One cold fall day,' she records, 'he had the urge to go down to the river for one of his trips, so he clothed himself warmly, wearing his high rubber boots. The little boat was skimming over the water and the Captain was comfortably settled with the helm under his arm and peace in his heart. Suddenly, as he rounded a point of land, a contrary squall of wind capsized the boat. Because of his excess clothing, he was unable to swim and only with sheer grit, and the help of Sport, was he able to reach shore.

'Sport started barking then ran up to a farmhouse on the side of a big hill and barked and barked and barked until he attracted the farmer's attention.' This achieved, 'the dog would start down the hill, looking back and stopping to make sure he was being followed, then go on,' continues Elsie. 'My brother was found on the beach, trying to get up, drenched and somewhat waterlogged. He was led to the house by the hospitable farmer, whose good wife made him comfortable both inwardly and outwardly, and Sport was a hero.

'After that, the Captain grew older and his trips down river grew less frequent,' concludes Elsie's most affectionate memoir. 'He spent most of his time on his front porch with his faithful friend by his side. Sport, too, became ancient and ailing, and one day he simply disappeared. The Captain never talked about it, but we had our own ideas.

'Shortly after,' she attests, 'my dear brother Adam received that clear call, and "Crossing the Bar, put out to sea".' According to the portrait that outlived him, crimson cheeks and the deep web of wrinkles splayed out on each side of his eyes served as a testament to the muscle of many a grainy ocean blast during his time at sea.

And this accounts for Elsie's pride in his dying which, as she was wont to put it, seemed a fitting end to a comfortably rounded life, a life which had been lived well.

'How many can say that?' were her last, proud words on the matter.

Now, if Captain Adam Pengarth had a youthful habit of sailing close to the wind, there was one other, entirely unconnected to him except, posthumously, by a great-grand-daughter they could both lay claim to, had it been possible to peer into a future that far ahead. Co-incidentally, this other one's life was also sculpted by the sea. He was one Jack Fitch, a merchant who himself had a wife, Kate, and three small daughters back in Acton, England. In the early years of the new century Kate Fitch became despondent as she pondered long on what on earth had happened to him. In the end, she had to assume he had disappeared into the hinterland of some foreign port, as some of his colleagues had done, to be with a woman, or on the scent of a fortune to be made in undiscovered parts, and so he had decided to abandon them.

But no.

The fact was that Jack Fitch "crossed the bar" himself in 1905 in a most untimely and utterly ignominious way, mid-Atlantic, following a disgraceful episode of drunkenness one stormy night, during the process of which he lurched, un-noticed, from the poop deck of his vessel, the Albana. No-one knew he had gone missing until roll call the next morning, which was way, way too late for this particular sailor. Poor Jack Fitch thus became invisible at a stroke, unlike his Canadian counterpart. A letter from his captain was later sent to Kate's first home in London, but when she moved to Rothschild Road she neglected to leave a forwarding address. While Adam Pengarth's seafaring was charmed with good fortune, it was misfortune that dogged Jack Fitch's career, latterly.

Towards what submerged canyon or marine mountain might the newly sightless, sense-free body of Jack Fitch have drifted on its downward balletic spiral? Into what dark, yet-to-be-discovered Atlantic ecosystem might the remains of his existence have begun to fragment, aided by passing strange creatures and the blind tube worms which grub about in the ultimate blackness where very soon – within hours, in fact – no earthly trace of him will remain?

And yet, it is possible – who can know for sure? – that a *sense* of this long forgotten sailor, destined to be forever unidentified, still surfaces from time to time in a fleeting patch of phosphorescence dancing through a breathing wave – in the same way as when, on dry land, a passing cloud will send a shiver along a grassy field, altering the quality of light thereabouts, and someone, or something – a hare, a rambler, a descendant – is suddenly startled by what can only be described as a mysterious prescience which stops them in their tracks. Consider this: whenever his great-great-granddaughter (Sunny is her name), shuffles to her feet in her stiff green school blazer along with her class at morning assembly to join in the chorus of the stern hymn that goes: 'Oh, hear us when we cry to thee, for those in peril on the sea' – to the bracing accompaniment of the school piano – a surprisingly vivid sensation, like icy seaweed, grips her stomach.

Poor Lil, Jack Fitch's middle daughter: she could have done with a father at the time he drowned and for a long time afterwards, hoping against hope that he would come back soon and stop the imminent disintegration of his family.

Well, then: one sinks, one swims: maybe it all depends on the quality of the navigation. Joint descendants of Captain Adam Pengarth and Ordinary Seaman Jack Fitch will find themselves on the whole craving peaceful lives in obscurity during times of unprecedented change (no notoriety, no sudden difference in circumstances, no extraordinary feats of dare-devilry, no enforced upheavals, no unexpected disaster – just ordinary normality, thank you very much). But these two progenitors chose the watery way of uncertainty.

One sinks, one swims. Fate seems to decree that it mostly boils down to this in the end, if the sea has any say in it.

7

Canada and England, 1914

Edward Pengarth, youngest son of the late Captain Adam Pengarth of Chebogue, Nova Scotia, is at present living in Montreal where, as a graduate of Queen's University, and after a period of indecision, he has been working as a teacher in order to fund a growing desire to be a doctor. For this purpose, he is enrolled on a part time basis at McGill University's medical school and burning the candle at both ends, work wise, as his father, the Captain, would have said – not without pride since it had been one of the Captain's guiding principles never to fund any of his children (Edward was the youngest) whilst letting them know that the once ample family pot of his merchant adventuring was far less abundant than it had previously been. Anyways, he had been the kind of father who always wanted his sons to make their own way in life – to kick 'em out into the world, so to speak.

Edward's 25th birthday falls barely three weeks after the news of London's declaration of war on Germany in 1914, and things are changing fast over here in Canada, too. Some nagging desire, some incipient sense of duty or just plain curiosity makes him respond to the early call put out to the colonies, and he enlists in the Canadian Army Medical Corps on the very day of his birthday, coming out of a recruiting booth with a new title ("Private"), following a successful medical examination at Valcartier Camp, the fulcrum of his country's new and suddenly frantic recruitment drive. Valcartier had been hastily built especially to process the first wave of 25,000 men of the Canadian Expeditionary Force, of which he has now become one. Along with all the other rookies, Edward is duly given a typhoid jab and presented with his full kit.

In early October 1914, after a wait of less than two months at Valcartier, he is one of the volunteer soldiers boarding the SS Meganitic for England. This ship happens to be the largest sea-going vessel built in Canada to date, a single-funnel ocean liner born of the Dominion Line Steamship Company. It seems solid, to Edward, who has maintained some knowledge of boats from his youth (though less than you might imagine). Sleek and slim, this ship's maiden voyage was in 1908, he learns, when it was deployed to carry pioneering passengers between Liverpool and Canada, and it cruised that route for six years without incident until being called into service as a troopship. In the event, it was nimble enough to escape an early submarine attack and to survive the First World War, after which it underwent two refits in order to provide accommodation for peace-time travellers between Southampton, London and Canada and, much later, economy voyages to the Caribbean. Unbeknown to Edward or to any of his fellow soldiers at the time, this very ship's moment of notoriety was yet to come when, hot on the heels of the fugitive Dr Crippen and his mistress, Inspector Dew of Scotland Yard ran the pair to ground in Canada and triumphantly transported them back to England for trial. The hardy liner made her last Atlantic crossing in 1931 after much hard service, during the course of which the sleek bloom of her early days became merely a memory inscribed on an old postcard. After two desultory years with silted sea water clucking idly against her ageing flanks, she was finally sold for scrap in Osaka, Japan. So ends the honourable life of a big ship which died a good death (of old age, the natural way), its crumbling gangways and decks taking down with them the roar of the ocean and the songs of thousands of soldiers – many of whom would never return – as well as the chatter of wave upon wave of strangers who formed intense but passing liaisons in the casual intimacy that has always found a ready reception in the libertine atmosphere infiltrating life on board an ocean going liner.

Yes, muses Edward as his eyes track the long curve of her bow, she is in the service of all we folk in the business of passing by, or passing through, and we, too, shall no doubt be discarding onto her decks some of the unwanted stuff we bring with us – our dreaming and our anxieties. To be a part of that "we" feels portentous to him.

A little later, Edward tries hard not to look down at the sea from his position by the rail on the main deck. His stomach feels like a football bobbing about on an unstable oil patch. He has inherited neither a single trace of his ancestors' sea legs, nor his father's tendency to flirt with danger. In fact, he has his Irish mother's soft brown eyes, and unremarkable hair that has simply been deemed "OK" on his service sheet (OK for what, he wonders?). He has volunteered his religion as "Methodist". The Pengarths were typically low church through the ages – unsurprisingly, given their possible Puritan origins in England; they would sometimes describe themselves as "Free Baptists" at Chebogue Point.

On the Meganitic, now pushing eastwards across the Atlantic in choppy autumn weather which continues to test the security of Edward's centre of gravity, there are drills at 1.00am and at 2.00pm, regular marches, and comfortable lectures on first aid, most of which he is all too familiar with from his medical training so far. Edward turns up at sick parade on several mornings, enfeebled by nausea. Notwithstanding this minor setback, he forces himself to run a mile round the middle deck at night when, inexplicably, his body seems no longer to operate like a gyroscope. He times himself between the lanterns suspended from an overhanging awning which illuminate nothing of the pitch of the ocean but instead serve to force the mind back in on itself whilst the body is in motion. One or two of the other fellows are beginning to boast that they can manage up to fourteen miles at a stretch in this fashion, but he is content with far less, competing against himself alone.

On arrival at Southampton, Edward, who has been assigned to the 9th reserve battalion of the Canadian Army Medical Corps, is immediately dispatched by waiting train to Salisbury Plain, his antennae at full reach in this new country – new continent, in fact. He makes a mental note of the gentle undulations of the countryside thereabouts, surmising they must be characteristic of England. Recently scorched or newly ploughed stubble fields roll out in generous waves that he feels, weirdly, he is riding upon, since it will take his body nearly a week to feel comfortable with the leaden stability of walking on dry land. Until then, he must learn to accommodate the curious sensation of walking weightlessly, apparently in slow motion, following more than a week at sea.

He is mildly surprised to be promoted to sergeant a month later, though it takes a further year to gain his commission.

'Well, here we are,' murmurs Edward to no-one in particular, one day not long after his arrival in England.

A thoughtful person by nature, he is soon tentatively but happily exploring the kind of comradeship which fires up between fellows who find themselves in the same boat, as it were, quickly forming relationships calibrated to the exciting aura of a keenly sensed common fate binding them in such an unusually heightened way. One day, out marching along a narrow Somerset lane, he spots two old timers from afar, smoking their pipes while leaning motionless over a fence, their eyes following the progress of the newcomers entirely without expression. It must be odd for them, he figures, if their slow agricultural pursuits are suddenly invaded by the rumble of allied artillery, limber and transport wagons, not to mention the clattering hooves of mounted soldiers and the sharp clack of marching infantrymen. So Edward makes sure he nods at them in a friendly sort of way as he passes, not waiting to check for a response as the march has a momentum of its own, bearing him onward with the rest.

Later, bonded through the grunted exchange of wry jokes, bearish teasing and the necessity of generally lending a hand when summoned, he learns he is to be billeted at somewhere called West Down North with a detachment of others assigned to the Canadian medical corps, and in no time at all they are setting to and pitching their tents, as instructed.

For two days the weather is kind to them, as he duly writes home with much to record in a scribbled series of terse remarks – 'Clear and cold to start, becoming warm midday and slowly declining into misty evenings here,' adding with an optimism in keeping with all he relates: '…our tents are certainly not uncomfortable, particularly being boarded, and the palliasses they use for mattresses feel snug at night, I'll say'.

Then, with the mean-spiritedness they have been

warned that English weather possesses, it turns with a vengeance, producing day after day of steady rain resulting, almost immediately, in oozing mud underfoot, several inches thick. Never mind, thinks Edward, it's only to be expected. Except that on the night of October 20, while the camp slumbers, the guy ropes and the canvas of the tents – by now entirely waterlogged – begin to contract, and one by one the tents start to collapse, causing great confusion all round in the pitch dark.

Perhaps this incident persuades those in charge of camps which had been entirely "dry" until then to allow the rookies limited periods of moistening, with alcohol to be consumed within a designated hour at noon, plus three bonus hours during the evenings – strictly beer only. It is well known that since their recent arrival the Canadians have acquired a reputation for buying quantities of forbidden liquor at the nearby villages, so this compromise to bring it out in the open is welcomed by all. In the temporarily "wet" canteens, Edward and his comrades can now relax in hot, reeking surroundings fogged with smoke, singing songs and telling their stories, glad to listen to an impromptu orchestra of Jews' harps and mouth organs, or to join in a clog dance, or to accept an invitation to play a game of chess. Alternatively, some of them are equally happy to queue for a vacant chair at a writing desk in the "dry" canteen, until the bugle signals it is time to return to their tents.

Well, it rains without pity all that autumn and they grow used to being in damp, spongy uniforms that lose their shape and shrink and become lumpy. Edward learns first hand about the particular unhealthiness of English damp, coming to know it as a kind of virus-hatching evil for incubating debilitating colds and 'flu that begin to speed around the camp. He notes how these ailments can quickly mutate into more serious pulmonary complaints and it isn't long before he gets to know one or two men in the bleakness of that first camp who go on to contract spinal meningitis. News of such serious illness chases infection across the camp faster than gossip, wiping the smiles off people's faces and making them sombre, as though it might be a harbinger of what is to come, whose moving finger is even now poised for fatal selection, were they to know it.

Then, in early November, they are treated to a visit from the King of England himself, and what a boost this turns out to be. As this small man of great presence, in full uniform, steps out to receive their salute, a kind of miracle occurs, or at least a good omen, they all agree: the sun bursts forth from a temporary rift in the clouds and flashes like a searchlight across a sea of gleaming wet bayonets. This is the life, thinks Edward, warmed and cheered. Morale is undoubtedly rising.

It needs to be, because the 2nd Stationery Hospital, to which Edward is now assigned, is about to be shipped to France.

Barely four days after the king's visit, in the early hours of the morning and by the dull glow of candles and misty lanterns, their packing starts in earnest. In the pouring rain which, it turns out, has only paused to honour the king, lorries are crammed full, each with around forty tons of camp supplies and hospital necessities, to envious cheers from those who must remain on Salisbury Plain, reduced to watching from their blotting paper tents a development which can't help but bring home to them the serious purpose of why it is that they are actually here.

Awaiting the 2nd Stationery at Southampton they confront a stately Indian liner, its markings barely discernible. Once loaded with men and freight, it finally shivers almost noiselessly from the harbour under complete darkness, as is customary in times of war.

On board, there is no question of taking a nap, despite the previous night of broken sleep. Edward slopes against the railings, eyeing the lifeboats. Mercifully, for him, the sea turns out to be utterly, eerily calm in the English Channel that night, once they get underway. There is no sound at all apart from the gentle hissing of the ship's languid wash and a soft groaning from the direction of the engine room, somewhere deep inside and below where he stands.

During the next few hours, a sustained hush envelops the sleepy men on the deck, most of them gazing out in anticipation of the dull glow which appears before dawn, just as ghostly shapes begin to emerge to stern. A whisper goes round that these are the torpedo-carrying destroyers which have been deployed to escort them, becoming vaguely recognisable as the sky begins to turn a greenish grey. The searchlight on board shifts from larboard to starboard without ceasing, back and forth in a manner that under other circumstances would surely have lulled Edward dangerously toward sleep, still standing, drawn into the sensuous rhythm of its sweeping of the sea's surface for signs of an enemy periscope.

At a certain point during this journey, he spots the ship's wash disappearing altogether just as all sound ceases, apart from the pulsing huff of the engine. All Edward can surmise is that they must be at "dead slow," watching and waiting in extreme suspense. He has a feeling that his father, Captain Adam, would be entirely at home on such a night, and imagines him frozen with concentration, pipe in his mouth but wholly unstartled by this development – unlike Edward himself. At a certain point, the big liner shiftily sends out a muffled burp on its siren, to be answered by tentative whistles from the pair of guardian ships flanking it. Inching forward, this tortuous crossing continues for a further day and a night while the fog thickens, and when they at last reach Le Havre it is to reflect that what was normally a twelve hour journey has taken an astonishing two and a half days. Lost days. Days at sea.

After landing in France, they lose no time in setting up a Field Hospital and soon afterwards commence their march towards the front, taking grim pride in the knowledge that it is the Canadians' main mission in this war to prevent the German army reaching the Channel ports.

By the middle of the month, after the heaviest enemy bombardment of the first battle of Ypres, the citizens of that town can be seen embarking upon their desolate, cowed exodus, watched from under cover by Edward and his Canadian colleagues in grave, horrified silence. Poisonous gas, in the form of a three mile wide cloud of chorine and bromide, threatens to descend upon these people. It is slow to clear, and will cause severe chest irritation to anyone unlucky enough to be caught up in it. Edward can scarcely believe his eyes. Unable to give the aid his instinct prompts him to do, and overwhelmed by the sense of a dreadful inevitability about it, he and his comrades can do nothing but observe this pitiful caravan of ordinary people displaced from their homes, carrying with them a crazy cornucopia of hurriedly assembled goods on their backs, in their arms, in prams, in wheelbarrows and in a miscellany of carts, some of them drawn by dogs because the horses have long since been taken for use by the army. It seems an unbearably dismal and shameful state of affairs, to Edward.

Two days after this event – as well as once more the

following August, 1915 – he is deemed ill enough "with 'flu" to merit two, then four days of discharge from duty. But he isn't a quitter. No, sir. And he is learning fast, this would-be doctor.

In fact, as he was later to relate in gruff terms to a few select medical colleagues back home, Edward's seminal experience during his first period in wartime Belgium had already been gained at a dressing station which was little more than a cavity dug into the bank of the Ypres Canal. Down the bank, during heavy periods of bombardment, he would receive the wounded as they were rolled below for treatment. They got used to proceeding quickly, efficiently, not dwelling on it but rather getting on with what must be done. It was astonishing and shocking, but there was no time for anything else, not even time for his mind to find a place for it within some kind of wider context. Given the nature of the bombardment, wounds were typically vicious and needed drastic, on-the-spot remedies. Edward found himself responding with the kind of urgency that he knew would never be replicated at McGill University back home, let alone in any training hospital back home in Canada. Broken people – yes, soldiers were still people, though often rendered unrecognisable as such – just kept turning up, with hands, feet, legs missing and bleeding stumps that required tourniquets prior to impromptu operations. In equal numbers came those with internal injuries: abdominal walls shot away, faces horribly mutilated, bones reduced to loose shards, fresh body cavities desperately filled by ambulance men with dirt and mud and bits of equipment and clothing – whatever they could lay their hands on to stop the flow of blood – while others raced for more sophisticated medical help. Thank the Lord, at least, for a nearby brewery which donated water for mass delousing. And for a level head, on the whole, though it rarely felt as though he was himself at all those days; a simulacrum, maybe, but an age away from the former Edward Pengarth, that pleasant, easy-going chap.

In November 1915 – following a period of some seven months of active service – it is time for him to be sent to the Canadian base in France for passage to England with a view to being discharged in order to resume his medical studies back in Canada, having done his bit. But just before Christmas there is a change of plan which, though he cannot know it, will alter the course of his life forever, though it takes a little while to unravel. This phase begins when he is made a Captain and transferred to Shorncliffe Camp, Folkestone which, he understands, is a key staging post for Canadians in transit to France. Random alterations to the direction a person *thinks* is his personal journey unsettle him no less than many of his colleagues, even though in the past he had always envisaged his destiny in the form of a strong black line, carefully ruled and pointing with confidence straight ahead. Now, the shape of that line is more like a collapsed elbow – and one that, despite all his recently gained medical experience, he is for the present unable to set straight.

On dry land again – as opposed to the disease-ridden mud in France (that brown porridge churned up by running soldiers, those craters where bombs had landed which instantly became quagmires of filthy pulp) he is about to be assigned to medical work at one of the Canadian Casualty Clearing Stations adjacent to Shornecliffe camp where soldiers too damaged to treat in France will eventually be dispatched.

It is instantly apparent to him on his arrival that all

along the south coast, extraordinary changes have been taking place since he was last there (which feels like a very long time indeed). It seems that the active war situation as experienced by civilians is, on the whole, still being borne with what he perceives as grumbling enthusiasm back here, if such an oxymoron can be made to hold water (evidently, the English are good at this sort of linguistic turn). But these are truly unusual times. He isn't the first person to feel that time itself goes through short phases of being obliged to stand to attention, given the constant cause for sudden alarm turning everything haywire and putting everyone on intermittent alert.

Local properties, he reads in a newspaper, are being hastily commissioned to accommodate the wounded as well as those struck down with an *epidemic* of venereal disease (there is a Canadian Special Hospital specifically set up for the purpose of treating the clap and syphilis, he notes, in an old workhouse building). Several Folkestone hotels have already been commandeered by the army. Further inland even local halls are being requisitioned: Masonic, Quaker, Anglican, Baptist – this war is no respecter of religion – parish rooms, churches, secondary schools and big houses – all of them at the ready, in order to gather in wounded men coming home on the boat trains, broken and in need of mending. Along with farm buildings, drill halls, mission halls …

Shorncliffe Camp, where the Canadians are based, is a fairly extensive settlement of modern brick buildings laid out in military lines adjoining Cheriton village and Folkestone itself, he discovers. On a clear day at Shorncliffe, outside on the high plateau, you can make out Dover and the Romney Marshes, while straight ahead lies the English Channel, unnaturally alive and bearing hundreds of boats of all sizes constantly busying themselves along the English Channel.

Faintly visible, on most days, is that hazy margin of land in the far distance which is the coast of France, and for Edward that place never fails to arouse a sense of almost supernatural foreboding followed, more prosaically, by the rumblings of nausea in his stomach at the dread of having to undertake any further sea journeys.

It doesn't take long for him to learn about what has become an apocryphal story at Shornecliffe during his absence. It is told like this: some time after lights out one night – unseen and unheard by the slumbering soldiers – a dark shadow insinuated itself between the moon and the base and hovered there for a short time before moving slowly off. The low sound it emitted may even have entered the dreams of some of the Canadian soldiers there, setting off sleepy images of unidentified sensuousness or impending doom, but it was barely loud enough to cause anyone to wake up fully. Next day, though, they were left in no doubt that this nocturnal apparition was real enough: it was a German Zeppelin intent on raiding London. In the event, it lost its course, dropping five bombs on Otterpool Camp nearby and causing a number of casualties. It is with this story in mind that Edward knows for certain that war is like the constant presence of deadly infection hovering round them all. He also knows that there will be no getting away from it of his own volition.

Of necessity – unconsciously at first – he therefore begins to seek out keener means of respite than the games of darts and lonely strolls along the coast to Beachy Head that have proven to be innocuous diversions so far.

8

Acton and Kent, 1915

On the face of it, what possible connection could there be in the trajectory of Lilian Smithyes's life so far between Birkbeck Road, Acton, and a surburban street in the small town of Cheriton, Kent? Nevertheless, eighteen months after Bill Smithyes left for Tottenham Marshes, it is here that she and her son Thomas have secured lodgings, and Lilian appears more relaxed than she has ever been, happy enough to laugh out loud with her large boy and lay down on the floor with no other purpose than to tickle him, from time to time. How her face is transformed when the thinly pointed bow of her lips expands into a smile, causing the forget-me-not blue eyes to sparkle. Do other people in her orbit know how sweet she looks when she laughs, how delicate and warm? Does *she* know it, herself? Hardly. Why risk exposure by relaxing her guard? No, Lilian knows better than that. There is a visceral intelligence about her, born of a rat-like will to survive at all costs which has not served her badly since her mother died. *I must keep my wits about me*: this is her first thought on waking, though not in words – rather, via a familiar, warning sensation floating into her consciousness. So it is that her lips – sealed against the world and all its potential hostility – *will* maintain their thin line of resistance, for the most part. After all, her wits are all she has, apart from Thomas. They must be made to work. Hard.

Soon after Bill left Acton Lilian's world seemed to perform a slow pirouette on its own axis. She had quickly become aware that young ladies who were not squeamish were yearning to become temporary nurses: it was all the rage. To this end, they set about acquiring rudimentary professional skills with whatever systematic resourcefulness and brisk enthusiasm their upbringing had provided them with. Others were equally energetic: knitting gloves and socks, selling flags, gathering books and other comforts to be dispatched to the soldiers. They were proving adept at commandeering Church Army and WMCA halls for their activities, such women, and forming new committees in support of the war effort. Lilian fancied *the idea* of being a nurse herself, mostly for the status that went with it, but she was clear in her mind that such a notion was only a silly, somewhat romantic whim. And so she opted to do what she knew best at that time – serving.

And Thomas? Well, he is used to a fair amount of chaos in his infant life, with new people bustling around him through these, his earliest London days – days so devoid of familiar routine that he might well end up asleep in his mother's arms on a mid-evening train from London back to Birkbeck Road, Acton. This is because his mother, alert for an opportunity, has responded to a leaflet pasted on a fence in Acton Park spotted on one of their customary walks. From now on, whether he likes it or not, Thomas will be obliged to walk rather than be pushed in his pram, fastened into a harness on a lead which his mother controls in her small gloved hand.

See him now, squatting by one of the trestle tables

behind which she stands, on the forecourt of Victoria Station. Becoming bored, he teases the white table cloth until the cups begin to rattle for a prank to while away the time, and for this he receives a summary slap.

It is Lilian's recently acquired role to boil up, and keep on the boil, water in a large metal urn. That is all. But it is a crucial task, because this urn will produce vast quantities of tea for the uniformed crowds and their hangers-on and loved ones milling around the station, periodically coalescing when a train approaches as they prepare for the daily embarkations and farewells that constitute but one aspect of the ebb and flow of the war. Part of her can't fail to be distracted by the mournful, uneasily shuffling dance of so many farewells. She is both drawn towards and repelled by the amount of raw emotion she witnesses, including the sight of children weeping in incomprehension at the exceptional nature of such a flurry. For instance, just look at the way the men hang out of the windows of the carriages – they don't normally do that – in order to grab somebody's pleading fingers for one last time. Soon will come the warning shriek of a whistle followed by a blast of escaping steam in the sooty atrium of the station, both harbingers of unimaginable journeys ahead.

Though exhausted and perspiring, Lilian – her small form folded inside an over-sized white, floor-length apron – is frequently taken aback when she realises that she has somehow managed to join a peripheral current of history at the very point when something important is happening, yet to be properly defined. That has to be an achievement of sorts, surely, for one who has been endowed with so very little. Doesn't it?

Thomas, his restraining strap tied round a back leg of the wooden trestle, bangs his head against the post, picks up a discarded sandwich and gives a rattle to the marbles in his pocket. He doesn't complain.

One day, as the clamour on one of the platforms subsides, Lilian allows her imagination to pursue one of the departing trains a little way on its journey out of the station towards who knows where, managing to conjure up a vaguely bucolic image of the south coast which she has never seen – the very area where her parents began their married life. She finds herself rather envying all those riding on the trains out of Victoria. She covets the simple excitement that surely might be had by going *somewhere*, anywhere.

But wait … Who is this? Here comes Nellie Fox in the company of a newly arrived group of women bearing fresh trolley loads of cakes. They are up for the day, it transpires, these boisterous Kent women, and they lose no time in setting up their own trestles to complement those already assembled. Their banter nearby is causing Lilian to prick up her ears, alerted by an almost faded memory of the sound of her own dead father's distinctive accent. When they begin to sit down and unpack their lunch from a large wicker hamper, one of the newly arrived Kent women – it is Nellie herself – beckons Lilian over to join them. 'Don't be lonely, lovey. Come and share with us, why don't you?'

Nellie and Lilian hit it off from the start, sensing in each other the common threads of kindred spirit. 'Is he yours?' enquires Nellie of Thomas, tipping his damp behind with her toe. 'Let him off the leash, poor lamb, just for a minute … Hal*lo*, dove,' Nellie beams down at him, after getting her own way. 'I might have a treat for you, young man. Now let me see …' She fishes in one of her voluminous pockets, eyeing him conspiratorially, preparing to surprise him with a stick of liquorice.

Thomas perks up. He, too, reckons she might be a kindred spirit.

That's always how Nellie was, mused Lilian some years later, at a time when she was putting all her mistakes behind her, or so she thought. *Coming up with something*: that was Nellie to a T.

At the same time, on this particular day Lilian is quick to perceive that the thing about Nellie, during their first encounter, is that despite having the friendliest, merriest soul on earth, she has no powers of discrimination whatsoever. Just a permanent, unquenchable sense of jollity and an ability to see the funny side of things. Lilian figures that such a nature will carry Nellie wherever the wind blows. In a way, decides Lilian, Nellie must be made for the times we are living through. She admires that ... is rather attracted by it. So much so that by the end of the afternoon, Lilian has learned all about a place called Shornecliffe, near where Nellie lives, and where, according to Nellie, they are always looking for women to work. 'It's a treat,' she confides, with a wink, 'having all those young soldiers on tap. Why don't you come down one day, ducks? Come and see. Come and stay, why don't you?'

Later, heaving Thomas into his bed at the end of another long day, Lilian can't help thinking very seriously about Nellie Fox's spontaneous (and no doubt very foolish) idea of her investigating this place in the vicinity of Folkestone which she understands is the epicentre for the big ships carrying colonial infantrymen across the Channel in order to join the fighting. But she can't contain a mounting urge to take Nellie up on her offer. It won't go away, propelled, maybe, by a subliminal imprint of her own mother's experiences at Portsmouth years before. It is the desire to *be there*, at the dockside, in the thick of it. After all, she tells herself, hasn't Bill just followed the same lure? Why not her, then?

So she takes Nellie up on her offer, spends an exploratory day on the coast with her, likes what she sees. Once she makes up her mind it takes very little time to extricate herself from Birkbeck Avenue, to purchase a cheap valise to carry essentials for both herself and Thomas, and to arrive with him at Victoria station with a feeling of self-importance – as one of the travellers this time rather than a perpetual onlooker. Is this, too, a foolishness? For now, she reckons not. It is enough to dispatch her from the foul vapours of Acton and the sad, murky streets of war-time London, a small figure with a child and a suitcase, soon consumed and rendered invisible by the unabated milling of the crowd.

And her new friend Nellie is waiting for her, as promised, at the station in Folkestone, full of glee that she has a new mate, a potential side-kick. She is something of a novelty – the first real friend that Lilian has ever had. Grabbing Lilian's arm – an arm less generous than her own and yielding a little stiffly – Nellie guides her towards a waiting omnibus. There's a narrowly averted disaster when Thomas decides to do an impromptu hop from curb to road, missing being crushed against a clattering horse-drawn ambulance by inches. Then they are off, embarked upon the short journey out of town to Cheriton, where a room has been secured for Thomas and Lilian in the house where Nellie herself lodges.

All the while, Nellie delights in clutching at Lilian's arm in order to alert her friend to the vast expanse of the Shornecliffe military camp as the bus drones past the hooded sight of row upon row of blacked-out low buildings, on a night entirely devoid of moonlight.

9

Kent, 1915

In due course Lilian, Thomas and Nellie arrive home – which has just become a roomy, semi-detached house in Cheriton owned by a master tailor, a Mr Farthing. This house also accommodates his apprentice, Wilfred Jones, a couple who take care of the house and its garden on behalf of Mrs Farthing, and Louie, a young laundress who also lodges here but is rarely seen, given her unsociable shifts. Lilian and Thomas are to share the room recently vacated by a horse trader in his twenties who has lately been called up. This just leaves space for Nellie herself, already ensconced in the attic.

On the whole, it turns out to be a hardworking but mainly jolly household – not unlike that of the Daltons in Ealing. It hasn't occurred to Lilian to inform anyone back there of her new abode. All but lost to her in recent days is prim Violet, the sister who witnessed her marriage to Bill Smithyes. How, then, is Bill Smithyes to keep track of his wife and son? Since settling in, Lilian hasn't allowed herself to dwell on Bill at all. How far away "all that" feels now. And there's so much going on nowadays that she has hardly the time to think, anyway. So many ties are being cut, it seems – whether temporarily or permanently. Who's to know anything, given the overwhelming uncertainty of it all? Life for women left behind in Blighty must proceed the best it can in this most uncertain of worlds, that's what the papers are saying. I am not the only one in this boat, Lilian reminds herself. This always clears her mind a bit, allowing her to concentrate on the more pressing necessity of making a fresh life for herself and Thomas.

'It could either drive you to suicide or bring out the best in you, I reckon,' Mr Farthing opines one day as his assessment of the current state of things, carving a Sunday roast (one of the skinny chickens which had lately been running around outside, long since half-consumed by its own state of neurosis prior to having its neck wrung). The two young women make him smile, for the most part. He is not their father or guardian, after all, and what girls get up to these days – well, best not to enquire. As long as they pay their rent. Which they do, Lilian and Nellie.

What *do* they get up to?

For a start, they both have jobs. Nellie works for one of the laundries serving the camp which houses 40,000 Canadians – ooooh, the never-ending washing – while Lilian (who, on principle will never, never, *never* again allow herself near the washing and ironing that had been the death of her mother) has found her way to the 30-bed military hospital for Canadian officers at Shornecliffe camp for the Canadians. It's only a short walk away. While deeply envying them their easy contact with the temporarily laid up officers there, she finds she can outstare any disdain wafting her way from the hoity-toity VAD nurses who sweep by in their floor-length uniforms, full of their own importance. But it doesn't take her long to manoeuvre her way into shifts that involve serving meals in the wards, rather than scrubbing them down, and it is thus that the small, fair-haired young woman with a carefully cultivated, newly clipped

English accent bears herself with studied dignity.

Thomas remains at Ashley Avenue with Mrs Farthing while Lilian works. She turns out to be a kindly soul who takes a shine to the large, unruly boy, not having children of her own. If Lilian is working during the evening, she seems happy to put him to bed as well. For his part, Mr Farthing lends Thomas his grand pair of binoculars now and again, and attempts to teach him how to identify the flotillas of ships large and small moving across the busy sea that they can gaze at from the elevation of the front room window. Mr Farthing does his own bit for the war effort by driving his motor car alongside the motley caravan of Red Cross ambulances, Canadian Army vehicles and privately owned local vehicles which help ferry newly arrived casualties from France to their designated hospitals when their ship comes in. If the portly Farthing Landaulet with its canopied rear end is called upon, then the likelihood is that Thomas, with unrestrained whoops of delight, will accompany him down to the railway station. 'We're on a mission, boy!' its owner likes to announce.

Another pastime that Thomas relishes these days is positioning himself in front of an upstairs window where he can sometimes take in the ever-changing drama of the street below – here, a pair of gossiping nurses, arm in arm; there, the careful preparations of neighbouring ladies who provide refreshments at Shorncliffe station; and there's often the bonus of spotting the fire brigade chasing some emergency. All, likely as not, making their way down to meet an anticipated hospital train from France.

Lilian, egged on by Nellie, it must be said, starts to lose touch with Thomas a little during this period.

But oh! It is a time in her life when, not yet twenty years old, she is aware of self-consciously navigating her way through so much that is unknown, unheard of and altogether unpredictable as she sets her compass towards entirely untested straits with a catching bravado that has become more acceptable these days. And she loves it! Not that she relinquished her core of natural caution, cultivated from earlier watchfulness in Ealing – absolutely *no-one*, apart from Nellie will be let into the secret of these new adventures. All Lilian knows is that she can't for one minute afford to take her eye off the roving tiller that is tempting her this way and that towards certain treacherous or promising – whichever way you care to look at it – side channels. But in truth, the most basic fact of her present environment – that which underscores everything else – is that the place veritably *throbs* with men. How can she not be aware of them? In an instant of self-knowledge, snuffed out quickly, she asks herself: could this have been the real reason she upped sticks from Acton when Nellie beckoned?

As for the current arrangement with her new close companion: what is in it for Nellie? Perhaps it is as simple as this: that every effervescent, scatter-brained person needs an accomplice. For Nellie, the unfolding war has always been a sphere of opportunity for being a little bit more daring than the life of a lower class female would normally permit, imprisoned by the oppression of a respectability not of her making. 'What luck,' she is fond of saying to her friend, adding a gale of laughter whose echo refracts a shock wave of daring (though she lets rip anyway). 'Come on, Lil. Don't a girl deserve a bit of fun every now and then?' '*Lilian*' her friend reminds her with patience, not for the first time.

So fun will be had, when they are not working and when Thomas is safely closeted with the Farthings. They can be seen enjoying picnics during which, emboldened by the presence of each other, they (mostly Nellie, to be fair) send out teasing looks towards passing soldiers.

They can also be spotted at the regular dances at the church hall on Friday nights, set up for uniformed men on leave as well as girls hungry for a bit of company. Girls just like them.

Despite Lilian's self-discipline, it has to be said that there have been certain indiscretions by the time 1915 comes to an end ('and good riddance to it,' is Mrs Farthing's opinion on New Year's Eve as the Ashley Avenue household indulges in a bottle of port to send it on its way). Let's hope nothing backfires, is Lilian's private wish for herself, with tightly closed eyes and ears almost blocking out the din of Big Ben on the wireless. And this is Nellie's wish, too.

That same Christmas-tide, the decorations have barely been packed away before Edward Pengarth, now a battalion Medical Officer in his own right and on leave, is unexpectedly admitted to Helena Hospital for Canadian officers, with a fever. It is an annex of Shorncliffe Camp, where Lilian is in employment.

An evening arrives in early January, 1916, when out sashays Lilian from the direction of the galley of this hospital, cutting a diminutive but resolute figure as she clears the makeshift curtain dividing the ward from the cooking area. For the last half hour she has been delivering supper trays to each of the bed-ridden invalids.

After three evenings of this he is sufficiently well to notice her – to anticipate her, even – aware of feeling a lift in his spirits as he follows her small footsteps across the wooden floor, efficiently clicking to and fro.

'The little lady,' he whispers to his companion in the next bed on the ward, who had been there longer than he. 'Who might she be, do you suppose?'

'They call her Lilian,' he replies, with a knowing smile

whose significance Edward fails to register because his eyes are trained in expectation until she swings backwards through the galley curtain once more.

On the day of his discharge from hospital, he takes his evening meal dressed in his uniform, sitting in the chair by his bed, as though to signal to all and sundry his return to health. 'Lilian,' he ventures, waiting for her reaction to his use of her name. 'Miss Lilian,' he corrects himself when there is none. 'I wonder if you would do me the honour of dining with me one day. But not here, of course.' Her composure pleases him, as does the small smile she allows to escape at his feeble joke.

It is Mr Farthing himself, now, who transports her in his motor car to a once grand hotel on the sea front, where Edward, smoking his pipe, is waiting for her in the foyer. The way she steps out of her rather fine "taxi" impresses itself on Edward's mind, as does her easy handling of the cutlery formally laid out in the dining room. Her Englishness endows her with a certain degree of formality, he perceives – there is an archness about it, which is not unattractive to him and seems superior to the more fluid manners and casual drawl of the Canadian girls he has known back home, even the richer ones whose brothers were his fellow students at med. school. He feels easy with her demeanour, able to address her without self-consciousness. To probe her in any way, despite his fascination with her, would simply be bad manners, and the little she divulges about herself on this first encounter only frees his imagination to add colour to the picture he is forming of her: the fact that she grew up in Ealing, a rather genteel village west of London, apparently; the fact that neither of her parents are still alive and that she is living now with an elderly aunt and uncle nearby; some well-placed French phrases which suggest she had a governess when she was growing up. None of it she denies. It adds up to a self-contained, quietly spoken young lady of taste and discretion who is modestly willing to be entertained by him.

Her lack of familiarity fascinates him from the start. Even her shy reluctance to meet his fellow officers or to introduce him to the aunt and uncle with whom she lives. No matter: this is the British way, he deduces. Fine, he'll go along with it. And it means that each time they meet they are likely to be alone, so that he can gaze at her discreetly that bit more closely.

He likes what he sees.

'Lil won't share her Canadian with anyone,' Nellie teases one night in the Farthings' sitting room. But this same Lil refuses to rise to the bait and gives her a cautionary stare.

'He sounds like quite a catch,' remarks Mrs Farthing.

'Da da da da catchee monkee,' chants Nellie somewhat enigmatically, squinting down at her knitting, a remark that sends Lilian's memory reeling backwards to a horribly crude remark her mother once made by way of instant, unrequested advice, with a leer that attempted, but failed, to generate a spark of intimacy between them, woman to woman, as it were. Easy-going Nellie, perhaps *she* needs that sort of reminder more than Lilian these days, having already explained to her friend that she possesses "ways" of making sure a girl will be "all right," including a makeshift rubber douche she has demonstrated to her friend, should she require one. All credit to Nellie, a generous soul at heart, she is without grudge or envy since Edward has come on scene, and quite ready to become invisible when required. What a lark! 'I'd do the same for you, Nellie,' Lilian has assured her, 'you know that. Just give it a little while, if you please.'

In April he treats her once again to a series of meals out in different hotels, and at one of these Lilian has cause to wonder if her number is up when an officer in uniform with one of the VAD nurses on his arm pauses by their table and Edward gets up to shake his hand. 'I say ... ?' ventures this officer, glancing down towards Lilian, as though trying to recall where they might have met before. She avoids his eyes and will not respond, causing him to complete his own sentence: 'well, maybe not.' Edward apologises to her when the pair move on. His colleague is clumsy: he made a mistake, embarrassing them all. Edward feels sorry if she felt assailed, he tells her, particularly when she was well-mannered enough to retain her composure. He does like that about her. He really does.

During May, on most Sundays as the weather begins to soften, it is their habit to rendezvous on the sea-front and wander down to Sandgate village not far off to stroll, arm in arm, along the beach. In June, she surprises herself with an unexpected wave of emotion when, on her evening round, she learns that he has been admitted once again to the officers' section of Shorncliffe Hospital. This time it is more serious.

She openly allows him to grip her hand while he explains from his hospital bed what happened earlier in the week. 'You know, dear,' he recounts, 'after we bid our farewells last Sunday I went out on a motor bike belonging to one of the fellows, and I guess I drove it too fast or I wasn't concentrating, or something like that. It was up in the hills on a narrow road and all of a sudden I found myself in a spin.' She listens intently, sitting still and straight-backed, offering him her full attention.

'I don't know ... I got up somehow and walked the two miles back, and that was fine, but there was blood in my water for two or three days and a helleva pain down my left side, right here. Yesterday morning, wouldn'cha know it, my batman apparently couldn't wake me up. He tried for about half an hour, then I came to but I was so dizzy I just fell over onto my knees.' Lilian is wide-eyed with solicitude. 'They reckon I had some form of convulsion in the night. My tongue was swollen, and my left kidney had taken a blow. So, my dear, I shan't be wanting that,' he gestured towards her supper tray. 'Only milk and water for your poor invalid for now.' She squeezes his hand in sympathy. She likes the sound of 'your', though he looks rather pale, poor thing. He won't loosen his grip on her hand, and looks into the summer blue of her eyes once he has had his say.

This incident marks a significant point in their relationship.

There is so much to fear now, they all agree at Ashley Avenue after scanning Mr Farthing's daily newspaper which is taking an increasingly bellicose tone about the need to 'THRASH THE HUN', once and for all. Leave aside abroad – there is much flux at home these days – you only have to look at the torpedo boats carving out their busy wakes offshore and setting up white criss-cross patterns in the water, as though these vessels were bent upon creating a macabre board game. Or walk almost anywhere in a town swollen by a constantly altering population of military people, whose purpose and destination you could mostly only guess at.

At the same time, Edward has been trying to rationalise his own impressions of the irrational lives they are all living, soldiers and civilians alike. There is a deceptively treacherous side, as he sees it, to the apparent freedom they are enjoying here in England. He fears his liberty could be snatched away at any moment. The only real certainty in his life at present is Lilian, here at the hospital by day, in his dreams at night, and by his side when there is free time. Before the summer is out he has proposed to her and she has accepted him.

What is she thinking of?

At first, she struggles for an honest answer to give both to herself and to Nellie, the only other person who has an inkling about the existence of one Bill Smithyes. But, for the life of her, Lilian can only come up with another question, growing more urgent as her meetings with her new fiancé progress, which boils down to this: how is Edward going to feel if he finds out he has been duped? The fear was in the equivocal 'if'. But no, he won't, she tells herself. Why should he? It's as though Bill Smithyes has ceased to exist. Maybe this is the truth of it: maybe he *has* gone for good, lost on some foreign battle field. A fantasy along these lines about a state of widowhood begins to act like an anaesthetic on her sense of reason.

It is not a wholly unfamiliar fog, this sort of self-denial, in fact it is rather like the fog that accompanied her back home after a certain day's work back in Ealing when she was in service (a chilly shiver ripples through her body at the memory of how she and Bill Smithyes clumsily seduced each other, back then). Still, the mirror of herself that Edward *will* hold up to her reveals someone else now: a pretty, fair-haired little woman with a slightly stiff and mysterious air about her, by no means all of it put on. She likes what she sees of herself in his mirror. If this could really be her, then it has value. It is the first glimpse of herself that suggests that *she* might have value.

He takes her into Folkestone and buys her a ring which she gladly wears in his presence only, for the time being.

After all, Bill Smithyes would have found her by now if he'd really wanted to. Wouldn't he?

10

They were married in All Saints Church in Cheriton, near Folkestone, in early 1917. Nellie witnessed the occasion, along with a lone woman who appeared to be deep in thought beside one of the graves that morning, sitting on a bench in the churchyard. *No ostentation*, Lilian had pleaded to Edward, not in war time. It wouldn't be right. He would have liked at least to include some of the men he worked and lived with in a muted celebration of the event, but was permitted to rope in only the best of them, a fellow he had got to know through his rehabilitation work at the hospital. She got her way with every last detail – claiming ethical grounds. So no photographs were taken, and instead of a reception the four of them sat down for the simplest of teas at the hotel where Edward and Lilian had enjoyed their first meal together.

The Farthings were not invited. After much deliberation, Lilian dealt with this in a carefully composed note to Mrs Farthing later that day, in which she pleaded, as she had done with Edward, her desire that any celebration would not be appropriate, as she was sure they would agree. Whether they took offence or not she did not wait to find out. One Saturday morning a car arrived for Nellie, Lilian and Thomas, and only one of them returned to the Farthing household that evening.

There was an awkward moment in the sacristy when the vicar routinely asked Lilian to supply details for a column on the marriage certificate headed "Condition".

'I have to ask you: have you been married before?' he queried, just as he had done many times before. 'Or should I put "spinster?"' Dependent upon what she replied, a number of fateful outcomes suggested themselves to Lilian simultaneously, one of which involved the image of a policeman. 'She's a widow,' interjected Edward. He had sympathy with his poor little lady's reluctance to talk about the Mr Smithyes he had lately learned about, father of the boy Thomas, who had evidently not been as fortunate as himself, since he understood that that gentleman was a casualty of the war. He squeezed her hand. The maiden name "Fitch" that Lilian began to write was duly crossed out and "Smithyes" substituted as Lilian's current (and about to be relinquished) surname. It was in this name that she signed.

So it came to pass, this most unlikely of unions between the daughter of Jack Fitch, ordinary seaman of Portsmouth, and the son of Captain Adam Pengarth, merchant mariner of Nova Scotia, Canada.

They had just three days together as man and wife before Edward was dispatched to the London Headquarters of the Canadian Army Medical Corps, where he spent the next fortnight in training, after Lilian and Thomas had been established in married quarters Edward had acquired for them within the camp compound which now took on the aspect of a wonderfully unassailable garrison to Lilian, who was only too willing and prepared to lay low until his return.

So far so good.

Once back, Edward was put on standby for active duty with the 9th Canadian Reserve Battalion based at Seaford, just west of Eastbourne, another base for around 3,000 men of the Canadian Medical Corps. The couple endured several false alarms but at the end of

June, 1917, the call finally came. Before he left, he made sure that Lilian, then expecting Dorothy, their first child, was comfortably established in what he intended to be a more homely first floor apartment in the quiet Meads area of Eastbourne.

Here, as elsewhere along the south coast, the locals warmed to the Canadian medics and she would enjoy feeling safe for a while. They recognised a certain confidence, an informal classiness about these serving men who came from the New World – which, in tune with the rules of progress, had to be a better place than where they were, unavoidably caught up in a vortex of disruption, enemy assault and food shortages. They liked the Canadians because they were reassuringly informal as well as being generous with goods from their well-stocked military stores. Equally, it was perfectly fine that the Canadians appeared to be more worldly than they were. A pleasing reciprocity grew up between the south coast folk and the foreign soldiers when the local people found they, in their turn, were able to put a few perks in the way of the Canadians and their entourage, which was satisfying all round.

Lilian, for one, was pleased to take advantage of the reduced bus fares into the town on the Meads route to which, as a brand new Canadian by proxy, she was entitled. Despite being weighed down by her pregnancy, she stood tall in her diminutive frame. It was unfortunate – yes it was – that her present state had necessitated "burying" Bill Smithyes, erasing him from her record as though he had never been. Truly, she bore him no ill feeling. It had been done not with unkindness, nor even much in the way of cunning. In the end, she had been obliged to employ a certain necessary ruthlessness when it came to dealing with annoying detail. That was all.

When she discovered there was a twice weekly coach

service from Eastbourne to the Grosvenor Hotel, in the area of Victoria, London, a dangerous whim tempted her to embark on a small adventure in order to peer vicariously at past haunts and maybe even make contact with her sisters, back in Acton, now that she was so auspiciously settled. Of course, it must remain pure fantasy. For one thing, her newly sensitive stomach rebelled at the thought of such a halting journey, made worse by the accompanying fumes of coal gas swiftly cancelling what had likely been a weak incentive in the first place. Her internal survival monitor also obliged her to caution why she would put at risk the good fortune she had lately achieved by meddling with what had indeed been consigned to the past. Anyhow, she was Lilian Pengarth, wife of a Canadian officer, one who was about to complete his qualification as a physician and surgeon back in Canada, once this damned war was over. She was a *doctor's* wife, for heaven's sake, a member of the professional class now, and she was entirely at one with him as far as making their new life together in another country was concerned.

Why look back?

She did not find it at all hard to pass the few months remaining, prior to Dorothy's birth, in almost complete seclusion in Eastbourne. Edward provided her with bills paid advance, some cash, and a daily maid. While her body grew heavier, her mind was lighter than it had ever been.

Before he left, he had taken the trouble to explain what she was to do if evacuation was suddenly ordered – grab what perishable food was to hand together with a kettle or saucepan and a mug and tie it all with string in a blanket around her shoulders, then get herself and Thomas to the nearest Parish meeting point to await instructions from the head special constable. Mercifully, the church bells never did herald such an event. Instead, Lilian and Thomas found themselves being simply mother and son together during the balmy days and early nights that autumn, a short-lived golden period for them both which would never again be repeated.

Halcyon days in Eastbourne ... There is plenty of activity in the air to watch while she and Thomas stroll along the front, wondering whether to stop for tea at the Winter Garden or at the White Corner Restaurant. Will a passing airship spread its shadow across the ground like a black silk sheet – only to be stamped on with much patriotic shouting by Thomas? The bi-planes from the pilots' training centre are constantly buzzing overhead and his sport is pretending – so loudly that Lilian has to shush him severely – to shoot them down. He revels in the band playing at the Royal Parade Bandstand, marching with exaggeratedly high knees in time to the music. He goes on to perform a kind of mime with enthusiastic cheers when they come upon a loud group of soldiers wearing their leather braces wide over their white vests as they play their game of six-a-side football. In such ways, Thomas lives out his own early destiny as boy-in-time-of-war on the home front. He seems happy enough. His antics even allow Lilian time for a lazy daydream or two while she rests her back on a bench.

By day, the pair of them often purchase fish fresh from the sea, courtesy of a permanent line of local anglers on the high groin. Formal rationing won't arrive until January, 1918 and they are managing to eat well, anyway, stocking up on vegetables and fruit from the nearby allotments for a diet quite unlike the meagre fare doled out at the National Kitchen for poor people down by the sea. They even enjoy decent bread, steering clear of the grey "national loaf" made with flour and mashed potato. Everyone seems to be involved in some kind of war effort apart from those women who are obviously expecting, like Lilian, and can't be called upon. 'Good morning,' she always nods in her softly dignified way to the women in strange looking dungarees at Lovely's Cavendish Place Garage when she passes. Not so long ago one of them offered her a cigarette, which she politely declined.

And by night, they both look forward to the crackling black-and-white films provided on Sundays once a fortnight at Summerdown Camp, thanks to equipment on loan from the Tivoli Cinema.

One November afternoon, following seven months in France – a tour of duty which included caring for wounded Canadian soldiers during the battle of Vimy Ridge – Edward, weighing nearly two stone less and appearing somewhat gaunt, arrives back in England, just four days before his daughter Dorothy is born. By Christmas, he is working at No 14 Canadian General Hospital, Eastbourne, the former Eastbourne Military hospital where he is required to start piecing together the best he can the battered bodies of those who have survived being shipped back. Some of those poor creatures are able to use the bowling rink at Gildredge Park, while others use the free sea-front deck chairs, Lilian notices. There are so many of them, their largely immobile, expressionless faces wrinkling against the constant breeze coming in from the Channel and wondering, no doubt, what could possibly hit them next.

In fact, there is nothing more keenly fastened upon than the idea of the future, at this point, expanding in the imagination of practically everyone, whatever their condition. The very essence of it seems borne on the sea air they breathe, and they take it in deeply. Surely, they tell each other, there will be the prospect of a better common goal when all this is done and over with?

Lilian and Edward find no difficulty settling down together as a new young family in Eastbourne during the first six months of 1918 when Dorothy, their new daughter, is an infant. These months have left them with something fundamental in common: a wholehearted desire to utterly put behind them the recent past. Edward, after all, is recuperating, and at Easter he spends two more short periods as an in-patient himself, suffering first with another kidney infection, then piles. He is finally demobbed in July 1918 and within ten days he is transported down to the docks in a local GP's splendid Sunbeam Tourer, about to set sail for Canada on a home-bound troopship in the company of several thousand Canadians, leaving Lilian with his solemn promise that it won't be long before she and the kids will be able to follow him.

In the event, it will be a while before this can happen, because their second son, Kenneth, is on the way by then and after the war ends in November it proves the devil of a job to secure a sea passage in the great rush of people westwards, though Edward, missing her dreadfully, continues to do his utmost from over there.

FULL STEAM AHEAD

11

At sea, 1919

What a sight! With a heightened sense of nervous tension, not at all unpleasant, Lilian fixes her eyes on the array of tangled paper streamers in perky primary colours rolling down the ship's shore-side flank, setting up a frantic chatter in the wind. Plucky little paper ringlets, thinks Lilian. It transpires that they are ritualistically tied to deck railings before a sailing and tossed out by those about to leave, in the general direction of friends and loved ones waiting on the pier far below to see them off. It's as though these gaudy strips of paper are the ship's passengers' way of half-heartedly bidding the great ship to reconsider its journey by fruitlessly attempting to tether it one last time to all that is familiar. Of course, in reality it's impossible to hold a ship's departure or even delay it for one second longer than necessary: streamer throwing is ultimately a flimsy, sentimental gesture since those going and those staying all know very well that there is really no point in trying to alter a course already set.

As she ponders this and much else in passing, Lilian considers the enormity of her position, for she has to be embarking on the journey of her life, and she knows it. She revels in it. She allows herself to wonder whether, thanks to this very sailing, she will at last be able to mount a real challenge in the face of what, on the face of her own internal barometer, had always pointed to a lesser destiny. Here she is, one-time Lil, about to ride the outgoing tide of a century barely out of its teens: no wonder she feels mad with excitement. And the restless, gurning water down below begins to tremble, the ship's engines throbbing into action in a most encouraging and confirmatory way.

At last, the streamers fray and tear, some flying off in curlicues on an up-current, the rest, tangled and forlorn, eventually trickling down to the quayside. Even though there is not a single soul who knows her on the slowly receding jetty, in tandem with all the other passengers on board Lilian casts her eye across the crowd of well-wishers, pinning two of her children to the front of her legs up against the railing to keep them safe. They are Thomas, now aged six, who appears on the ship's manifest as "Thomas Pengarth", and little Dorothy. At the same time, she manages to cradle baby Kenneth, barely six months old, in the crook of her left arm.

As the ship lumbers at what feels like a crustacean pace, edging its stately bulk away from land, Lilian can only applaud … *Goodbye England, glad to see the back of you. I've done it! Nobody can catch me now!*

The one-time scullery maid is one of some 200 passengers travelling second class on the SS Scandinavian, a sprightly passenger liner, powering towards open water. In a true spirit of modernity, it occurs to her that there is a certain brash pride beaming from the wooden panels of its staterooms and the spacious boardwalks on several of its promenade decks. Far, far below and out of sight there is enough room for a further 800 unfortunates to squeeze into steerage. *But not me*, exults Lilian, *not me*, and she feels for one ridiculous moment like Britannia on the English penny coins, daring to indulge some fancifully dangerous words that enter her mind: *I shall rule these waves … My time has come.*

After tea, when she notices that the last crust of dry land has flattened into the sameness of sea and nothing but sea, she proceeds to establish her bearings by sniffing out the whereabouts of the remaining 200 passengers – those who are travelling first class …

A day later, the popular quoits deck is effervescent with spray. The spume mesmerises Lilian, who notes how it creates a rolling mist above the boards until it encounters the decking, only to be tossed up again by a fractious gust which splays it out in filigree lines. It is lightness itself compared to the weight of the sea, thinks Lilian. Indeed, it is too feeble to survive at all. Where does it all go to, she wonders? It seems to just vanish into thin air, the scant residue of vapour it leaves producing a sense of lost-ness, of ghostly absence. But since sailing commenced, Lilian's predominant mood has been a fascination with learning to ride the waves. When she has a minute to herself, she keeps an eye on the dense eddies of sea water clinging to the belly of the ship, weighted with such monstrous energy, reminding herself over and over: *it'll all be alright … I am set fair now.* Out here, she is but one of a thousand people on board whose stories are caught between lateral currents sorting the non-solid from the apparently solid. Little wonder she delights in entertaining the spirit of being a nomad, a vagabond, a person of no fixed abode whilst on this ship. It is true to say that the *terra incognita* that lies ahead holds few fears for Lilian at this stage.

One evening, when she squints for long enough to

confound her sense of distance, the sea manifests itself as a series of blackened undulations from horizon to horizon, as though submerged monsters might be lurking within its slow, watery swayings and tremblings, in eerie counter-point to the palpable reality of the geometric cross-hatch of passengers in silhouette strolling quietly across the deck in the fading light like small puppets, thanks to the artificial illumination coming from the salons. Concentrating upon these people, she senses a hidden frisson of energy in the blank spaces between them and wonders what a journey like this is contributing to her hazy notion of progress. Are she and her fellow travellers in some way progress itself? How utterly thrilling it all is.

At the same time, there is no denying the odd notion of being surrounded by miles of watery *nothingness* as the ship approaches mid-Atlantic. It's compounded by the early evening shadows the liner projects, giving her an impression that out there the ocean must be heavier than the thickest oil at a depth almost too overwhelming to contemplate, and it occurs to her that drowning must be the worst – surely, the most hellish – death, because for a brief while you would surely be fully aware of what was happening. This is when Lilian unfastens her grip on the deck railing – a grip so tight that it has turned her knuckles white without her being aware of it – and hastens to her cabin where Thomas is old enough – just – to be trusted to keep an eye on Dorothy and Kenneth for a few minutes, allowing her to get a breath of air.

During this, her maiden voyage, Lilian is perfectly happy eating sardines with the children in the late afternoon. She has also taken to affecting an interest in games of shuffleboard on deck and shows her appreciation of the winners with a dainty clap of her hands.

Then, on a day towards the conclusion of the voyage, there is a brush with danger, the nature of which she dreads more than any other: that of being found out.

'My dear!' Her head swings round and upwards towards the source of this invocation, a female voice which, it seems, is in the process of offering her a greeting. So quietly and skilfully has she acclimatized to the surprisingly easy familiarity of on-board acquaintance that she at once offers a mild smile to the lady who she recognizes as one who was sitting next to her in a row of deckchairs that very morning and who, it appears now, has just emerged from the first class lounge. 'So glad to have bumped into you again,' the woman persists. 'Good news: I've managed to make up a four for bridge and you are one of it. Play commences after tea today.'

How brisk such women are, notes Lilian, swiftly weighing up three possible responses open to her. She *could* stare at this woman as though a mistake had been made, then make a quick exit. But that would mean denying herself the rare prospect of an entry into what might turn out to be a promising group. Another option would be to own up that she has no idea how to play bridge, but Lilian hasn't the confidence to do this, any more than she wants to make a fool of herself – any more than she wants to risk appearing to be a chancer, an *arriviste* who pretends to be more than her background warrants. With barely a five seconds' delay, she takes the third option: 'I am so glad. That sounds delightful. I hope we can play tomorrow, though, because I am having my hair done today.' It is a smart move, buying her a little time.

Despite knowing she has less than twenty-four hours to accomplish a working knowledge of this arcane card game, the more she thinks about it the more she feels satisfied that the risk is worth it. If the worst comes to the worst and she can't master its fundamentals with speed, she can always plead the children, and beg to be asked on another occasion. But there. She has a strong feeling it won't, and on this occasion she will be proved right. In the ship's library it doesn't take her long to pop into her bag a copy of the stalwart "Bridge and How to Play it" by Archibald Dunn, and, on second thoughts, the rather breathily titled: "Bridge Whist: its Whys and Wherefores. A Progressive and Clear Manual of Explanation and Illustration of the Game, and How to Play It, etc" by C.J. Melrose, long dead – just in case she needs to cross-reference anything she doesn't understand in the first volume.

To be one step ahead of the game, just one. Nothing must be allowed to block the way forward – this is the first rule of survival. So she will teach herself how to play bridge, even if she has to knuckle down throughout the night by the light of the moon beyond her cabin's porthole while the children sleep and an obsidian sea drifts by, its presence ignored. During those long nocturnal hours of study, she reminds herself that her new bridge partner, Nora O'Hara, is also heading for Montreal, where Mr O'Hara is an attorney, endowing her endeavours with the promise of a social investment.

What a pretty pass, Lilian muses – her very last thought as lines of print begin to turn into squiggly black entrails on the page – that I shall be in a position to introduce Edward to someone of merit! Thoroughly exhausted, a gale of hysterical laughter builds inside her at the anticipation of it.

After six days and several games of bridge, during which

the children are minded by a nurse on the crew, the pleasant respite offered by the fluidity of ocean travel has quite run its course, and they duly arrive in a new country, on a brand new continent. It has been a successful and largely happy journey, as far as Lilian is concerned, during which the drifting, curling trail of the ship's wake has increasingly suggested to her the possibility of a fresh blending of cultures, which only complements a rising sensibility of her own state of becoming.

Every docking has to be a kind of homecoming in itself, however alien the land is. It is proof of travails overcome and a safe conclusion, she reckons. But what would "home" turn out to be now?

Oh, look, here come the streamers again. In a slightly cranky way, due to her excitement at the thought of seeing Edward again as she confidently tosses out her own, Lilian figures that she and the SS Scandinavia itself on which she has just sailed – now painstakingly negotiating its way into its narrow berth – have something in common. Tiny and insignificant though she may be in contrast to the bulky liner, she feels herself in the process of being carefully steered towards her own landing point in a ceremony of arrival which contains within it a celebration of herself. The last traces of those maritime moments involving a sudden occlusion of clouds, the unpredictable play of shadows across a choppy sea, the blast of a sudden cool front, a barometer continually on the change – all of it is abandoned in a trice: none of it will be of any account whatsoever from now on.

At the end of her first sea journey, her only apprehension is a vague notion of what she privately terms upper class "purity" as a result of her socialising – it's the only word she can find to describe that rarefied and desirable state personified by her new friends, the O'Haras. Their natural poise, their sense of balance, their apparent lack of loose ends – this couple must be a guide for her own future security, and she badly wants to acquire a veneer of their "purity" for herself.

And so to arrival.

Down the gang plank she steps, searching for Edward in the welcoming crowd, utterly sure that he will be there. She discovers that she is easy about her own invisibility in this new country. *I am nobody*, she reflects as she dexterously gathers up her three children, almost exulting in the thought. But that is fine. One way or another, it is of no account. It really does not matter at all, because soon the process of crystallizing into "somebody" by virtue of her marriage to Edward must begin in earnest.

12

Montreal, 1919

The Doukhobors loved Edward, they truly loved him. They had a plain slogan by which to live and it went like this: "toil, and have a peaceful life". Maybe it was a coincidence, but this was more or less what Edward had in mind for himself and his family, now that the war was behind them. His whole memory of Europe was by that time like a collection of cold ashes fused into a concatenated hardness which sometimes felt like a solid brown tuber lodged in the region of his stomach, where it must remain, as long as he didn't agitate it. Confining that war more or less exclusively to the absolute privacy of his own mind – other than on the odd occasion when something of what he had learned in France came up during the course of his medical practice – he resolved to squeeze down that tuber a little each time it threatened to become engorged, rather as you might do if you were milking a goat, making it less resistant as its malodorous contents were bit by bit drained away.

Since they had been apart, he had been turning his spare energy towards the Doukhobar community, deciding to pledge what support he could to these fugitive refugee people who had settled in down-town Montreal.

One day, he paused to catch what was being said at one of their outdoor meetings, slowing down to appraise the Doukhobor women in their distinctive white headscarves. He quickly learned how they'd come from Russia, supported by those other peace lovers, the Quakers, and that Tolstoy himself had donated the royalties from his novel *Resurrection* to boost their migration fund after the order went out that they were to be expelled from their homeland. They had been subject to systematic persecution for their pacifism, this gentle Christian sect, and to add to their troubles they also found themselves at odds with the Orthodox church in Russia, not to mention the authoritarian tsarist regime of the time. In their search for somewhere safe they consulted a map of the world and hit upon the great open spaces of Canada.

It is a cough which starts him talking to one of the Doukhobor men on the fringe of the crowd today (Edward knows a thing or two about the treachery of coughs by now). 'Hey, that sounds rough,' he ventures. 'Want me to have a listen?' As a newly qualified doctor, he mostly carries his case about with him. As a matter of fact, he is just on his way back from a long shift at the hospital, so without more ado he draws out his stethoscope and very soon makes a diagnosis from the symphony of sounds he hears coming from that man's pulmonary cavity. 'This needs treating,' is his verdict. But the man only shrugs and makes as if to move on. There is no money for doctors amongst the Doukhobors, let alone even the most rudimentary medicines. 'OK, then you come and ask for me by name at the hospital tomorrow,' Edward urges him, recognising the reason for this poor man's reluctance to take him up on his offer. 'Don't worry, my friend. I will take care of it.' At this stage, his first thought is to make sure the fellow doesn't spread his infection further.

Lilian is not happy about his involvement with the Doukhobor community, which only seems to expand, judging by how much time he seems to spend with the outcasts. 'How can people be so *needy*?' she puts to him. 'If you give in to one, Edward ...' No, she is constantly urging him, it should be society people whom he cultivates, those who will pay him an income, rather than those Doukhobors who push into his hands a handful of eggs for his troubles from the malnourished chickens who roam their back yards, or a barely edible flat cake.

Ever since he set up home for his growing family in an apartment on First Avenue, Montreal, lack of regular income has become *the* issue that has been testing them both sorely. Since he is at the beginning of his medical career, Edward works six days a weeks and as many nights, too, if necessary, in order to establish himself and keep those for whom he is responsible clothed and fed and warm, especially during the extreme cold of their second winter in Montreal, when waist-high snow in the gardens and parks didn't start to melt until late April. There is less time than he might wish left for his family, once his charitable work with the Doukhobors is done, on top of everything else. But this would change, he would make sure it did.

Nevertheless, they seem happy enough, this growing family. In years to come Sunny, Lilian's grand daughter, will find herself perusing a number of studio photos in sepia or black and white from her grandparents' pioneering time in Canada after the first World War, only to wonder why it is that in only one of all the photographs featuring her does Lilian display a full, open smile? Lingering on this one because it is different, she will conclude that her grandmother must be having fun on the day it was taken, squatting down to be on a level with her small children in front of an enamel basin with a scarf tied in a fashionable way around her hair, all of them apparently messing about washing dolls' clothes. Most of the other pictures show Lilian's gaze offering an expression which appears frozen, or slightly dazed, according to Sunny's reading of them. Then something quite shocking drops out of the pile for Sunny to pounce upon: in one group photo, pencilled "drama club" on the reverse in her own hand, Lilian – or someone else – has systematically scratched out her own face. Uncaptioned, undated photos like this don't tell any story at all, Sunny concludes, in frustration. You just have to accept that they're just moments which have ended up in a dry place.

For now, Mrs. O'Hara – Nora – is proving a useful friend, being able and willing to provide a ready-made network of initial contacts for Lilian, which proves satisfying and useful. Unexpectedly, Edward is dubious at first about her ready-made friendship with the O'Haras, a reaction she hasn't anticipated and doesn't understand at all. 'With a name like that?' Edward queried. 'They have to be Catholics, don't they?'

'Dear, Nora's husband is a *lawyer*, Catholic or not. Does it matter?' returns Lilian.

But he is not in the mood for explaining residual, historical prejudice, already in the process of fading away as the French begin to regain ascendancy in eastern Canada. Anyway, just because they must have come from Ireland at some point, given their surname, it didn't *have* to follow that they were Catholics. He was wrong, anyway, because at the first opportunity Nora introduces Lilian to the local United Church where she is persuaded to join the drama group and she starts by showing them all how artistic she is, especially with her nimble running up of cast costumes on the new sewing machine Edward has bought her. There is a warm welcome here for the new "English lady" who seems so well versed in much admired old world etiquette which makes their simpler, chummier manners look somewhat gauche and loud: this is the consensus amongst the ladies of the drama group, anyway.

Nine months after their arrival in Montreal, Lilian's three children – Thomas Smithyes (now Pengarth) and Dorothy and Kenneth Pengarth – are joined by Elizabeth (known as Betsy), the newest arrival. 'What a picture she is,' Lilian shares with Edward one morning – just as Thomas brushes past her like a … like a *dromedary* is the word that comes to her mind, though she's not entirely sure what a dromedary is. It just sounds big and awkward, which fits Thomas exactly. Edward glares at the boy, as he often does, and bends down to pick up the linen bag the unsophisticated child has just caused his mother to drop. He makes no excuses for Thomas, but neither does Lilian these days, on the whole, sensing that Thomas represents to Edward an unwanted burden, though one that he is willing to tolerate, within reason.

As far as his mother is concerned, Thomas is like a piece of fruit that rather spoils the symmetry of the bowl. No doubt about it, he is not like the other children. You just have to look at them to see at once that Dorothy and Kenneth and even baby Betsy have finer features, and the older two seem so much more able to assimilate, naturally, habits of good deportment and manners under her strict guidance. But Thomas – oh, Thomas, Thomas. She sometimes despairs – he seems to tower over the other children with his wide grin and clumsy ways, and can't be taken *anywhere*. He goes to school now, where he fails to distinguish himself in any particular way though his cheerfulness is remarked upon by his teachers. In winter, he is employed running errands and helping out around the home and he takes responsibility for keeping the driveway clear of snow, shovelling it into heaps away from the front of the house in readiness for the melting time.

That summer, he carries baskets of home-grown berries and apples to be pickled and preserved in jars in preparation for the next period of cold weather, and he stacks those jars in the basement when the time comes. It seems right that he does these things, not by way of earning his keep or justifying his presence in the family, exactly, but because the older children (soon to be followed by yet another, Edith, the youngest and last of the four Pengarth siblings) do not regard him as a brother at all. Instead, they are given to understand that he must be a cousin from Nova Scotia.

For now, he is just there, hovering on the outskirts of the family.

And yet, can it be just Thomas's bumbling bluster and general loudness that so grate? His difference seemed to be magnified incrementally with the birth of each new child, and by the time Edith was born the balance had well and truly tipped between the perceived normality of Thomas's presence among them and his undoubted strangeness. What began to chaff Lilian most of all was how the boy seemed to deliberately surround himself with the atmosphere of another place and time – just as she was in the process of discarding all that once and for all. It troubled Lilian that he persisted in carrying such an aura of *elsewhere* about with him – it was distinctly audible through his accent, for one thing, which had never become entirely Canadian as it should have done by now but pawed the air with its out-of-place vowel sounds. Hardest of all, this son of hers was a daily reminder for Lilian of the ghost of Bill Smithyes.

Not that she was unkind to him: he was her son and if anyone from outside the family looked askance at him her protective instinct reared its head every bit as strongly as it would if any of the other children were the victim of a slight, intended or not. Neither could it be said that Thomas was neglected. Rather, it was in the folds and creases of daily existence – the breeding ground for all their moods and routines – that his estrangement began to take root. Even a seven-year-old child as apparently disorganised and perpetually cheerful as Thomas must sooner or later register his mother's recoil when she is called "Ma", by mistake, as of old. Gradually, he developed a new address for her – "Scuse me" – to be employed whenever he needed something. It was more acceptable than "Ma", yet on the whole it failed to mollify her. In fact, it made her bristle with distaste because it sounded to her like a passive criticism. At the same time – and how headache-making this was – she was cross with herself for not being able to fathom quite what it was that made her feel so very contrary about him at times. Perhaps it was that she, who had once been required to defer to others, found his ready acquiescence a weakness, and weakness was on no account something Lilian was prepared to tolerate, either in herself or others. All of this added up to a persistent, low level of impatience with the boy as he became a kind of tinnitus in her ears, from which the other children seemed immune.

Neither Dorothy nor Kenneth retained any recollection of a journey across the Atlantic in their infancy and Dorothy was led to believe she was the first child of her parents (which of course she was). It was something she never questioned – why should she? But her position of responsibility burdened her at times and made her out to be an anxious child. Such juxtaposition between herself and Thomas meant she was never required to look up to him, as the younger ones were encouraged to do to her. On the contrary, although he was physically bigger than her it came to seem natural to her to look out for him, young as she was. The other children learned to adopt their own attitude towards him, of not exactly rudeness, but something which may have appeared mildly curt or dismissive to an outsider. He was an idiot, after all – Lilian and Edward openly confirmed it in all their dealings with him. Or maybe it was mostly disinterest, in the end, that dictated their manner towards him: *Uh-oh, there goes Thomas again.* Mostly, he did not get in the way too much. All too quickly their little lives began to fill out to become their uppermost concern.

Meanwhile Thomas, if he's lucky, gets to hover around the lives of those more important people he lives with, whistling to himself until he gets on someone's nerves and is told to shut up.

Perhaps this partially explains why Dorothy did not find what was soon to befall Thomas particularly scandalous, either at the time it happened or later in her life. Just perplexing and ineffably sad, such is the way that a sensitive four-and-a-half year old manages to contain misfortune when it lingers close at hand, though it is quite beyond her understanding or control.

Watch Lilian stirring, then, two or more years after her arrival in Canada, just as the sun aims an early morning dart across her bed one sunny morning in late August. It is several hours since Edward left for the hospital, to be followed by an afternoon of being out and about, making the rounds of his newly acquired handful of private patients. He hasn't abandoned his Doukhobar friends – far from it – but he has at last been persuaded to undertake more lucrative work as their mainstay. Ah, here comes the nursemaid with the latest baby, their fourth, beautiful blonde Edith, followed by the housemaid who leaves by the bedside a silver tray with today's mail on it. Sitting up, Lilian nestles into her child for a moment or two, inhaling the aura of fresh loveliness which radiates from Edith, who offers her a cute lopsided smile in return … the baby feels so good, so entirely fresh and untainted. She casts an idle eye over the letters and decides to leave them until later because the light coming in is kindly and warm, and this is home.

But just as she settles a burst of adrenalin floods through her body, resulting in a trickle of clammy perspiration running down her spine. She has caught sight of an envelope bearing the grotesque and threatening sight of familiar writing from a time she has almost committed to oblivion.

Only clearly it isn't.

She wrenches the envelope open.

'Dear Lil,' Bill Smithyes has written in the inelegant but careful cursive ink strokes of an office clerk. *I am not, NOT Lil, I am Lilian*, she inwardly corrects, while forcing herself to read on to see what he has to say. Why now? What slip of hers could have led him to be on her scent, over here? What cruel twist of fate is reaching forth to catch her out, after all this time? 'I write to send you greetings although you have treated me like a wife should not treat her lawful husband,' he begins, in an even, if petulant tone. 'To summarise, I was taken prisoner of war in France and kept there for three years. I was ill and it took a further eighteen months to recover. I searched for you but other folk were living at Birkbeck Avenue by the time I returned. What happened, Lil? Could you not wait a little for your man? You wrote to your sister Violet but not to me.' Ah, there it is – *the slip*. Yes, without much effort she remembers a photo-card sent to Violet on an impulse, showing herself in the midst of a group from the church drama group. In a daft desire to show off she must have stamped it with her Canadian address, without thinking. Oh, a rare slip, just one, in one moment of stupid, self-indulgent vanity. How she curses her carelessness – because the day she had been dreading at the back of her mind is here *now*. To her discomfort, she finds she can almost sense his nearness.

She fears there will be consequences.

But wait a moment. She is "married" now. She has given birth in quick succession to four more children since Thomas. It has to count for something. Surely, this fact alone outweighs any old claim he might have, doesn't it? War time, and all that? People disappearing? Mistaken assumptions?

She forces herself to read on.

'I am on my way to Canada,' he writes (with no preamble, clumsily, just like their son). Her stomach clenches and something resembling heartburn sends a pain shooting upwards through her oesophagus. 'I shall be pleased to see you again, and young Thomas of course. With affectionate wishes, Yours sincerely, Your husband Bill Smithyes.'

Oh dear God. What exactly does he know about what she has become? Will the law descend upon her? Can her new friends be expected to stick by her? Must they find out?

Her mind curves away from all such speculation since it is plainly unanswerable. The immediate question must be: how can this man be deflected? She glances at the top of his letter and spots that he calls where he is writing from "On Board". It is now clear to her that in her haste to read what he had to say she failed to take in the official logo of his ship. Underneath it, the date he has written is "18.x.21". Good grief! *Four days ago!* He must have landed at the same time as this very bit of mail!

Her eyes stare straight ahead while her coffee, untouched, begins to cool. The new baby beside her wriggles its hands experimentally and stares towards the ceiling, following the progress of an upside down fly.

Think, Lilian, think.

When the Second World War was declared eighteen years after these events, there was a period when little seemed to be happening, although much was running through the minds of the people, and it didn't take long for the establishment of a home front while a state of phoney alert established itself in the popular psyche. Right now, during the hour following her reading of Bill's letter, Lilian feels as though her own phoney war is about to come to an end, prior to the flaring up of open hostilities. All the trappings of ordinary life – the ordering of ice from the drugstore, an afternoon out with the children, a note to be written for the gardener about fixing a broken plank in the fence – assume a completely different aspect, meaning that everything must now be viewed for the very first time in its new, true light. As her concentration intensifies, both her coffee, now stone cold, and the baby patiently toying with its own little limbs in complete safety, represent the innocent delight of a fast-fading state of being which remains *now* but is queerly in the process of holding itself in suspension.

How we sleepwalk most of the time, muses Lilian, nursing her misgivings. Until something like this happens to wake us up.

What is to be done?

She opens the porcelain cigarette box on her bedside table, fishes absently for a cigarette, strikes a match.

The telephone rings, its silvery trill an assault on the still air of the home. It sends a morbid shudder of sound rippling through the room. She waits for the maid to answer it.

It turns out to be Edward, just to say he expects to be delayed at the hospital and will not be home until eight o'clock that evening.

These are still pioneering days for Edward and Lilian, though they recently managed to move to a bigger, ground floor apartment, on account of the latest baby's imminent arrival. It is fair to say that Lilian feels she's beginning to acquire a measure of Montreal, so that she can confidently set her sights on their next move – it would have to be to a house rather than an apartment – somewhere she can start entertaining in earnest. In fact, to look back, to remember, to accommodate anything from a bygone formative age or a once familiar neighbourhood or landscape has become utterly passé to her now. It just doesn't fit with the times.

So why does that man drag himself over here to my territory, she wonders again, this time with resentment – why now? What on earth can be done to head him off?

It may be that Lilian is actually at her best when her privacy – her most prized possession – is under threat and she is put on her mettle. She fetches out a modest wooden jewellery box she keeps well hidden under a number of silk under-garments folded into a drawer in her bureau, a receptacle which neither Edward nor the maid would think of delving into. She makes a swift inventory of the contents: a piece of yellowing crepe paper enfolding a precious trinket, an art nouveau necklace, never yet displayed or worn, which she passes over; the birth certificate of Thomas Smithyes (now Pengarth); her marriage certificate to Bill Smithyes; a few recent photographs, none from her former life in

England. Next, she does several oddly violent things in succession, prompted by a build up of irrationality during the limited time ahead when she might expect to be granted the freedom to act, moved by a pressing desire to *do something*, in the face of adversity.

Firstly, as if to defy the past, she reaches for her wrap, calls for the nursemaid to relieve her of the baby, takes the documents down to the furnace in the basement and proceeds to burn most of them. This helps a little, lightening her load. Then, returning to her bedroom, she scrutinizes the photos – both the cherished snaps of her children in familiar family poses, and the more formal group shots of herself at the drama society. He shall not – nobody will – take all this away from me, she vows, a brief surge of unwanted sentiment causing her eyes to fill with tears of impotence at the unfairness of it. She then rummages for a pair of scissors and sets about scratching out her own face in each of these pictures, which portray her as both an amateur actress and as a director of several plays. I will remove myself from any nosiness, she tells herself, as though any of these actions had the power to somehow render her subliminally invisible to Bill Smithyes when he calls, as she has no doubt he will. She lingers for the merest few seconds on an unthinkable alternative: coming clean and abandoning herself to Edward's mercy. *I never meant any harm. I will go, if that's what you want.* But no. That wouldn't do at all. It would not do the trick.

She emerges from her room eventually, dressed and with her face made up, just as the maid's shadow approaches from the direction of the kitchen. She has already waved away any thought of lunch.

She registers the groan and click of the front door of the apartment, followed by the nursemaid heaving the pram out over its lip, accompanied by the banter of the other children. 'Quiet in the corridor, please,' admonishes Lilian, her customary composure quickly re-asserting itself. 'This isn't the first time I've asked you.' The nurse administers two sharp taps to the back of Thomas's legs behind the knees where the flesh is sensitive – he is always regarded as the catalyst of any unwanted loudness – and sweeps all the children towards the kitchen, avoiding the gaze of her stern little mistress.

"*Asked*" … 'I've asked you.' Did I just say that, Lilian wonders? Now there's a word. In Acton, once upon a time, Lil would have said "orsked", no doubt about it. Now, it seems the word has travelled towards the middle of the Atlantic to become the softer "ass-ked" which is neither wholly Canadian nor precisely English, but has been consciously modelled on the young Bette Davis at her Hollywood snootiest during an interview heard on the wireless – a tone haughty enough to be top-of-the-range indigenous with the added mystery of old-country class about it. He would tease her about that, would Bill Smithyes. The thought of being teased by that man makes her shudder.

The *intimacy* of it. He has no right.

13

It takes Bill Smithyes a further two days to make his presence known, effecting a brisk, military knock on the front door. Having braced herself for this, Lilian has positioned herself, at some inconvenience, to be the one who answers it, her newest baby in her arms like a shield. For maybe fifteen seconds the pair eye each other with mutual caution.

'What do you want, Bill?' Lilian demands eventually, in the tone of calculated weariness she has been practising. 'Why are you here?'

He takes offence at the rebuff.

'Can you be the same person I married?' he tosses back, with an attempt at defensive sarcasm.

She shrugs. 'We all have to move on.'

' "We *arll hev* to move on," ' he mocks, inaccurately. She shrugs. 'Come on, Lil, don't you even want to *know* what happened to me?'

There is another brief pause while she gathers herself.

'Well,' he resumes, 'I came back to Acton after the war and you were gone. You left no forwarding address, did you? Now I ask you, is that a way to treat a soldier?'

'I'm sorry, Bill. I really never meant to hurt you.'

'Well, you did.'

Footsteps approach, and all at once the shadow of a bigger man covers Bill's own shadow on the vestibule wall.

'Hullo?' says the doctor, much as he would to anyone, whether Doukhobor, nurse, fellow doctor, friend, or tradesman. One pleasing thing Lilian has discovered about social relations in Canada is that all you have to do is keep a straight back and look people in the eye and generally be yourself, whatever the situation, to be regarded with equanimity.

'Shall we go inside?' continues Edward in a neutral voice. Clearly, there is not enough room for three people to remain, inert, by the front door. No move is made by Lilian to stand back from the space she occupies, in the hope that Bill Smithyes might register her manoeuvre, do the decent thing, pay his respects – as he is obliged to do now – and maybe introduce himself as an "old acquaintance" or some such, who was just passing by – then take himself off.

A vain and rather desperate hope this proves to be.

Instead, he leans close to her in a meaningful sort of way, then swivels round to shake hands with the man of the house. 'William Smithyes,' he announces, 'Lately of the Middlesex Regiment.' This is accompanied with a hearty (bordering on the presumption of a matey) smile which makes Lilian recoil in horror. 'Wouldn't you like to catch up with some of the news from home?' he persists, facing Lilian once more with raised eyebrows, his hands behind his back.

That which ensues during the next ten minutes or so is surely one of the most uncomfortable interludes of her entire life so far. It takes place behind the door of the sitting room, firmly closed after baby Edith has been removed by her father from her mother's arms and deposited firmly with the nurse, giving the strictest notice that they are not to be disturbed. Goodness, thinks Lilian at a tangent, correctly calculating that events are now moving swiftly beyond her control – the staff will think it's a visit from the bailiff or worse. Heaven knows, these people were in the habit of gossiping amongst themselves.

'Will someone please explain to me what is going on here?' queries Edward in what sounds like a menacingly reasonable voice as soon as the three of them are alone. Like Bill, he declines to sit, and Lilian surreptitiously eyes the two men she has married, resting her hands neatly in her lap from the place on the settee where she has arranged herself. The last script is being written, then, but not by her. She can only sit and watch them create it between them.

Scuffles, a shriek of laughter, the sound of bags being dropped – not long after the sitting room door has been closed the three older children can be heard in the wings of an adjacent theatre: their nursery. Evidently, they have just arrived home from school. One of them – Thomas Pengarth (once Smithyes) – flings open the sitting room door with his customary carelessness and clatters in with something on his mind he can't wait to share, it seems. But even Thomas, her first born – so distressingly unruly and spontaneous – can't fail to feel the density of the atmosphere in the sitting room, and to register that whatever is happening in there is exclusive to those three adults. 'Leave!' commands Edward, pointing to the door. But Thomas, who is used to Edward's summary instructions, has anticipated this and is already backing out, the grin on his face slipping floorwards.

Lilian scrutinizes in turn Bill, then Thomas as he recedes. It seems that there is no shred of recognition on Thomas's part, although his father knows instantly who the boy is and responds with a short intake of breath, allowing his lips to part but no words to issue forth. Thomas turns and runs off, slamming the door after him.

'Is anyone teaching that boy manners?' demands

Edward of Lilian, feeding his wrath into a secondary source as he often does when he has been working long hours.

Sometimes, a cornered animal will simply freeze rather than run on further, if faced with predators who have it cornered beyond any hope of escape. All it has left is to trust that – immobile – a camouflage of imaged invisibility might save it as naked fear transforms its eyes into vacant stones fastened onto the one who is closing in on it. Is this how it is for Lilian? Will she manage to insinuate herself into the regency pattern of the settee's upholstery and become invisible? For sure, she would find solace in such an altered state of being. Is this what accounts for her strange composure? She is in deep, deep trouble and yet, illogically, an alternative picture forms in her mind, unbidden: of a gaping sea shore bathed in the aura of a sunny day. It acts as a necessary balm whilst she tries to un-hear what is being said above her head. She contributes nothing as the afternoon wears on.

He came. He went.

After less than half an hour, in a puzzling scene her memory will not retain for long, Dorothy, who has been hanging about in the hallway squeezing a doll in her hands, pauses to stare when the front door is opened by her father in order to let a stranger out. She is the last Pengarth to set eyes upon Bill Smithyes once he reaches the street outside and strides off towards the high road where a street-car soon buzzes by, obscuring him.

Inside, the ramifications of his unwanted visit start to get underway.

'Did you know about this?' Edward challenges, returning to the sitting room after he has seen Bill Smithyes off the premises, to discover that Lilian has not altered her position at all. 'Did you?'

'Of course not.'

'I don't believe you.'

'Edward.' His name is conjured up in a low voice, with gentle reproach, a tone he usually associates with seductiveness. But she has made a misjudgement because what this does is infuriate him further.

'It's not being made a fool of I object to most,' he begins – though the white tension around his chin and lips suggest otherwise. 'Jesus, Lilian,' he spits out – he who never blasphemes – 'are you aware that this could be *bigamy?* Have you any idea what that *means*, in *law?*' She reaches out to touch him, seeking, perhaps, to re-attach herself to a promontory of solid, undefiled land she senses is in the process of disintegrating.

'No, no, no, NO – don't you say anything,' he yells, shaking her off and leaving her unmoored and effectively marooned. 'Let me *think*. I need time to think about this.' With that, he picks up his hat and bag and heads for the door, turning around once to glare at her with his hand on its handle to declare: 'Is this how I am repaid?' He makes his exit abruptly, not waiting to witness the deep flush rising from her neck to cover her face, nearly knocking a tea tray out of the maid's hands, which had been re-set for three in anticipation of the visitor still being there.

'Here,' motions Lilian with a sigh, 'Over here. Put it down here. There's only me now.' Nothing can be more excruciating than being confronted with the truth and having to deny it. By turning his back on her, at least he has spared her that.

Edward's thoughts about the matter emerge in unpredictable spurts over the next few days. At night, he ignores her completely, coming in late and turning his back on her in their bed where he sleeps soundly.

'You told me you were a widow,' he challenges, the next afternoon. 'Why did you do that, eh?' But he refuses to listen when she attempts to explain.

Two days later, his sense of raw anger has developed into something sharp-edged, often cynical, and quite out of character for this most even-tempered of men. 'You know what? I think you set out to trap me, didn't you? You made me think you were *all alone in the world?*' He puts on a mimsy voice for this. 'You must have thought: "aha, here comes a patsy". Oh, and wasn't I just? I fell for it alright.'

Time and again she attempts to interject placatory words, but any attempt to move closer to him only serves to provoke him further. 'How *dare* you!' he thunders finally, backing away from her as though she were infectious. 'Get away from me, you *cheater*.'

One morning soon after this, she decides to wade in before he can shut her up, having rehearsed her appeal in advance. 'Edward, let's be clear: Bill Smithyes is not going to trouble us. Remember what he said?'

'That he is on his way to South America? Making a new start for himself? Oh, yeah. Until he needs money or something. Then he'll be back. You'd better believe it. I know the sort.' This has been preying on his mind, as well as a growing revulsion towards the man he is frustrated to concede that his wife probably still belongs to, technically. 'Thank you, Lilian, for a lifetime of looking over my shoulder,' he throws at her, not ready to let up. 'Was this your *dowry*?' It concerns her to hear this and only confirms the gravity of the situation, should she need reminding. The lack of any material contribution to the marriage from her side had never been an issue before, even when they were struggling through their first year in Canada and he was working towards his finals before fully qualifying as a doctor. She knows it is meant solely to put her down further. Can't he appreciate that she is smarting, longing to be able to hold her head up once again and re-inhabit the more comfortable self of old?

'What if he informs the police?' persists Edward.

'Why should he?'

'For revenge? On you?'

'I am the mother of his child. He wouldn't do a thing like that.'

'I'm glad you're so sure. For myself, I am not.'

The dreadful issue of Bill Smithyes which has at last come to light develops further during the following days, before which there is a short impasse between the couple. Since no more bitter words pass between them during this interlude, it now takes on the guise of a tangle of malignant threads winding their way into the common arena of their lives to choke off further communication on the matter of *that man*, creating invisible knots in the air which it is hopeless to try to unpick. As days pass, the thickness and complexity of the situation insinuates itself into the very fabric of their home, causing the children to become subdued and a little shifty, as tense with it as their parents are although they haven't an idea what it is all about – only that life is becoming deeply unsettling for reasons they cannot begin to imagine. Neither Lilian nor Edward offer to the children anything by way of an explanation for this, although Lilian finds herself apologizing for their affectionate Papa's unusual distancing of himself, explaining that he has to work so hard for all of them, therefore they must be patient with him. She attempts to carry herself in front of the nursemaid and the housemaid as though nothing at all out of the ordinary has been going on, though she suspects they are agog to know who the un-named visitor was, the one who had arrived without notice, leaving behind him something bad.

One evening a little later that autumn Lilian finds herself summoned by Edward to sit down with him after the children have gone to bed and the maid and the nursemaid are both off duty and therefore guaranteed to be away from the premises. She perceives that he has something to say to her. Not to *discuss*, as he makes plain from the outset, but to *say*. The conclusion he has arrived at is, quite simply, that Thomas Pengarth – no, let's not call him that any more – that Thomas Smithyes – must go.

'Go? Where?'

'I am telling you this,' says Edward. 'Do not make me repeat it.' Of course, he has the advantage of having it all figured out. 'I will not have that man's child in my house any longer,' he announces finally.

'But why? What's he ever done to you, or me, or anyone?' she protests, while in disbelief she takes this in. A short period of unease follows, prickling with resentment on both sides. But Edward has made his mind up in advance and he will not budge, eyeing her squarely to gauge her reaction. In her heart of hearts she has always known that he had taken the boy on because he was a gentleman and also a kind man, and in the beginning one who was so besotted with her that it ignited in him a sense of chivalry towards his little lady and her "orphaned" child. In returning his implacable stare, she wonders whether having her grand bluff called in this shameful way could have destroyed the innocence of his love for her, once and for all, and that she might have infected this wonderful man with certain of the blemishes she feels have always marked her.

'We have four other children, Edward,' she pleads in a lowered voice. 'Thomas is their brother.' But as she says this she knows it to be the weakest of appeals.

'I have made my mind up, he replies, sounding more shrill than he would have wished. 'I want him out.' It is hard, now, for him to look at her directly, but he meets her eyes as he adds one more thing: 'However, I will not ask you to give yourself up. This "marriage" will continue, for the sake of our children, and let's hope that you – that *we* – are never found out,' he said.

'But he must go.'

Later that day, Lilian pays particular attention to her eldest son crashing around the cellar on his roller skates, where the great furnace thrums as it circulates hot water through a labyrinth of heavy radiators above. The warmth down there and the throbbing of the cast ironwork never fails to remind her of being back on board ship with a permanent, hollow roar in her ears and the ultra-dry smell of its interior in her nostrils. Edward has never really taken to the boy, she has always been aware of that. She considers whether it might have affected her own feelings for him. Poor Thomas. Yes: he is difficult to control, absent-minded, prone to making a lot of noise and letting out those dreadful caterwauls of inappropriate laughter. But following his progress in the basement where she reaches up to squeeze a sheet, testing its level of dryness, she can't help but notice that he is entirely unaware of her scrutiny, and a desire to reclaim him comes over her in a passing stab of pity for him. Despite it all, he remains her very own son, after all, whose father had been within touching distance of him just a few weeks back, a father he was never likely to encounter again. Her son.

She claps her hands together as he whizzes by, whirling himself around her as though they were attached by an invisible rope. 'Thomas, Thomas ... Look out or you'll bump into that pillar!' ... Which, of course, he proceeds to do, and sits down with a bruise about to form on his elbow and a reluctant grin on his face. Her son.

He doesn't know it, but moves are soon afoot to transport him back to England. Lilian has duly taken matters into her own hands and come up with a drastic plan, bracing herself to make contact with her sister Violet once more, this time with a bit of a story. There are too many children now, she will plead. If Violet could look after him for just a few years he would be able to make his own living before she knew it, and would be off her hands, too.

To be sure of this, she encloses a generous money order made out for the purpose by Edward, a lump sum he has borrowed from the bank in order to have done with it. Very well, replies Violet before much more than three weeks is up: if Edward is prepared to pay for her train ride to the docks as well, she will be there to meet the boy. That's just as well, as it happens, because his berth has already been booked on a passenger liner sailing for Liverpool just before Christmas. A chaperone, who is also taking this passage, has been identified. Without further ado, Thomas will be "home" for Christmas.

Edward has inspected the tickets himself – does he not trust her at all? – and he begins to thaw a little towards her in acknowledgement of her having done a brave act on his behalf. Soon, they will be moving into a bigger house in a better neighbourhood and Nora O'Hara and the rest have been given to understand that Thomas is returning to his family in Nova Scotia.

Finally, the icy December day arrives when Lilian and Thomas stand huddled together on the chilly quayside where a large liner's outline is blurred by seasonal fog.

There must be no question of a change of plan, Lilian has known that from the start. Neither she nor Edward could stomach sending Thomas to a Canadian orphanage, the only other viable option she came up with. No, it wouldn't be right: from Edward's point of view, the boy would remain too close for comfort, and from Lilian's, such proximity, concealed from his half brother and sisters, would stand as a dreadful betrayal of all concerned as well as the continuation of a lifetime of watchfulness.

Today, the boy is wearing a kind of satchel on one shoulder which Lilian, on second thoughts, automatically pops over his head, knowing that otherwise he will lose it, for sure. He holds a small square case in hands which are being kept warm by large mittens, sewn into his overcoat on a length of elastic. He stamps his booted feet and blows out clouds of white, cold air, watching it disappear with wondrous concentration, as though he has just managed to create something precious, a dream miraculously made palpable. Both Lilian and Edward have long suspected that there is something odd about the boy, something unconnected, something you can't quite put a label on. How else could he be so apparently accepting of what is happening to him?

'Now then, young Thomas,' says Lilian, when the time comes for boarding. 'This is an adventure, eh?' He nods, in that exaggerated way he has that Edward always finds so irritating, and she, distasteful. And yet she does love him, in her own, pinched way, and hugs him close for as long as she dares, covering his face with kisses until he breaks away from her of his own volition, taken aback by such unusual affection. Without a second look, without all the questions his mother knows he ought to be asking of her but in his simple, trusting way fails to do, off he romps up the gangplank. 'Goodbye, darling. Good luck, my sweet,' she calls out. She wants to tell him not to be afraid – as much to console herself as the small figure bounding up the gangplank, to wrap him round with a belated blanket of motherly concern, to scoop out of the pit of her stomach the dread of a bad conscience as he becomes fused with the boarding crowds.

With that, Thomas Pengarth, once again Thomas Smithyes according to his new passport, takes his leave of Canada.

There is only one person who is overly concerned about the unruly boy's sudden exit, but she is too young yet to piece together what "missing" someone might mean. It is his sister Dorothy, a watchful child who was for a short time his friend and ally, setting up little games they played together, bringing food to his room in secret when he was in trouble. Following his sudden departure, whenever he enters her mind while she is growing up he will be wrapped up inside a grey cloud of undiluted melancholy. She hasn't a clue why this should be but in time such a burdensome feeling comes to suggest the nature of bereavement to her. She believes he *hasn't* actually died, but it feels like that to her. She hopes he is happy, back in Nova Scotia, because he had spent such a very long holiday with them.

'Won't Thomas be lonely, without us?' she ventures to ask Lilian one day as the two of them prepare to bake a cake in the kitchen.

'Why do you say that?'

'I don't know,' says Dorothy. 'I think I would feel lonely if I lost my friend.'

'That's a silly thought, Dorothy.'

'But he seemed to belong here.'

'No, dear. He didn't,' says Lilian.

'But he was my brother.'

'No, dear, Kenneth is your brother,' says Lilian, with a brittle attempt at patience. 'Oh, goodness, Dorothy. What things you come out with,' she adds, hoping to put a lid on it.

'Will his mother be there?'

'Mother? No ... he doesn't have a mother, I believe.'

'Did she die, then?' Dorothy asks in almost a whisper, tilting her head back so the big tear forming in her eye won't spill out.

Lilian must now busy herself with searching for something deep inside a cupboard, refusing to answer any more questions. 'I don't know. I don't know. You must stop pestering me.'

By the time Dorothy is eight, however, and able to write reasonably well on her own, she gets an idea, triggered by coming across an old peg doll Thomas had made for her once upon a time. On a scrap of paper she writes: 'Dear Thomas. I miss you. Lots of love from Dorothy xxxxx'. She creeps into her father's study, steals an envelope from his desk and addresses it: 'Thomas, Nover Skosha', passing it to the maid to post, as she's seen her mother do on many occasions. The maid places it in her apron pocket, carrying on with her chores until she is able to hand it over to Lilian with a conspiratorial snigger.

About a year later, hearing nothing at all from "Nover Skosha" and putting it down to her childish spelling at the time, she tries again one day. 'Please write to me, Thomas. I want to know how you are getting along.' This time she posts it herself after school one day, having bought a stamp out of her own pocket money.

Nothing.

Could he have forgotten her? She has not forgotten him. She thinks she probably never will. So she tries once more, and this time a fuller address is discovered under multiple entries for 'Pengarth' in her father's weighty address book when she takes a sneaky look. It must have been the wrong Pengarth family it got to, she figures, because after this attempt Lilian was obliged to put her most firmly in her place after the embarrassment of receiving a short note from one of Edward's relatives asking: 'Who is Thomas? Why does Dorothy write here?'

'You foolish girl! Whatever have you been up to, bothering these people?' admonishes a distinctly scratchy Lilian at this point, waving the treacherous document Dorothy had dispatched for Thomas's eyes only over her head. It leaves Dorothy in no doubt that she is in big trouble, sly sort of trouble – for indiscretion, or bad manners, or eccentric behaviour – who could guess what it was? Who would dare to ask? She therefore hangs her head in silence, which seems to her the proper, expected thing to do.

'Well?'

'I don't know.'

'That's no answer. This really has got to stop.' She gives the evidence, the offending missive, a little shake before rather theatrically tearing it up, to emphasise her point. 'Really, Dorothy, there must be no more of it.'

'But mother, why won't they let me write to him?'

'Oh, my gracious, what *is* this? Let the boy alone, give

him some peace, for heaven's sake. Boys don't take to girls writing to them like this anyway.'

Dorothy did as she was told, though none of it quite stacked up, to her way of thinking.

When she was around ten a large, hearty sort of man from Nova Scotia visited and was introduced as Uncle Percy. Each time Dorothy looked as though she might be about to ask after Thomas her mother managed to interrupt her, but Dorothy was more persistent this time. She followed Uncle Percy around the house while her father was out and her mother was entertaining her lady friends in the sitting room, finally pinning him down and coming right out with it before there was a chance of being caught: 'Uncle Percy, can you please tell me how Thomas is getting along?'

He peered at her over his newspaper.

'Thomas, you say? Who is this?'

'He used to live here, you know. For a very long time.'

After a moment of reflection Uncle Percy told her: 'I don't know anything about anyone called Thomas,' before his face dipped down out of sight once more, cutting her off.

Dorothy lost the heart to pursue it after that.

Before this, whether it was related directly to her disappointment about losing Thomas or not, a heaviness wrapped itself around Dorothy in the days following the boy's departure and it remained, invisible to everyone except herself, for nearly half a term, causing her teacher to report her for being prone to bad moods. Her mother fully concurred with this, apologising for her daughter's contrary nature. Only her father noticed that maybe Dorothy's heart had been a little broken by the boy's departure, but although he was a gentle and loving man where his children were concerned he never permitted her to explore such feelings with him, even when he scooped her up to snuggle with him in his easy chair from time to time, spotting that she was preoccupied by something that troubled her.

Then one day, out of the blue, lightness returned to raise her spirits and she put the long winter of "not being myself" almost out of her mind.

But she never did shake a suspicion that his going had something fishy about it. Since no-one would help her out by supplying her with a convincing story, she felt her parents' judgement had been exposed as faulty, and that she had been violated in some way by their caginess regarding Thomas. As time passed, she was able to develop a thicker skin and would discover that children who began by naively believing all their parents said were almost guaranteed to be disappointed, all things considered.

Perhaps Thomas's disappearance contributed to her way of keeping her own thoughts close to her as she grew up. Stubborn, she was: that's how her mother described her at the time.

14

All too soon, it is the heady month of June, 1934.

With her children in their teens, the new house is now satisfyingly full of attractive people and stylish nooks and corridors leading towards generously sized rooms. This house represents what a sense of achievement really feels like, to Lilian, vindicating a lifetime of skilful manoeuvring – apart from one or two lapses. The house has a grand veranda running along two of its sides at right angles so that anyone may sit out in the sun through both the morning and the afternoon. The whole solidly detached building is exclusively Pengarth territory and its rooms and corridors echo to the sound of clipped voices, the occasional peel of female laughter and the distant rumble of traffic from the main thoroughfare, which is a comfortable way off whilst at the same time leaving them fashionably central.

This morning, no-one but Trudi, the dog, registers another, all too familiar sound from outside: a pneumatic and rather sensual squelch of tires as Edward, a permanent pipe clenched between his lips, swings into the driveway at the front of the house in his black four door De Soto sedan with its spare wheel somewhat eccentrically attached to one side of the protruding nose of its bonnet. Returning briefly from his consulting rooms, just as he often does at this time, he turns the car around with practised ease on the generous expanse of gravel at the front, carrying a list in the pocket of his seersucker jacket of the addresses of six of his private patients who are about to take up the rest of his day.

Lilian, meanwhile, is still in bed where she intends to remain for a bit, scanning the Montreal Daily Star whilst smoking her second cigarette of the day, her spent breakfast tray aslant on Edward's side of the bed. The maid is about to bring up the morning's post for her to sift through, just as she always does. This is how her daily routine begins, now that Edith, the last of their four children, is thirteen years old.

It doesn't take long before the maid's footsteps can be made out on the landing, whose timber floorboards creak like an elderly gentleman clearing his throat, resonating stability. Such sounds are associated in Lilian's mind with the filigree of wrinkles spreading from the corners of the maid's own eyes: both have a sense of mature sunshine about them, it occurs to her, blended with a hint of woodland.

This morning she expects to learn by post the important news that their annual reservation by Lake Champlain has been confirmed, meaning that at some point in the next few weeks she will have to take the children on a seasonal shopping expedition down to Ogilvy's, the new department store on St Catherine's Street where she has long held an account, in order to replenish their summer wardrobes. Ah – maybe there will be a concert in the shop's Tudor Room on the fifth floor – in fact, she decides there and then to make sure they time their visit to chime with a day when there is. She has developed a shy enthusiasm for chamber music since an unfortunate feud at the drama club caused her to withdraw suddenly from her theatrical hobby. Anyway, she had become restless with it, if the truth were known: too many newcomers, fashionable youngsters, were taking it over for her liking and she had been irritable with them until they froze her out. Well.

She doesn't need it anymore. Her musical preference is for pieces played by demure quartets and quintets and trios – such a picture in their formal evening wear in the middle of the day. She likes the symmetry of such ensembles, and she mostly likes it when, completely untaught, she can identify whether the music is meant to be witty, or romantic or tragic – or simply *of itself*, like something which has been so carefully thought out that it would be inconceivable to present it in any other way.

In this way, the interim years of their lives together are set on a steady course, Lilian and Edward, those years book-ended by two world wars. Not helplessly, not without hope, as she had once feared, but with the rhythm of an old fashioned cart stalwartly drawn by an anonymous horse at walking pace, its coopered wheels taking on and shrugging off the springtime mud, crackling over the dry stoniness of summer and squeaking out new tracks in the winter snow, round and round and round. And who is to know – really know – beyond the signature creak and groan of this particular cart and the brief unshuttering of a casual camera aimed at capturing a moment in its travels – the whole picture? Lilian often wonders this: what does anyone *really* know about anyone else beyond the few public episodes by which they are defined, those set pieces caught briefly in the momentary glare of a street lamp that relegates to the shadows the mystery of its wider context?

To the post, then. Oh, my – the O'Haras have sent a card – from Europe! From Switzerland! Goodness! How smart they look in their tweed jackets, posing on a verdant hillside alive with Alpine flowers. Lilian admires their enthusiasm for travelling but nothing on earth could entice her to move from this house, from this country of hers, apart from their summers by Lake Champlain. In fact, she feels so thoroughly Canadian now – has done for as long as she can remember – that the odd memory of other times that surfaces occasionally like an alien air bubble from some ancient hinterland, feels exactly this: out of place. So it is popped at once. Such memories seem to visit her less and less these days.

What else is there in the small pile? So automatically that she is scarcely aware of doing it, she occasionally checks for two things: that there's nothing from either Violet or from Bill Smithyes. Not that Lilian ever wrote to her sister to make further enquiries about Thomas or invited reports from her sister on his well-being: she trusted he was in safe hands over there. On balance, it was best to assume everything was going as planned so as not stir up potential problems. Best to imagine the boy in a place she had cause to believe would suit him much better, back in England, so very far away. As for Bill Smithyes, he, too, had more or less slipped her mind entirely. He was gone. He would never return. Why pick at old sores?

Does her sister even have their latest address? It crossed her mind, but really she knows: there is no-one here in Canada who could possibly have given it out apart from herself. That particular fortification is in place, then, and it cannot be breached, as far as she can see. She has learned to keep her feelings for Thomas close to her chest, and it has been a bitter lesson. But her return to anonymity has made her feel safe again.

It seems that the auguries for their marriage turned out to be rather good, after all. Edward, not a man to bear grudges, had to concede at the time that asking a mother to give away her child was about the highest price he could have exacted from his wife in recompense for her deception. As a result, he took pains to show her that he respected her acquiescence, mainly by behaving with deliberate courtesy, which he intended to be restorative, given time. Very little had been discussed following the dismal December day when Lilian arrived back from the docks, alone – not waiting for the joyful ceremony of the streamers which had once so entranced her, not once faltering – apart from one final terse exchange with Edward in the hallway of the old apartment whilst she removed her hat and coat, still smelling of the cold outside from the quayside where she had left Thomas. On that occasion, she sensed him skulking in the vicinity to check whether she had managed to do it, or whether her nerve had failed her at the last minute and she had brought the boy back with her. Or, as he would put it, whether he was about to witness another display of her disloyalty towards him.

'Are you satisfied now?' was all she said. Her eyes, which in angry sadness became a darker shade of blue – more like hyacinth than forget-me-not blue when troubled – started to lacquer with tears, but she faced him out, determined to hold her head high.

Upon which he turned and walked towards the small room he called his den, where he drew out his pipe and set about lighting it with much huffing and puffing.

And yet, at a fairly mature stage in this, the latest chapter of their marriage, life is feeling mildly auspicious, as it mostly does to Lilian these days, now preparing herself to get up out of her bed after one last cigarette, since it will soon enough be coffee time and she remembers that she has invited people round and they will be calling before she knows it. The Pengarths are in no way out of line within their circle in their routines. Men work. Women oversee the household, practise a narrow range of social interaction, offer acts of charity from time to time, executed mostly within, or in line with, the confines of their group: that's about it. None of these tasks demand that a wife needs to be up early in the morning. Lilian has her own repertoire of innocuous diversionary activities to ensure that one thing elides into the next, in the same continuous way that she reads the paper deliberately slowly, in bed. She is not about to complain.

Stepping out from the roomy house, the whole family is in the habit of attending the United Church on Sundays, and on the way home Edward treats the children to popsicles of their choice – pistachio for Kenneth, orange for Dorothy and Edith, lemon for Betsy: a tart flavour that matches her rather precocious personality. This is his contribution to the family day, a trade-off for mid-afternoons when he always goes out alone in order to deliver medicine and check on those patients who can afford constant home visits. Except that he doesn't. Not exclusively, anyway. Lilian has been aware for some time that he has a mistress on the other side of town, a Doukhobor woman, probably, given his interest in those people. Perhaps he knows she knows, since he has not gone out of his way to be overly discreet, but she hopes he doesn't. If he did – if this had to come out as a *known fact* between them – then he might indulge in a bit of gloating and that would be a set-back to the bridge-building both have been doing over the years. No, it is best for her – for them both – that disclosure does not occur. She knows that as the first to deceive, no right remains for her to criticize his behaviour. This is her burden, and hers alone. It may be unequal, but she has a feeling in her gut that at bottom this is probably right.

Nevertheless, it has to be said that over time he has come to admire his wife's gathering confidence and poise, and – yes – her pluck. It was a brave, though necessary, thing she had done, sending the boy back to England, where, in Edward's opinion, he truly belonged – he would never shift on that. But from each of them towards the other, a kernel of respect is the result, though any promise of the deeper closeness they shared from the early days in England was the first casualty of their truce.

From time to time Lilian has taken a peep behind the lines of their marriage, recognising what was tacitly established from the time of Thomas's departure. She has come up with an image of this marriage of hers as smoothed out, comfortably oval-shaped, and she can track a finger idly around its closed circumference. Lilian concludes that if her marriage lacks the bruises and triumphs, the sheer bliss and the occasional splinters that total union with each other might otherwise have yielded, such messy unpredictables are really not necessary. This has long been proven, as far as she is concerned.

And it has to be said that Edward does love to watch her dancing so daintily at the Royal Society of Physicians' and Surgeons' winter ball, appreciating the sharp little features of her face, the high summer blue of her eyes, the artistry of her gown and the way she always undertakes to customise it herself in small, telling ways, to her best advantage. Not to mention the nuanced make-up she wears increasingly in such a ladylike manner.

A few weeks later, the De Soto is parked on the driveway once more, crammed to the roof with luggage until it sags on its axle. They are just about ready to leave for Rousses Point, a village only a mile from the USA itself, where the border between New York State and Vermont crosses Lake Champlain. With Kenneth sitting up front beside him Edward makes a final check that he can just about see the road behind him using his side mirrors and Kenneth, his arm resting on the window sill on the passenger side, maintains a healthy beam on his face that he turns to share with his dad from time to time, as though seeking affirmation from his father. He can't wait to get down to the marina and grab a sail boat: it seems that he is a born seafarer, just like his late grandfather, the legendary Captain Adam Pengarth. Built like him, too. Edward admires the boy's pluck, never having been a natural sailor himself. The plan is that Lilian and the girls will follow by train and Edward will pick them up at the local station later, once the bags in the car have been deposited at the white-painted rented clapboard villa on Lake Street they just about regard as exclusively theirs.

'Dad, I really want to make it to Grand Isle this time – on my own,' Kenneth announces as the car glides off.

'And I'm sure you will, Ken. Yes, I am. You must pick a good day for it, that's all.' Edward is confident about the boy's navigational ability – they've been coming to Rousses Point for the past six years and he had taken to the water immediately. Edward is well pleased with his son and can barely resist showing it. At nearly sixteen years old, Kenneth is developing into something of a friend in this overwhelmingly female family.

Rousses Point is not really that far away from where they live – in fact, it is no more than thirty miles or so south of Montreal. It's a peaceful village where the girls can make free use of the lakeside beach, and where Edward himself can stroll by the water to chat with the people out fishing on the jetty. It's also where Kenneth can sail to his heart's delight, as though the day does not progress through hours, as normal, but in a state of eternal present-ness, inside which his impression of the borders of the lake, the sky and his own consciousness are allowed to drift in and out of each other in a tranquil and most gratifying way. The entire family enjoys breathing in the pure air here for the whole of July and August each year, building up inner resistance against harsh winters back in the city when temperatures stick at well below zero for weeks on end, and in the basement the great furnace is tuned to send its energy roaring around the house at full blast.

A day or so after their arrival, with a brand new summer just awakening, it feels good to each of them to be able to step out and re-acquaint themselves with Lake Champlain together, gazing across water that seems to glitter in the sunlight with something akin to pure glee, and to spy on the boats moored in the marina, lined up neatly with their sails rocking from side to side in the breeze. And to eat the freshest fish for supper, caught that same morning, after a quick walk to familiarise themselves again with some of the inlets and promontories near where the lake itself becomes the Richelieu River.

As with most of the visiting men folk that summer, Edward only comes at weekends, obliged to hurry back on Sunday afternoons on the daily train to Montreal with half a dozen or so other men – the attorneys, the accountants and one other doctor – leaving Lilian with the car for the week. But during those precious weekends he makes sure he and Kenneth spend time together exclusively. Right now, they are beginning to talk man-to-man for the first time, and these conversations are a source of great satisfaction to both of them.

'Dad?' ventures Kenneth one morning as they make

their way to the marina. He has been kicking a small ridge of sand at the water's edge when a thought occurs to him.

'Hmm?'

Kenneth has been thinking about the way whole armies of shells and small pebbles and – oh – all the leftover stuff that lines itself up on shores like this acts as a reminder that no high water mark ever remains the same, despite the lake being tide-less. He attempts to put this to Edward. 'Isn't that right, dad?'

'Why yes, I suppose it is.'

'Dad?' he tries again.

'Uh-hu?'

'I love it here.'

'Good. Me too.'

'I love the way the lake *itself* doesn't change.'

'Oh, I don't know about that,' says Edward, whose surgeon's eye delights in the play of light across the water at different times of the day when the colour of old slate can be transformed into emerald green in an instant.

'What I mean is, it's enclosed. Sufficient to itself and all that. I kind of like the peace of it, I suppose.

'I know what you mean there, son. That's why we're here.'

'Dad?'

'Yes, Ken.'

'Do you think there will be another war, Dad? I mean, would I have to go and fight? Like you did?'

'We must pray it doesn't ever happen again,' is all he can bring himself to say. Because although there have been disturbing signs from Europe it is more than he can bear to imagine – that his son could one day be fighting for his life on that dark continent he himself has never had the slightest wish to revisit.

And so the summer begins to mature this year, as it always does, rendering much of the foliage by the lake ragged in its darkening greenness, rude and overblown.

There is one particular Saturday when Lilian and Edith decide to spend the morning idly playing cards at a make-shift table erected on the lawn of their villa, occasionally waving at a passing neighbour.

How relaxed they all are by this stage of their vacation, even if Lilian tends to use Dorothy as her helper now that the maid is having her own week off back in the city.

In fact: 'Let me show you how to iron,' she offers suddenly after the sixth or seventh hand, switching her attention from Edith to Dorothy – who, if the truth were known, would rather carry on reading her latest Jalna novel, a long family saga drawn out over a number of volumes which is all the rage amongst her friends this year.

Without waiting for a response from her eldest daughter, Lilian disappears into the kitchen, stands the ironing board up on its legs and plugs it in. (An electric iron! How her own mother, poor thing, would have rejoiced at such an invention.) She is utterly confident that Dorothy will be docile and follow her. As always, she is proved right.

'Don't slouch, Dorothy,' she can't stop herself remarking as the girl duly drifts in. Spitting on the iron to test whether it is hot enough, she makes a mental note that Dorothy will need to be coached to think more about her posture the minute they get back to Montreal. That, and this episode of diversionary ironing: it's all part of her assiduous coaching of Dorothy for marriage, which is now underway. She is, after all, nearly seventeen-years-old.

'Now then, just watch me do this shirt of your

father's,' instructs Lilian. 'I will demonstrate. See, it's not the easiest garment, but you'll get used to it once you've done one or two.' Dorothy leans over stiffly, as bidden, and follows her mother's movements in a manner she suspects could be registered as perfunctory, the whip and click of material being so deftly manipulated by Lilian reminding her of a magician's sleight of hand. She puts this new skill down to her mother being artistic – until that awful row with some people at the drama society she was the one who not only acted, but could run up costumes in such beautiful detail, and she would always make their Christmas tree quite magnificent with her hand-made baubles. Dorothy notes such things. At this point in time, she is on the lookout for ways to follow in her mother's footsteps, keen to improve herself and earn some approbation from Lilian.

Frowning slightly as she tackles the next shirt on the pile by herself, Dorothy manages to leave a burn mark on the cloth of the ironing board. 'Clumsy, clumsy girl,' scolds Lilian. Failure annoys her greatly and she has no patience with people who are slow. Dorothy lowers her head and presses on. No point in answering back. Anyway, there are many, many things Dorothy knows she will have to learn, for the future. It kind of all makes sense to her, on balance.

For example, almost immediately after they return home at the end of summer, she knows she will start work as a teller at the Doric-columned Bank of Montreal on Place d'Armes. True adulthood will surely begin there, she has been forecasting, without knowing quite what to expect of it. She is a thin, neatly presented girl who can handle figures: that's what she can do. The throaty marble echo of this austere place frequented by business people and well-to-do families – many of whom were known to her already as they criss-crossed its wide foyer under her gaze – intimidated her at first when she was taken there by her father to investigate what her prospects might be. Yet, she has already been driving the de Soto for two whole years – the same as all the other girls. Like them, she has been kitted out with proper evening clothes, too: a couple of tailored gowns with separate shoes and neat little pochettes to match each one. It is all part of growing up and she rather takes it for granted. She has no doubt she *will* be married eventually, takes it as given. Just how such a thing is to come about is far too strange to cause her much apprehension, although her reading of romantic novels has been giving her certain ideas. But no, she has no real worries about her future: her mother will be taking care of that.

Nevertheless, Dorothy often feels mildly *useless*, like today. While she irons, she allows her mind to stray around foolish notions, impossible to define, which are lighter than the moving shadows created by branches of a tree just outside the window where they coil about each other, distracting her. Everything today is feeling unfinished, to Dorothy, in a languid sort of way.

'Concentrate, Dorothy. *Concentrate*, please.'

'All *right*, OK, mother. I am. I will.'

'Now, I am going to show you how to fold a shirt.'

'Is any of this important?'

'Important? Of course it is. Do you think I would allow a daughter of mine to appear slovenly in front of her mother-in-law?'

'But *maids* do the ironing – '

'And smart girls know how to, so they can keep an eye on their maids. OK?'

Dorothy pouts thoughtfully.

At eleven o'clock Edith makes them all a pot of coffee on the stove, of her own volition. She is a quiet, kindly child.

'Thank you, dear,' says Lilian, just as the ironing is completed. 'So which of you young ladies will join me back out in the garden?'

Now Bets, that sporty girl who tells anyone who will listen that she intends to become a ballerina, is outside already, performing expert cartwheels on the lawn, tripping in and out of the shade. Years later, one used to being vigilant, like Dorothy, is able to track each of these moments so that in retrospect it will seem as though they were being purposefully staged, as though part of a pre-scripted pageant.

At just after noon the delivery man comes with two boxes of groceries. When he leaves, Lilian loses no time in retrieving a side of cooked ham from the refrigerator. She slices half of it, puts potatoes on to boil and washes lettuce, tomato and cucumber.

By ten to one, when the steam from the potatoes has long subsided, it seems likely they are going to be late back from the marina for their lunch, Edward and Kenneth.

Notwithstanding this, Dorothy sets the table while a pleasant aroma of warmed, melting butter sliding over the hot potatoes only serves to increase Edith's appetite. In fact, she is now mouthing '*come on, come on,*' through the kitchen window towards the road, drawing circles with her finger in the mist her breath creates, making a squeaky sound on the glass as if this could be enough to draw her brother and father home. 'Stop it, Edith,' orders Lilian. 'Don't be annoying.'

'Sorry, mother,' replies Edith, re-positioning herself.

Although her children have all overtaken her in height by this time, it has always been plain to them that their mother must be obeyed in all matters, unequivocally. She is quick to snuff out any answering back and tells them how ungainly and unattractive such behaviour is, which they accept. She requires a show of impeccable manners of them at all times, even when they are alone together and ostensibly relaxing.

'Where's Bets got to?'' Lilian calls out with a sigh, placing a lid on the potatoes to keep them warm, though she prefers it when the butter is not left to seep into them because it makes them soggy, and this will surely happen if lunch is delayed much longer. The sound of a jazzy tune from the wind-up phonogram on the veranda answers her question: the fourteen-year-old is now dancing, as she will do whenever she gets a chance, flinging her arms wide and inventing fancy arabesques of her own.

At one-thirty, Lilian instructs Dorothy to start serving up while she pours herself a small sherry. Edward and Kenneth will just have to have plates made up for them and put by so they can eat whenever they turn up.

At two-thirty a police car draws up.

At two-thirty two Lilian is spotted by a neighbour – alerted by this unusual visit – getting into it, while the three girls, all gathered in the doorway as though framed in a group portrait, pause for a moment to watch the car cause a minor dust storm as it speeds away.

'Like I say, there's been an accident, that's all I know right now,' says the nice policeman once they are on their way. 'What we have to do is get you there as soon as possible, lady,' he adds with the lazy, sideways smile he employs which is intended to be comforting, his arm on the back of the seat so he can keep an eye on Lilian while he is keeping up a steady stream of chatter. 'Don't you worry too much right now.' What lovely, self-assured voices Canadian men have, Lilian thinks, so comforting. She is prepared to allow this man's voice to stave off a pinch of concern about the way things are developing. 'My husband is a doctor, you know,' she informs him, with confidence. Edward will be dealing very well with any accident, she is sure about that too. But why do they need her?

The scene at the lakeside appears to be just that as they approach – a carefully arranged backcloth made for a drama. But who are the players? Why is she here? Then, all of a sudden, her mind begins to join up certain clues. The man in the car might have been trying to prepare the way for this a little – who knows? She was not really listening to any of his talk – only the sound of it – and she hears nothing at all right now as she runs – dashes – to where her husband is kneeling on the boardwalk, appearing to hit a body with his hands then turn it over in order to haul the arms backward. She can't make out who the unconscious figure is. Yet at the same time she knows very well.

'What happened? What is happening?' she appeals to Edward, who refuses to acknowledge her, so intent is he on the task in hand.

When two men in the crowd come forward and try to raise him up Edward lets out a ferocious 'No!' both in response to them and as if trying to rouse the body in front of him. This inert, this perfect body, is his son, Kenneth. 'Come on, man, you've been at it for over an hour,' whispers someone who has been kneeling next to Edward. To no avail whatsoever. He keeps right on pounding at Kenneth's water-logged chest.

He works on until he can physically pump no longer and when he slumps back on his heels, his head bowed low, the futility of his efforts is plain for all to see.

They back off in the end, Edward and Lilian, too

stunned to speak. Lilian lets out an involuntary groan which shoots out a painful root that curls around the people standing by, though she attempts to hold it in with one hand in front of her mouth. She notices Edward's panama hat on the boardwalk a way off, a forlorn object drifting in a light breeze. The hat just carries on – unlike Kenneth – she muses, illogically. A feeling of deep, irrational pity for the hat suddenly melts her: it looks so vulnerable. She slowly picks it up and grips its rim.

He will not be reached. Neither of them will be reached. The small crowd waits to see if anyone can help but it is a long time before either Lilian or Edward can bring themselves to recognize that there are people there.

She turns and wanders a little way off.

Alone, she grips a flagpole hammered into the end of the jetty and a moment of clarity assaults her with the intensity of a physical blow. In a flash of white light, she sees for the first time the sheer folly of it all – of *being here* in Canada without her dearest Kenneth, surrounded by a heap of artful subterfuges that now seem so have been pointlessly crafted and sustained over the years. For a minute or two she experiences the whole artifice of her mannered existence as a mocking accusation rising up before that loss that she is yet to wholly confront, back there on the jetty. She sinks down, dizzy with the force of it, barely aware of being eased gently up by sundry others. She shrinks from their prying hands, but eventually yields with something like a snarl on her face – the snarl of a cornered dog: bloodied, uncomprehending, defiant. Then she shakes them off entirely and strides back to Edward, who is talking to the police, and takes her place beside him.

Much later, when it is evening and she can't settle, she returns to this spot alone and stands close to the water's edge, listening to the dull stupidity, the pointless entropy of tiny waves clumping over and over themselves: flop, flop, flop. In the way of waves, they are declaring the passing of another day, but they also seem to be bitterly mocking her with the banality of their leaden inevitability. There is nothing, nothing, after all, she can absorb from the sight of such wavelets. All beauty, all happiness, all loving kindness – it's all been an illusion feeding on the treachery of borrowed time. The thin line of the horizon, sharp as a knife, appears absurdly unblemished, despite this tragedy. There are no signs, no portents there, only whiffs of weather, puffs of cloud promising rain later, maybe. There is no memorial to be had for that dear, lovely boy, no stain on the water or rift parting it to declare and honour where he had gone under. There is no pity here in this place, and this hurts her to the core because it feels so disrespectful towards him.

The autopsy records that he died by drowning, brought on by a sudden, unpredictable brain haemorrhage.

Not one, but two lost sons, then. Is their beloved Kenneth the price to be paid for getting rid of the first? Without leave of appeal?

ALL AT SEA

15

Canada, 1945

Hey! Here they come!

A small group of friends are eager for the emergence of the bride and groom, forming an arch with their arms in readiness outside the church just before the cheer goes up. The newly wedded couple is soon followed by a medium sized crowd of guests in formal clothes trailing behind the pair, who will be leading all on foot to the reception at a hotel nearby.

But what on earth can this be? As she squints against the sudden contrast of sunlight a strange fizzing starts up in Dorothy's head, gripping her new husband's arm now that *the deed has been done,* and the irrefutable proof of the matter has been lodged in the certificate entrusted to her safe-keeping barely twenty minutes previously. There can be no turning back now. Is this how a bride is meant to feel? She does not know about that – how could she? She's never been a bride before – and she is certainly not about to share such odd sensations with anyone else, especially those friends who organised her shower, who seemed so worldly wise all of a sudden, spraying her with their homely darts of advice. Is this why it is called a shower, she wondered at the time? Surely, the last deposits of pre-wedding doubts should be gone by now? It's as though she cannot quite keep pace with all that's happening, let alone relax properly into her new status, despite trying hard to keep in step.

When all is said and done, it does feel as though it might have been a little too … quick? One moment she was a young woman; next, at the stroke of a pen, she has become a person who from henceforth will be regarded as "Mrs Robinson". It sounds hugely different, this new name, and suffers from both its strangeness and the added weightiness of such a title. The surname she has just acquired comes from one of the other officers on the air force base who pursued her in a flattering and, in the end, irresistible way. So where is her smile? Are these very private feelings making the bride look as though she might want to stop the clock and wind it back to earlier in the day, to when she was "myself" and not this newly espoused creature?

Well, tough, thinks Lilian nearby (accurately reading her daughter's bewilderment, as she invariably does). She has been watching Dorothy like a hawk to make sure she doesn't faint or do something else inappropriate (Lilian knows a thing or two about bringing off a performance). Look at her right now, fiddling with her veil in such an awkward way … gauche, distracted girl. With her small, gloved right hand, Lilian flicks out an irritated "stop that" sign towards Dorothy. Instinctively on guard, the girl casts a guilty glance at the brand new husband standing right beside her, as though he might be about to reprove her as well.

Without quite being able to put her finger on it, Lilian felt a touch suspicious of the rather hearty man Dorothy had chosen. It probably wasn't entirely the fact that he had red hair – though that certainly did nothing to enhance her view of him. It was more that he came with the scent of England about him – a place with which she neither wished nor intended to have further dealings. But there: a small fortune has been invested in a smart hotel for the reception to cover a three-day stay in Ottawa for herself, Edward and the girls, over from Montreal for the occasion. And whichever way you look at it, the eldest of their girls is married at last and that's a relief. Lilian counts this as a personal accomplishment.

It has to be said that he who is *Mr* Robinson wasn't Dorothy's first choice either – this red-haired Englishman. No, *he* was the Canadian Air Force pilot whose plane had gone down on his very first mission over in France the year before. He had wavy light-coloured hair, that dead beau, parted on the side, and you could guarantee it would always be immaculately oiled into place. So stylish, he had been. And with the sloppiest, sweetest smile as he held her in his arms for all eternity, according to the black and white photo she treasures and never, *ever* intends to do away with, despite being joined to this other one now.

By this, her wedding day, she has managed to build a comfortable enough mythology around the man who will be Sunny's father (or at least the *idea* she has of him) as some sort of "gentleman" from the old country. For one thing, he is the owner of a Cambridge Blue, whatever that is: it sounds important, anyway. But here she is – she has just married him and her parents seem satisfied with this state of affairs, if not exactly jubilant. In the knowledge that her mother, in particular, has been appeased, she feels let off the hook somewhat, and for the very first time ever in a position to cut loose and embark on a life she feels she has managed to claim entirely for herself. How exciting it all is, but mighty daunting, too.

Right now, she is aware, primarily, that she is very

new at it.

Let's be plain, though: Dorothy's sole ambition from way back has undeniably been to marry, just as she was given to understand that her mother's had been. It was, for sure, the correct and dignified state for any girl and there was some complicity between them on this issue. Not that it was ever discussed in plain terms, as a concept; it was more like an unshakeable understanding they both shared. Dorothy came to view it less as a rite of passage than a *duty* to one's family. And of course to oneself. (To Sunny, the daughter she will soon conceive, such a notion will come to sound like the laziest abdication of self-hood there could possibly be. At the very least, her parents' marriage as a goal in itself will strike Sunny as a gross omission on her mother's part, an anachronism and a feat of self-abandonment which is amplified by seeming so careless, given the course it would take. Maybe Sunny will be proved wrong; it is possible that she might be missing the real point. Only time will tell.)

Meanwhile, as far as Dorothy is concerned right now, from way back it was always made plain in ways both subtle and blunt that she could never fully *let go* until she was married. Oh, how desirable as well as necessary that hazy state of relaxation appeared to be as it crept up on her, promising to become an end in itself. If she ever felt the need to seek confirmation, all she had to do was look about her and be in no doubt that *all* the other girls were set on getting themselves married, too, without exception, and most of them had done it already.

'Come on, Dorothy, remember that you are *someone* in this city,' Lilian had drummed into her eldest daughter each time she tapped her back (Dorothy was prone, as a teenager, to round her shoulders). 'Look at you. You'll get a curved spine and you won't like that'. Or, when she caught Dorothy peering idly around her when they were out in the street together: 'Don't stare, Dorothy. Look *past* people. It does no harm to make them wonder whether they're worthy of you'. Or, if Dorothy forgot herself and behaved in a frivolous way then, Lilian was in the habit of lowering her voice to the coolest point on its register and command: 'Behave, please!' And without fail Dorothy would leap up to correct herself.

She was twenty-seven years old on her wedding day – virtually on the shelf.

A little later, while picking up the knife from a silver salver passed to her for the purpose of executing the first slice of her wedding cake, Dorothy suddenly remembers spotting a newspaper clipping in the silver mail tray in the hall by the front door, back home in Montreal not too long ago, announcing that some British high-up, a rear Admiral, or something, called Sir John Fitch, was visiting Montreal at that time. The way this clipping was openly displayed made her think that this undoubted "someone" must be some sort of relation of her mother's since her maiden name had been Fitch, and therefore of hers, too. Maybe he'd been invited? Looking around, she doesn't see evidence of it. They'd been so busy with the detail of wedding preparations and now she wishes she'd taken a note of the Admiral's name, maybe with a vague idea about making contact with him back in England. Perhaps that was why such a newspaper item had been left out, for all to see. Of all the many things Dorothy has neglected to ask her mother before getting married, this is but one.

It is too late now for questions. That time has gone forever. Soon, all too soon, she will be sailing to England.

Isn't it just extraordinary the way that whole

populations seem to be on the move now the war is over, for the purpose of starting all over again – just as she, herself, is soon to do? Flotillas of big ships must be, at this very moment, she supposes, making waves across the surface of the ocean ...

Concentrate, Dorothy, projects Lilian towards the bride, who accepts she cannot escape being under all kinds of scrutiny on her wedding day, being the star of the show.

A little while later the newly married couple are required to freeze in a number of set poses for a small collection of classy photographs. They are both air force officers – she in the Canadian Air Force, he in the English.

It shall all be accomplished properly. This has been Lilian's sole challenge and triumph during the busy months leading up to this wedding. She has shepherded Dorothy through ritual trips to Eaton's in preparation not just for the wedding but also for her trip back to England as a wife. In several departments of the Montreal store, a young lady (for this is what Dorothy undoubtedly is) can be kitted out with virtually everything she needs, including a whole new set of clothes for her trunk. It was on one of these sorties that she had taken possession of a shiny black snakeskin vanity case full of the latest Elizabeth Arden toiletries. If Dorothy herself sometimes appeared to be sluggish about such choices it was because she wholly acceded to her mother's judgement and taste in everything laid out before them. She had an absolute belief that her stylish mother would know exactly how a person should be equipped for a voyage to England and, importantly, for the moment she makes her debut over there.

Some nine months later, the time for that trip is upon

them. The day arrives when Dorothy must say goodbye to her family, perhaps for ever – who knows in these uncertain times, when foreign travel is such a major undertaking? From the window of the train taking them on the twenty-six hour journey to Halifax from Montreal, she aims a final, all-encompassing wave towards her parents and sisters on the platform, squinting at each one of them for the last time as though laying down the sharpest possible image in her mind, lest she ever forget *exactly* what they look like. They've all come to see her off and smiles are a little tense on all sides, given the momentousness of the occasion and the time it takes for the journey to get started.

It's plain to Robert that she is preoccupied, leaning back in the compartment as the train pulls away eventually, aware of the unknown that lies ahead, and he wonders whether her anxiety about leaving her family behind might also be affected by the early phase of her pregnancy. Too embarrassed to share much of this with a man, let alone one she has still to get to know thoroughly, she retains mixed feelings about all that is happening to her under such circumstances, and it feels to her a bit like being lured into the slipstream of a driverless vehicle. Frowning, probing the gathering darkness outside, she summons all her senses – somewhat frozen after the drama of that final, *final* letting go – and comes to the tentative conclusion that all will (or must) be well in the end. Somehow.

It isn't until evening the following day that Halifax comes into view and as it does her mood lifts. 'Hey, look there,' she points, spotting the crowds of local people who have climbed Citadel Hill to watch the loading of one of the big ships – maybe theirs? – feeling delighted that for once she might know something that her new husband doesn't. One thing she is starting to figure out about Robert, now that it is just the two of them, is that he has a way of making her feel stupid. She knows it isn't necessarily his fault – he can't help it that his head is full of untold amounts of arcane knowledge which can erupt randomly during the course of a conversation – but when this happens it disorients her, putting her on her guard and tempting her to make silly, bluff responses as she attempts to hold her own.

To prove to him that she is not entirely dumb, she goes on to remind him how Halifax was the main hub of marine transport between Canada and England during the recently ended war, the setting off point for an important and sustained mission – that of supplying his homeland with food and other essential goods. Lately, the steady flow of people arriving here has been gathering momentum for a different purpose – and look here: coming into view, is Pier 21 itself, that big waterfront shed through which, during the next year or so, nearly fifty thousand war brides from Europe are expected to pass, bringing with them some 22,000 children. 'Enough to populate a small city,' exclaims Dorothy, warming to her theme – all intent upon starting new lives with the Canadian officers that they'd met and married back in England or elsewhere in Europe. At the same time, it isn't lost on her that they are all heading over *here*, while she is undoubtedly going over *there*, a notion that prompts a frisson of worry as she wonders for a second whether she might have somehow *blundered*. Does this make her impending journey eastwards the *wrong way*, then? As their train rumbles past Pier 21, she realises that she has no idea whether or not there are other Canadian women in the same boat as she is (well, a different *actual* boat, of course). She suspects not, because there weren't many allied serving men like Robert based in Canada in order to support the training of new pilots for the war. She wonders what English war brides about to settle in Canada are like. She wonders, too, whether there will be an opportunity to meet up with any Canadian war brides at all in England.

During her wedding shopping, she'd come across a Canadian cookbook written especially for such British brides moving to Canada and the United States, and made a point of leafing through it. On one randomly opened page she paused to learn: 'The average Canadian dislikes boiled fresh meat almost as much as he dislikes suet pudding, though he usually likes meats that have first been corned, cured or smoked.' OK. True. But in trying to reverse this in order to figure out what British men's appetites might be like, she came stuck over "suet pudding", clearly an English speciality dish. Also, she was well aware that people didn't seem to drink coffee in England. Mingling with officers on the English base in Ottawa had introduced her to a viscous dark brown liquid pretending to be coffee called Camp, made from chicory. She sure would miss her Canadian coffee, if that's what they drank over there.

A taxi takes them along a jetty where lights are coming on, blunting the last remnants of daylight. Heck, it *is* rather exciting, coming to land's end like this, finding oneself on the very edge of things. The curving coastline seems to cast a single protective arm around the country she is leaving behind as they travel on towards the big ship named on their tickets. It feels to Dorothy like arriving at the ultimate place, taking her to the very brink of her own imminent becoming. But she does not care too much to gaze out to sea like he is doing with a grin on his face, as if he were in the act of drawing himself away from here.

Eventually, the Robinsons find themselves face-to-face with the towering bulk of the SS *Aquitania*, securely moored, raising their eyes to appraise its passenger decks way, way above. She will never forget her first sighting of the distinctive red funnels of the ship. They were like giant pillar boxes, Robert offered, apart from the black banding around the top. This great vessel, launched in 1913 by the Countess of Derby on a special public holiday in Glasgow, contained the very first onboard indoor swimming pool, Dorothy is pleased to read in the leaflet given out with their tickets. *Not that I will be using a swimming pool in my condition, of course, but it might be fun to go and see it* ... It turns out, as she had suspected, that this ship has a rich history of its own: it thrills her to imagine the incubation of thousands of partial stories within its cavernous hull all the years it has been commercially afloat. For the last thirty of them it has reliably brought westwards the young, the adventurous, the curious as well as a phalanx of displaced travellers on the run from a decadent and troubled Europe during the years leading up to the Second World War: Germans, Jews, Poles, Scots and Irish in the main. She has read about them from time to time in Montreal newspapers and given a thought to the desperate people fleeing what sounds like unimaginable poverty and exploitation, exhausted by the escalation and complexity of troubled times brewing over there on that other dark continent. This big ship, she surmises, must have seemed like a crucible of hope for them – as it must now be for her, too.

This may be why Dorothy is by no means the first traveller to issue a deep sigh of relief when it is her turn to set foot on one of the gangplanks linking ship to shore, because at the very least there is the promised respite of being *nowhere at all* for the eight days of the voyage, in the middle of the supremely fluid nothingness of a seascape and wholly in the hands of other forces and influences, giving her soul a little time to float freely and prepare to adjust.

Conservative by nature, she pays real attention to the lifeboat drill instead of pretending she has done it all before, like she notices some are doing. It's the first thing they're required to do – assemble on deck to be shown the lifeboats slung against the ship's flanks and to try on their heavy lifejackets while the ship is still in dock. "We will not stop if anyone falls overboard" heralds a sign. *And I'll bet they mean it*, Dorothy thinks to herself, with a grimace.

The *Aquitania* glides gently out of Halifax at last in a bit of a squall, which confines the newly weds to their narrow cabin on B deck. 'It gets calmer, mid-Atlantic,' Robert announces. He has, of course, done the journey once before, in the opposite direction. 'I certainly hope so,' she replies, because she is definitely feeling queasy now.

Once at sea, she comes to favour a place by the rail on the middle deck in her new, dark green gabardine raincoat with its wide collar turned up and both hands tucked into stylishly expansive pockets in a pose which could have come from the pages of Vogue magazine, though it is perfectly natural to her. She discovers that to feel the sea air almost assaulting her face is actually quite exhilarating: its energy may be harsh, but it is also purifying. It dampens her face with its *petilance,* a fine mist of watery air calling out to her own tiny bubbles of anticipation, reminding her of the expectation brought on by the first sip of a glass of champagne. She prefers to be out here alone, because conversation becomes laborious and exhausting when words must be shouted over the perpetual maritime gale, making them sound unintentionally terse.

She finds herself thinking about things, out here, in a newly philosophical way.

It is strange, for example, the way that hope and fear become almost indistinguishable to one in the first throes of exile. One moment, the reality of her leaving rises up in a shade of pearl. Then, without warning or break in continuity, it shades into charcoal, perhaps in collusion with the rhythm of the waves. She feels it would be indiscrete to raise any of this with Robert, and wouldn't know how to find the words without feeling awkward and afraid that he would laugh at her. Instead, her imagination produces occasional sentences which float free of her more troublesome thoughts. *Truth is, I don't know how I feel ... Truth is, I must wait and see.*

There will be changes to be made, for sure. But for now her anxiety, when it arises, is the fault of the slurry of memory wrapping itself around the first quarter century of her life so far, and it is small wonder that it rises up from time to time on the swell of the powerful Atlantic waves. Day by day, as Canada grows further away, she is surprised how a rag bag of recollections begins to slip almost naturally into the recess of her mind marked *then*, compressing itself into what, if she only knew it, is about to be transformed into an *impression* of Canada – home's bigger picture rather than its reality. By the time they become used to the ocean and its ways it is as though Canada, no longer visible, is in the process of slipping slowly down (off?) the face of the globe altogether. Notions such as this strike her with poignancy, turning her home country into a vision of a lover who is no longer available – like the deceased wartime beau, perhaps: forever beyond reach.

Nevertheless, by the end of a mercifully uneventful trip and with a determined effort, she almost manages to convert what might be described as rising apprehension at the approach of a foreign shore back into a sense of mild and largely trusting anticipation. After all, she tells herself, in a way I *am* going home, recalling the fact that she had been born in Eastbourne towards the end of that other war, the one they called "great" which her father had played some part in.

And on a warm June morning, here they are, finally, in Liverpool, England – *at last*, because Dorothy has been experiencing morning sickness with embarrassing regularity in their foetid little cabin during the past few days. Still, it's not too hot in England, despite being summertime. It's not even that breezy down by the docks, where staid white cumulous clouds balloon above the water's edge like inflatable airborne sofas, creating a series of bulbous shadows on the water.

She summons the patience to edge slowly forward in the crush of the disembarkation queue. Somewhat tensely steering her by the arm is her husband – lately squadron leader Robert Robinson, once more plain "mister" of that name – who, very soon, just like her, will be knuckling down to the business of reclaiming a peace time sense of his own identity.

Why, wonders Dorothy, looking all around her as the next leg of their long journey gets underway – why is it that everything in this new land is so lumberingly *slow*? This is her first impression of England. She is wearing a long fur coat, far too bulky to store in her trunk, which she has left unbuttoned, exposing a tailored cotton dress underneath covering the neat bump which is Sunny.

Should anyone have been waiting for them amongst the crowd of greeters and photographers by the dockside, that someone might have perked up to give his neighbour a nudge and remark: 'Look, here they come,' on recognising Robert. Then, turning expectantly towards his new wife, there could be no doubt in anyone's mind that Dorothy, his bride, is utterly beautiful, though in a distant, understated sort of way. Also, that she is entirely unaware of this fact.

Though her beauty is not underscored by the kind of prettiness that stares people in the face in cheeky awareness of itself (occluded, as it is, by habitual reticence), for some time now it has been regarded with respect and admiration by new acquaintances. Sometimes, it's as though they need to step back a pace to appreciate her fully (which she typically mistakes for their revulsion or suspicion, and has to consciously resist curling into herself, her eyes cast down). She has bright, clear, cider coloured eyes and is noticeably small-boned, yet tall for those days – around five feet seven inches – naturally slim, with long, bony hands and a shock of thick brown hair, swept back fashionably from her face. Maybe – since she wears her clothes so well, so effortlessly – she could be described as chic, but no: this would make her too worldly, too self-conscious, and she isn't at all self-conscious. Rather, she is utterly, impenetrably, self-contained. What that lovely carapace contains is not to be probed, least of all by herself. (At a later date, Sunny would find herself rather unkindly comparing her mother to a perfectly shaped but hollow Easter egg, one which manages to mask a dent or two under the housing of its brittle, silvery covering.)

It doesn't help matters that she has been programmed

for marriage as a kind of stasis – an arrival in itself, an end point that surely requires no more effort on her part.

Robert peers this way and that, on the lookout for a porter. As it happens, he is prone to anxiety by nature, just like Dorothy, which typically finds expression in short-lived displays of irritability – she is already learning about this side of him, the nearer he comes to being home, and she has made a private vow to herself to stand up to it. *That's what mother would do, surely.* At such times, words between them are like tiny, sharp-edged pebbles that hit home then fall away awkwardly, as though lacking the grout to seal them in place.

She places first one then the other elegant court shoe on *terra firma* and observes, to herself as much as to him: 'Oh boy. Land at last.' And the way she pronounces 'last' is, it strikes him, almost Liverpudlian. For the present it will be "land" and not "home" because she needs to reserve judgement about that.

A couple of hours later her body is swaying pleasantly on the well-sprung seat of their second class carriage in the train carrying them south. And here's a thing (this is Dorothy's second impression of England): how *small* everything in England seems to the girl who has grown up with her soul calibrated to the wide Canadian prairies beyond to form her perspective on what "space" amounts to. The oddly shaped fields here, the funny little terraces of houses – they all flash by, as well as other narrow trains heading in the other direction which pass with a cheery *whoosh* and a white blast of steam, making her jump and temporarily obscuring her view.

For their first night, he has booked a hotel in London by Liverpool Street Station. Upon arrival, she falls asleep instantly with a sense that she has earned her place as a full member of that exclusive community of ordinary people caught up in the extraordinary process of changing places for good, giving her a tentative boost of reassurance that lifts her spirits a little at the thought that perhaps she is not entirely unmoored, after all. Maybe not.

The following afternoon, it takes less than two hours to arrive at a dinky little village station on an East Anglian branch line half an hour or so north of Cambridge where she is astonished and a little embarrassed to see what appears to be a welcoming party out there on the platform, evidently curious to meet her. As the train takes on water through a spitting pipe attached to a tank by the signal box, she prepares to be guided down to the platform by Robert.

'It's *Dorothy*, isn't it?' booms a robust young woman of more or less her own age, bounding forward to pump her hand in rather an alarming manner. Is the extra emphasis because her name identifies her as peculiar, she wonders? The stranger that she is? She can't stop herself freezing, at first. The whole ambience is so different from what she is used to that it causes her to recoil ever so slightly and respond with a one-sided "Yankee" sort of smile with her lips but not her eyes. They are fond of him, of course they are. He is one of theirs, and probably they want to like her too, to honour her on account of him, to give a good impression, to take her into the fold, if she will let them. This woman is one of three of Robert's acquaintances, she is given understand as she is introduced, perceiving a kind of welcoming party. Once more, she reminds herself to suspend any hasty judgement.

And now, finally, for home itself, the end of the

journey. Has ever a word been pumped up and primped and cosseted and decked out with such expectation?

It turns out to be a square Victorian house which has seen better times, with its rugged looking façade on the north facing side of a village green, its ageing walls a pattern of red bricks and flint stones. Their home. It soon transpires that the house is already inhabited by Robert's mother, who lives there. Waiting in undisguised excitement also are three of her sisters who live nearby, up for this very special occasion. A large pot is boiling on the stove in the kitchen, containing something tied with muslin. The steam issuing from it smells humid, meaty and well done.

'This is it, then,' announces Robert to his new bride with evident pride as he opens the back door for her (only the postman, she will soon learn, goes to the front door, along with unfamiliar visitors). Dorothy can see that he is in a very good mood indeed from the broad smile on his face as he waves his left hand in a wide arc that proudly invites her to take it all in.

'Well, hullo,' ventures Dorothy, her eyes adjusting to the red and white coconut matting on the floor of the living room in the dark interior, and a mean little fireplace containing an empty grate. A mottled glass lampshade suspended from the high ceiling by a chain catches her eye, too, as well as the pair of mock Chinese dragon vases on either end of the mantelpiece, whose open black mouths gape back at her.

'Oh, my, oh my, it *is* good to see you both at last, home and safe,' gushes Maud, Robert's mother, barely able to contain herself (she had sent not one, but *four*, telegrams for their wedding back in Canada, just to be sure *something* arrived and not trusting the state of the mail). 'Go along, Robert, go and get the bags in,' she instructs her son, with a wink in Dorothy's direction.

'The table is laid. I expect you'll be hungry, dear,' she adds, with no pause between any of her opening statements, grasping Dorothy's arm as though afraid she might run away. Recoiling instinctively from such gauche enthusiasm, Dorothy has no intention of being unmannerly and recovers herself quickly. But here it is: this is probably the moment when the first splinter of real, rather than suspected doubt digs in, taking its place not as a visitor but a permanent resident under her skin. While her mother-in-law's rough hands still twist into her skin, Dorothy begins to sense that far from being the proper gentleman her imagination had constructed – a vague concept to do with manners, with class, with exclusivity – Robert Robinson has, in truth, turned out to be something a little more ordinary. She sees it plainly, now, written across a page turning over in her mind and falling in place. At heart, he is a rural boy made good, one unlikely to want to distance himself far from his origins right here in this house, not from the hearty way he is hugging his mother, anyway. I must hold my nerve, she thinks, blaming herself for such a failure of perception whilst there had still seemed time to get to know who he really was, way back in Canada. Was this the true reason why her mother had never wholly warmed to him? Well, it's too late to find out now, for sure, and Dorothy is not certain she even wants to, anyway, because if that were the case it would only make her own idiocy shine out of her like a beacon for all to see. A small tremor – part dread, part stunned confusion, part quickening of the child inside her – appears to pass unnoticed by those assembled in front of her, well masked as it is by her loose maternity dress.

Glancing around her, Dorothy views the other three people in the living room, figures who appear to be in some kind of startled coma, as if her presence has caused them to be uncertain how they should behave, finding themselves face to face with an exotic from the colonies. Two of them are identified as Maud's cousins, the other a sister. One, she notices, subliminally mouths Maud's words as she speaks. They wouldn't miss Robert's homecoming for the world, she is told – and of course, the opportunity of getting a first look at the bride. For a brief moment, she wishes the younger ones of the welcoming party at the station had stayed a little longer.

Will Dorothy round on her new husband later, as the walls of their small bedroom close in on her at the end of such a bewildering day? (Maud to Dorothy, as the couple prepare to retire: 'You shan't be wanting a hot water bottle in this weather, shall you, dear?') Will she accuse him of false pretences? Will they face each other like players in the process of unravelling the rules of an unfamiliar game? Both are the keenest players: she of bridge, he of cricket. They are already familiar with the irresistible scent of a potential contest. When she sits down for a rubber of bridge, which she has learned well from her mother, Dorothy knows how to play with covert cunning, making smart moves to disable her opponent's hand. As for Robert, his cricket is performed like a gladiatorial conquest. It is the creative centre of his life, as she will soon discover.

The trouble is, in marriage he is not cut out to be a team player at all. Any more than she is.

16

Right from the start, it is Dorothy and Robert's habit every Saturday night to meet a group of his local friends – including the loyal welcoming party – for drinks at one of the pubs in town. And what do they do? As one, they guide themselves back to the recent past, to those few, increasingly concatenated years of war which were finally rounded off the previous year, although their embers still smoulder in the hearts of the people. So here's what they do: they re-live, through a stream of anecdotes and old songs, the war just ended, because it's still very much alive in their minds and refuses to be boxed up. Maybe this unprecedented wedge of time *needs* to be re-played, and in the doing of it partially refashioned, in order that their collective memory can create a folder into which, eventually, those war years may be safely placed, once lingering trauma is finally defused. It is at such gatherings that Dorothy senses these people's search for a lost centre, fractured by time and last experienced, in truth, way back during the 1930s.

Here they are again after the first few rounds, swaying arm in arm and side to side, humming along to an old piano in the corner. Dorothy finds she is occasionally able to join in, picking up a tune or phrase she's learned. How they all love to reminisce, especially the men, as though they have suddenly become born raconteurs, officers of the story rather than the regiment. How they whoop with laughter at the absurdity of stylised, cartoon images that come to mind, readily indulging in the clipped dialogue of incidents which, as reality is recalibrated and reinterpreted, increasingly seem inconceivable or absurd in retrospect. Time and again, these meetings produce a profound gratitude amongst them that makes them cling to each other as they remind themselves that the boat in which they'd been sailing until that point had not been entirely shipwrecked after all.

Week days, left to herself, Dorothy remains somewhat vertiginously convinced she has landed up on another planet. Even the word "continent" – as in "The Continent" – that's what they call Europe over here, just as her father always did – has a mythical ring to it, representing all that is unknowable, dark and ravished, out of sight yet shrunk to being just over there, across the narrow English Channel.

Here, on Planet Abroad off the western edge of The Continent, there can be no guarantee of ever again landing back on the version of earth she has been familiar with before marriage on that other, faraway landmass: so much is by now certain. For her, Canada has become little more than a discernable shape since the other continent, mainland Europe, naturally assumes much more of a day-to-day presence in her life these days, being the constant focus of ripples of the news from the ashes of early reconstruction. These two continents – America and Europe – it sometimes feels as though they are a pair of walls, and she has become someone who is in danger of slipping away into the invisibility between, suspended somewhere in the middle. To make matters worse, both have a whiff of "then" about them as well: two half spheres of a roughly etched globe, one smelling of her own past, the other of a collective past being re-assembled in the wake of recent conflagration.

Only the most fragile lines of communication are in place between the two continents, going back and forth in the form of "aerograms" on wafer thin blue paper which must be folded and licked at the edge on three sides after being filled with spindly writing that more often than not scampers up and down the margins in order to cram into the mean space allowed every wish, every last bit of detail, every important sentiment. All the chatter of magnificently mundane everyday life and the rituals that embellish and bind folk must be mustered to make sense within the limited space of these vital, feather-weight communications. This is how her sisters keep in touch with her, but Dorothy finds it almost impossible to compose such missives herself, though she dutifully tries. This is because instead of feeling fertile with curiosity about her new homeland, the truth is that she senses that she has entered a *museum,* causing her inner seismogram to all but flatten out. 'Dear Bets,' she writes to one sister. 'I baked an apple pie here today. I wonder what you are all doing at home?' What else is there? She taps her pen and waits for inspiration.

What she is careful *not* to do in any of her stilted communications home is to pour out in crude terms any of her partially articulated feelings to her mother or her sisters. To put it a slightly different way: just as the maintenance of her face and body matters a lot to her, so does *keeping face.* No-one – she has absolutely promised herself – no-one back there shall suspect that a mistake might have been made in coming here, with all the associations of personal failure that this would imply.

Robert is not at home very much. The university, typically loyal to his past sporting glory, has rewarded him with teaching scheduled in such a way that he can coach the cricket team, which involves weekends away from home and some touring. This is the period when, as her pregnancy progresses, she often finds herself left at home with Maud, whose solicitousness she finds suffocating.

She begins to suspect that her chosen strategy of defensive withdrawal might be distorting even her own image of herself at times during this tricky period, though none of it is entirely clear to her. Most of all, it makes her suspect that she must be an odd creature. There is a sense of the uncanny about the days drifting by, as though her own originality has been diluted and turned into something lightweight and strange to her. She manages to resist such worrisome sensations only by degrees by persuading herself that it is actually Maud, her mother-in-law, and all the other locals who are out-of-kilter rather than her; yes, it is *they* who are hopelessly old-fashioned and living by the precepts of an earlier era as this new, modern time begins to unfold.

Nevertheless, when Sunny arrives in late October that year – her thick red hair gives her a permanent name rather than "Linda," which remains on her birth certificate, unused – Dorothy can still be heard taking refuge in any reference made to Canada, and even the United States (all part of *her* continent), referring to both as "home" with a certain defiance, even – if truth were told – when she doesn't altogether feel that way about it any more. She has a fundamental notion of what home should be, and surprises herself to realise that it forms one of the most essential aspects of who she is. She can't help herself: the fact is that Canada seems the better place, the *superior* place in all regards, a place about which it is acceptable for her to interject a hazy, collaborative "we" into a conversation, as in: "No, no …we don't make pastry like that at home". If not exactly in mourning, bereft of nation and with repetitive and unidentified longings, she just about recognizes that she is in danger of turning her former life into a kind of idealized hallucination – even when she knows deep down that in reality such a mutinous thought is probably a little wide of the mark.

If she could but make one or two connections from the heart, here in her husband's village, how less threatening and bleak the milieu onto which she has become artificially grafted in exile might seem. But she will not make the effort to open any of the doors that remain ajar during these early months of her arrival. In her heart, she will not permit herself do so, for fear of being subsumed once and for all into Robert's culture. As yet, she is far from ready for such a degree of assimilation because she fears it would risk disappearing for ever.

Who on earth am I, now? It perplexes her to pose such a question, as though it is too fundamental, too bewildering to pursue. What is to become of her, then? Why, instead, does she allow the worm of perpetual uncertainty to squirm so, making her vexatious at the very slightest perceived provocation or misunderstanding? What is it really made of, that submerged centre of selfhood, buried deeper than anyone so far in England has been allowed to penetrate? Maybe she has been fishing for clues lately – gingerly, as though negotiating her way across stepping stones laid into a shallow stream – not trusting herself to receive favourable messages – all the while defending herself against stalkers of that uncertain prey she believes she represents to outsiders.

Over and over she tells herself she has no choice but to let the dust settle, and then settle some more. Let it harden into gravel beneath her feet before making irreversible judgements.

Naturally, kindly feelers were put out at first to encourage her to join in, from Robert's friends who hovered for a while expectantly, but none of it felt like what she was used to back home so she became known for being stand-offish, and as time passed people began to give up their efforts and leave her to her own devices.

The days, weeks and months that pass after the birth of her daughter find Dorothy still on her guard while the infant Sunny, passed lovingly around amongst the coven of elderly aunts, begins to focus her eyes and in due course commences the painstaking process of getting her own bearings on the world from the depths of her pram.

Standing in the queue at the butcher's shop one day, Dorothy finds herself next in line behind an Austrian woman, brought back by one of the returning local conscripts after the war, who lives with him now in one of the new council houses in the village. A tight smile of tentative recognition might have been exchanged between these two aliens once, but there is enough protocol in place – amplified by Dorothy's own caution (as the wife of an ex-officer) – to make sure that any potential acquaintance between them is unlikely to arise. Instead, Dorothy, the doctor's daughter, concentrates on her little pickets of resistance, just as this Austrian woman can be witnessed vigorously and cheerfully crashing through barriers, quickly adopting not only the English language but a game approximation of its local dialect.

On the subject of language, despite English being her native tongue, Dorothy, quite unlike this Austrian lady, finds English a source of constant vexation. All the bewildering ways they have of expressing simple things, with their blunt and often ironic delivery ... *do you pass me them 'taters, love,* for example – a request made in the greengrocer's queue. Then again ... *that it isn't,* they say when a disagreement occurs, and: *she was in a right puckaterry yesterday* … Puckaterry? What? And the pronunciation! How is she to know that the person she's been calling "Mr Hard" is actually a Mr Howard? Why do they giggle when she calls a vase a *vorse*, heedlessly over-compensating the vowel sound in an attempt to absorb some "proper" English she's been picking up from the wireless. Oh, yes – and do these people not know that *herb* loses its "h" when said aloud?

She makes every attempt to keep her sights above the stifling dreariness and cramped conditions of the house they live in at first, and the essential manual work she is expected to do, which naturally increases when the baby is born. Robert occasionally succumbs to exasperation, calling her resistance stubborn, because as far as he can see there is a continuous blizzard of help being offered by his mother and her sisters. What's wrong with that? But apart from allowing them to walk Sunny in her pram, as a new mother she finds such offers claustrophobic and threatening, preferring to keep charge at least of *something* herself.

This is round about the time when Dorothy slips into what will become a life-long habit of pouring herself a Scotch whisky (or two, even three if the day has yawned its course out too tediously), enlivened with American ginger ale, before the long hours of the evening begin, bereft of games of bridge and the banter of her sisters.

A crucial obstacle blocking any of her tentative attempts to set up distractions for herself turns out to be transport.

From the first, she doggedly made a play for her own use of the car – only to encounter unexpected conceptual as well as practical reservations in return. Who drives cars? Men do, of course. Women who drive attract the tut-tutting controversy attached to such a self-assertive, mannish sort of activity in this fenland backwater.

Dorothy herself has been covertly eyeing the village's sole female motoring enthusiast, a racy character, with a mixture of scorn and envy. Look, there she goes again along the back road, speeding scandalously with the driver's window wound down, wearing a fashionable turban and gripping a cigarette between lips pursed in a flighty sort of leer. Such *loucheness*, such rebellion. It isn't Dorothy's style at all.

Another obstacle is that the Canadian driver's license she'd gained naturally at the age of fifteen in Montreal holds no sway in this country, so she makes her way to town without delay, takes the British test, and passes it. Just in case an opportunity arises. She figures there is no harm in being prepared.

Unfortunately, windows of opportunity to actually take the car out on her own ('oh, please, Robert, just so I don't get out of practice,' she regularly begs) are for the moment extremely rare. Robert leaves the house by 7.00am and returns at around 5.00pm, dashing all hope of using the car. Well, sometimes he does, but more often than not he has "something on" in town during the evening. *Lucky him*, thinks Dorothy to herself. No, not lucky – selfish, she revises, after another long, lonely evening shut up in their bedroom with a magazine, listening out for Sunny, rather than crowded round the fire with her mother-in-law and the sisters who always seem to be in attendance.

In her view, not being a possessor of a set of car keys of her own as she had been since she was a teenager comes to increasingly rattle her, especially as to be able to drive places – any places – would be so darned handy with Sunny now in tow, all of which Robert seems to find bizarre.

'Look, why do you have to be so awkward about it?' she thrusts out one evening, striving to keep her voice neutral, to keep the topic alive.

'Because you know you don't really need the car. And I do. It stands to reason'. A tangle of hidden rage grips her, exacerbated by her suspicion that he requires her to contain and suppress any rebelliousness regarding the one-sidedness of it all.

The car … The latest vehicle to sit on the drive is a modest and toughly built Ford Prefect, black and temperamental. Many are the early mornings, especially in winter, when hoar frost whitens the garden and Robert fails to crank it into action and has to shout for Dorothy to come out from the kitchen and *push*, to her incredulity, in her dressing gown. It lurches and stops and lurches again in a series of hesitant spurts towards (with luck) full ignition – with little Sunny and Maud viewing the uncertainties of this cliff-hanger from the kitchen window. When ignition does occur – which is by no means guaranteed – he lays into it with a blast on the accelerator that sends out a plume of blue smoke which leaves a sour smell on the sluggish early morning air and is slow to dispel, so that when Sunny leaves the house in hand with Maud a little while later to buy groceries she associates this odour with her father's crossness. Dorothy treats these necessary antics as a personal affront, groaning at him and his damn car and all that she is forced to do in this primitive place. It doesn't help matters at all when that Austrian woman acquires for her sole use a thoroughly decrepit, smoking old banger which she takes enthusiastically about the village, where it sends out loud reports from the perforations in its exhaust pipe, making old ladies jump as it passes.

There is one incident, when Sunny is around six years old, when fate, embodied by the car, intervenes. By this time, driven by impatience bordering on recklessness, Dorothy does something quite radical and extraordinary: without asking Robert's permission, she acquires a job as a flexi-time market researcher after successfully answering an advertisement in the local newspaper, meaning that she will be *obliged* to use the car some evenings, taking herself off alone to nearby villages with her bundles of forms and essentially knocking on a lot of people's doors in order to meet her targets. With a signed contract in her hand to place in front of him, she privately congratulates herself on managing, at last, to deliver a *fait accompli* to her own advantage.

The sheer pleasure of driving, of setting out on a journey, of doing something that is familiar from "the old days" back "home"! But as it turns out, this current job lasts for no more than half a dozen such expeditions. Right from the start, it is plain that Robert is twitchy when she is out on her own. It doesn't seem right, to him, to have a wife who has paid employment, although at first he prided himself on having the forbearance to "give in" to her.

One evening, on what is surely to be the last of these trips, as the clock creeps towards half past ten and she is still not back, it is not hard for him to conclude that he has reached the point where it all has to stop.

'Right, then,' he announces, to no-one in particular, slapping both palms down in a purposeful way on the arms of his easy chair and leaping from it abruptly – to be overheard by Sunny who is startled into momentary wakefulness from the first flush of deep sleep by the loudness of his voice and the crack of the chair as it grazes the wall of the adjoining room.

He decides there is no alternative but to phone the police and ask them to search for her, which he proceeds to do, observed in silence by his mother.

'I just lost my way,' she sighs as she helps Sunny with the buttons on her small blouse the next morning, and Sunny registers the sadness of resignation in her voice without understanding what it signifies. 'You know what? I spent about an hour hunting for a darned phone box to let him know I'd be late, but I just couldn't find one.' She shrugs. Sunny shrugs in sympathy. Nothing more is said. It has shaken Dorothy – both the sense of being lost in the dark and Robert's recriminations after the departure of the policeman who had eventually found her and led her home.

In the end, it adds up to an important discovery, for Dorothy: that she is far from modern enough to buck any of the established conventions here. So she resigns from her "little" job, and the forms, most of them still empty, are briskly parcelled up and sent back.

17

Coming up to the mid 1950s, there is a general feeling in the village – as elsewhere in the country – that people are weary of dancing to the tune of an unknown future, restless for it to begin. When will the tautness of austerity – of holding themselves in, undergoing the inhibitions of rationing – come to an end? There can't be much more of it, can there? As a result, an incipient light-heartedness is surely putting out its first spontaneous shoots – you can feel it in the air, Maud observes one breakfast time, over her newspaper. More than once that summer a black-and-white tabloid splash featured a man in a jaunty fedora with a cigarette hanging out of the corner of his mouth, snapped as he triumphantly cooked an egg on a sun-fired pavement, wielding a scoop in one hand and a plate in the other. As though this were news. As though cooking an egg really mattered. It never fails to raise a smile in the Robinson household, and farther afield.

With regard to herself, Dorothy is not so sure.

In the unravelling skein of the early years of marriage, the terms of their engagement seem almost impossible to define: both parties are capable of initiating a skirmish following a perceived slight from the other, with offence taken at the slightest provocation, as if both harbour a desire to have a pointless pick at the open wound of their marriage. These hostilities seem to arise from a combat of wills – his, for acceptance of all he is and represents (which he is not prepared to alter one iota); hers: the humiliation of always being the weaker party in their disputes, which inflames her sense of injustice.

Maud shrinks further into her chair in the corner of the room and declines, in some discomfort, to "interfere with" the plateau of mutual incomprehension inhabited by Dorothy and her son, composed of silences so solid with obstinacy on both sides that it makes her want to reach out and squeeze them both dry of their mutual antagonism. Or just to knock their two heads together.

Just lately, there have been more than the usual volleys of words between the couple – hasty, visceral and short-lived – amounting always to abbreviations of something deeper. But all Sunny registers is the way the air stiffens around them all as though it has suddenly acquired scales, while her ears strain like a hare's, sensing danger. It isn't the words themselves that are important to Sunny – it is the tone of them: bitter … scrappy … lurching … *angry*.

Neither party is naturally inclined to give in.

When the dust settles after one of these episodes, Dorothy is left with the frustration of being emptied out by the irresolution of it, and slightly ashamed of herself. She attempts to undermine him, in her own limited way: 'Why, oh why on earth do we have to live like this?' is a repeated opener. It transpires that she now wants a modern kitchen for the house, one with fitted cupboards instead of an arrangement of random sideboards and an elderly table with rickety legs. She wants a refrigerator instead of that wretched contraption they call the "safe" – a wooden hutch with a wire mesh door located in a gloomy corner of the pantry where milk, if it is left out, goes off a bit less quickly than it would if it were kept in the kitchen. She wants – God help us – a *shower* to be fitted to the bath. She wants "help" in the house. She wants some form of central heating instead of the plucky little fires in the rooms which are fed by lumps of raw coal heaved in from one of the sheds outside and deposit oily dust on every surface. 'For pity's sake,' she insists, 'we had all these things back in Canada those years ago, and none of it is *that* special.'

Robert just can't fathom it. For a start, isn't it obvious to her that such modern effects are beyond his means? His salary alone from his modest post can never run to the costly luxuries she requires. Moreover, he just can't bring himself to understand why they should be necessary. After all, he is used to unheated male changing rooms and draughty gyms and lecture halls. Comfort, to him, is stoking up the fire until your cheeks become inflamed and begin to prickle with its heat, while treacherous little draughts on their circuit round the skirting boards ensure that people's backs remain chilly. But no: this is his answer to all her requests for "improvements". No. And again, no.

Dorothy tries to imagine what her own barometer of correctness – that is, her mother – would do, given such unrelentingly unpromising circumstances. *Rise above it, stand firm*, was always her haughty little mother's own guiding principle, when under duress. (Could you do both at the same time?) Concurrent with this, and often at odds with her other pronouncements: *hold your own at all costs*. These are the words Dorothy hears in her mind and they are steely and silvery at the same time, just as they always had been, though at such a distance of time and space they no longer hold out much help, let alone reassurance.

As for conciliation and compromise – neither well-tried, longer term strategy is in her repertoire, any more than it is in Robert's, and she becomes perilously undefended on all flanks, resulting in finding herself often driven to investing her energy in sporadic, freakish outbursts, tilting at windmills. Twice, recently, she has lost her head entirely, darting outside with little screams and stamping hysterically through the long grass at the far end of the green opposite the house where the neutrality of mature trees across the common offer the solace of their silent, eyebrows-raised cover for a while. *These things happen*, marks Maud to herself, powerless to approach her. Best keep it in the family.

Then, in the nick of time, a man who is every bit as much of an outsider as Dorothy enters her orbit, one day when she plans to unburden herself once and for all to one of the local doctors. He is a doctor himself, a man she instinctively warms to at first simply because he *is* a doctor, like her father, and all doctors are gods to her, possessing healing remedies for just about everything. She has a raw faith that he will conjure up a cure for the futile, unguided missiles she is prone to launch in her doomed attempts at self-determination. Not that she describes it that way to him. Instead, she calls it "the blues". It gives her great hope when his gentle nod seems to be in agreement with this description of what ails her.

The good doctor's name is Dr Strauss and, like her, he is from abroad: a Jewish refugee who talks with a thoughtful lisp. What luck: he is prepared to be generous with his home visits when everyone else is out and Dorothy has the house to herself for a time while Maud is somewhere down in the village (decidedly not Dorothy's stomping ground), Sunny at school, and Robert at work. This doctor has a most patient, sympathetic air about him, and an expression of quizzical compassion nestles in the wrinkles that haunt his face. And another thing: he doesn't take his eyes from hers when he listens to her, and he listens a lot. How could she not warm to him? How tense she has become.

'I was never like this at home,' she confides, but she does not offer – nor does he elicit – any detailed conversation about the possible cause of her feeling "down": it simply amounts to good manners on both their parts. Instead, by his very presence in her life he supplies a vital refuge for her anguish.

No, Dr Strauss listens to Dorothy as though he is really harkening to her, marking the cadence of her words with encouraging nods that encourage her to trust that he is genuinely marking time to the beat of her thoughts. And he *never* interrupts.

Sunny, if she happens to be around, doesn't need to be told to take herself into the garden when Dr Strauss comes calling. Occasionally during such visits she becomes distressed by the sound of her mother weeping indoors – a hollow, secret sound that makes her stamp about, bashing at the lawn with her toy spade and crying a little herself.

Dorothy finds that the kindly foreign doctor's listening alone is a kind of cure – but also that it wears off not long after he leaves. His greatest virtue is that he most generously prescribes small white pills ('they will keep you going, my dear') and she will end up taking these for the rest of her life. Depression, he calls it. Giving it a name provides Dorothy with a new perspective and she takes this as a form of vindication.

Around this time another listener arrives, another outsider who also happens to be Jewish, like Dr Strauss. She is Ruth, whose father, Dorothy learns, is a businessman of some substance. Ruth grew up with her family in London and recently married Bim, an American GI from one of the fenland bases nearby. Funded by Ruth's parents, the couple lost no time in setting up home in two cottages they knocked into one, an enterprise of flair and daring that Dorothy is drawn to with a mixture of envy and awe. To Dorothy, Ruth is someone her past experience instantly registers as familiar. For a while, beginning with the day they get talking in the doctor's waiting room (Ruth is pregnant, Dorothy is waiting for her repeat prescription), she doesn't feel quite so strange about herself, so bleakly alone.

It doesn't take long for lingering coffee mornings to take place in Ruth's new home. This activity usefully and most pleasantly covers the desert of mid morning. To Dorothy's delight, Ruth serves real coffee, courtesy of Bim's PX, with condensed milk from a tin to make it creamy and sweet. They dip into the biscuit tin and smoke cigarette after cigarette in this way until the air in Ruth's kitchen turns blue.

There's a brief period when, egging each other on like teenagers, they both develop a pseudo-crush on the local policeman who, they agree, bears a certain resemblance to Dirk Bogarde. But this is how Ruth will be most fondly recalled by Dorothy in later years: humming 'Que sera, sera' while she puts the kettle on, and for an occasional evening treat when both husbands are out just the two of them settle in to watch an episode of 'I love Lucy' on Ruth's television. *Ah, they were good times*, she will confide to Sunny in due course.

For now, this emerging friendship is like having a lost chip of her old self unexpectedly restored. It even permits her to be a little bit proud of her own difference in the battle against becoming one of the locals – unlike that ridiculous Austrian woman charging about in her car – and she is delighted and relieved to find how this easy friendship with Ruth seems, increasingly, to legitimise her own outlook.

Here they are in Ruth's garden, talking quietly so they don't wake Ruth's baby son, asleep in his pram with the protective cat-net dangling from its extended hood.

Quiet talk is sometimes an invitation to be pensive.

'Shall you be going to cricket this Saturday?' enquires Ruth. 'Goodness knows what we'll be doing. Bim's family are visiting from Ohio. I think Daddy is bringing over some tickets for a play in town. Then, I suppose, we might take a walk by the river on Sunday.'

To Dorothy, these plans have an enviably integrated feel about them. She nods her approval.

'I wish Robert would do something *cultural*,' she says. 'My mother liked music. We used to go to concerts.' Even if they were only held in a store.

'Do you ever get bored?' wonders Ruth, with unexpected bluntness (she finds Robert wholly uninteresting, herself). 'Is it that Robert is a bit, well, dull?'

'I wouldn't say that,' Dorothy shoots back. 'Just – he hasn't turned out to be quite what I expected.' Suddenly, it feels as though she is a seasoned married woman, a person of a different generation to Ruth though they are close in age.

After a short pause, Ruth resumes: 'What *did* you expect, honey?'

Dorothy asks herself. 'Well, something ... friendlier, perhaps?'

'You mean the people here?' Ruth replies, missing Dorothy's point. 'You mustn't let them get you down, you know. OK – the Mothers' Union and the Women's' Institute whatever they call them are not *our* cup of tea, but once you get to know people a little ... ?'

'It's not that I want excitement, exactly,' says Dorothy obliquely. 'But I look at Robert sometimes and – I don't know. I had this beau once, you know. He died in the war. I was so close to him.'

'And you're not to Robert? Is that what it is?'

Dorothy fears this conversation might be in danger of

becoming maudlin, or turning into a kind of confessional – neither of which she wants at all – but at the same time she is grateful for a chance to air her feelings a little, though doing so like this feels a bit risqué.

'I just wish he wouldn't ... I don't know, *put me down* all the time. I don't know how to explain it. I am not as educated as he is – fine – but I'm not so very *stupid*, surely, and he makes me feel like I *am*. It's not a good feeling to have about yourself.'

'Ever thought of going back to school?'

'What?'

'Or getting a job?'

'Oh, come on. Anyway, I tried that once and look where that got me. I'm married. I have a child. Would Bim let *you* to work?'

'Maybe,' says Ruth. 'Maybe not. Anyway, I'm thinking of getting some piano lessons. That's something I wish I'd done when I was younger. Hey – maybe you and I could join a tennis club. Do you play?'

How interesting it is to have a friend with ideas.

But it doesn't last.

I should never have made any such assumptions, Dorothy tells herself, on hearing from her excited friend six months later that an opportunity for Bim to take them back to the States has arisen. It was never meant to last, apparently, this gift of a friend. Oh well, then, Dorothy consoles herself after her initial disappointment, even more reason to be grateful for the brief respite it provided. At this stage, she is well aware of how once precious things tend to intensify in value once they are withdrawn. Summoning a reserve of effort, she resolves on the spot to try her best to share Ruth's excitement, despite a dreadful sense that a vulnerable part of her will be re-surfacing, as a result. She knows she will have to work extra hard at not giving in to any feelings of betrayal and abandonment in the time that remains for this most fleeting of friendships and there are days when it takes some discipline not to believe she is a kind of toy which Ruth is in the process of growing out of.

'We will keep in touch, of course we will,' insists Ruth, taken aback to notice from Dorothy's fugitive expression how much of a life-line she must have been.

Nevertheless, maybe it is Ruth's characteristic chutzpah that finally gives Dorothy the courage to wonder whether now might be the time to make a stand, calmly and reasonably. Towards this end an idea slowly begins to form, like a piece of dough for making bread that is rolled out on a floury board then squeezed and flattened many times in order to gather in the stray bits before being placed inside the oven for baking.

On an evening when she judges that the brief fiasco of her marketing job has receded sufficiently and she and Robert are in a period of truce, she braces herself, turns her chin upwards to signal that she means business, and announces bluntly: 'Robert, I need to go home.'

18

To Maud, the business of Dorothy demanding an exotic vacation is more than a betrayal – it is downright infamy, upping sticks and taking the child with her like that. But she buttons her lip (curls it under the other lip, actually, so that no lips show and just the hint of a sign is manifested for anyone who can interpret it, corroborating her feelings on the matter with a sharp intake of breath through her nose). Even when she suspects that the Canadian daughter-in-law she has made fruitless efforts to befriend might be mocking her – what with her hoity-toity nose in the air and that condescending smile she often puts on (yes, *puts on*, maintains Maud, for it is surely an act). Sign for sign renders no words necessary between Dorothy and Maud. Of course, she will have missed her family – Maud concedes, to a degree – *that* she can well understand, coming from a close family herself. But once gone, will her daughter-in-law ever come back? That is the question. And what about Sunny, with whom she has formed a special bond based on their love of walking the fields and discovering together traces of animal life amongst a feast of wild flowers with pretty names?

No-one really knows.

None of them will venture to talk about it for fear of causing an upset, given what is at stake.

Enough money for this crazy endeavour is scraped together. The few details on their tickets for the forthcoming sailing describe merely the scaffold of the plan, stating that return journeys are booked on specific dates for Dorothy and Sunny more or less six months after their departure. They are to set sail early in the new year and come back by mid-summer. Certain arrangements at the other end have been made in advance via a rapid exchange of aerograms and one specially booked telephone call. Sunny is to be taken out of the village school she's been attending and enrolled in a fee paying establishment back in Montreal that boasts a smart navy blue uniform with black and white piping round the blazer, to be paid for by her grandfather, the Montreal doctor. Robert has gone into a protracted huff, admitting he hasn't a clue what the exodus of his wife and daughter is all about. For a few weeks, they see even less of him than normal as his diary takes him to meetings and engagements beyond his teaching, both evenings and weekends.

In the house, they take to coasting around each other in an outward show of restrained politeness as the time of Dorothy's departure approaches. Sunny welcomes a truce in the house, but she is aware that it is an icy one.

And here they are now, Dorothy and Sunny, booked into a B deck cabin on the Queen Elizabeth, the original Cunard flagship. Prior to this trip, Dorothy works out that Cunard first took on the Atlantic crossing east to west with a mail service some twenty years before her grandfather, the pioneering sailor Captain Adam Pengarth, set out due south down towards Venezuela on one of his own epic voyages across the same broad ocean, opening himself to a world which seemed infinite with promise, back then.

It's plain to Dorothy that cruising the ocean at the start of 1956 has taken a different turn from the experience promised by earlier vessels, with vacationing families and well-to-do-honeymooners in the ascendancy on the passenger manifest nowadays who quickly set the prevailing tone on board, endowing their ocean voyage with a more docile, cheerful aspect than before. As ever, Dorothy feels her cheek muscles tighten as she discovers herself to be the odd one out again – woman travelling alone with child. Yet she is glad, on the whole, to be on board in the presence of groups of excited but far from unruly children threading their way through the perpetual promenade of strollers up and around the decks, and people who can never sit still, it seems, but must perambulate up and down the ship's warren of straight avenues and artificially lit corridors, always on the move. Holiday makers, all of them, taking advantage of a cheaper passage in winter.

It certainly helps that there is now air-conditioning and before long it forms a permanent descant to her thoughts, alongside the more distant rumble of the ship's engines. There's also a pervasive, claustrophobic smell everywhere of sweetish, cloying fumes leaking from the squeaky green lino of the passageways, fusing with the lavender-scented polish regularly applied to the ship's wooden interior panels. After a day at sea, this awkward combination of smells blends into something sharper, despite the swift attention of jauntily dressed serving boys with their mops and buckets. Mass vomiting, sometimes discrete but more often not, erupts on the operatic rise of a grand, winter swell that makes people lurch towards the nearest hand rail. It hangs heavily on the air, souring it. Somehow, it even manages to seep up from the cabins on C deck, just below them. There's no getting away from it. To Dorothy's irritation, Sunny turns out to be a poor sailor with a weak stomach, succumbing at once. It affects the child's balance, moreover, both on the journey and for nearly a week in the city afterwards.

After breakfast, Dorothy takes Sunny along with her for a stroll – 'we'll just pop out and see what's going on' – and after a while Sunny sometimes finds children to play with while her mother retires to one of the loungers set in place behind a glass enclosure which serves to mute the chilly hiss of the wind outside. Here, wearing a little used fur coat packed into her trousseau ten years before, Dorothy draws out a magazine and lays back to skim its pages, prepared to be not unpleasantly distracted by the frequency of passers by and rarely able to concentrate for long on any article.

There are sedate bingo games in the cavernous lounge after tea which she sometimes takes a peek at, before finally rounding Sunny up.

And Sunny's first days at sea?

One of the few conversational memories she will retain of time spent with her mother during this trip is Dorothy telling her an unintentional joke just before they boarded: 'Look, see that line painted round our ship? They call it the plimsoll line. It shows how low a boat can sink in the water and still be safe.' And how they both giggled the moment she said it – at the way that both this mark, and her school gym shoes, could have the same name. She remembers, too, the essence of the strange moment when snow began to fall one day, and the greenish whiteness of the sky seemed to descend like a gigantic blanket onto the deck, softening it – softening everything – and making the whole adventure seem comfortably phantasmagorical.

And the Kit Kat man ...

He is nice, decides Sunny. There is also something not quite right about him when he pops up from time to time, materialising close by her when she happens to be alone, as though by accident or through a peculiar coincidence they can confidentially share. 'Hallo, little lady,' he greets her, surprised but not surprised. He then leads her into one of the on-board shops. He asks her what her favourite sweets are and tells her to choose: 'pick anything you like – go on'. She takes him at his word and points, and he buys her a Kit Kat. This is kind of him.

One day, Dorothy frightens Sunny by suddenly dashing towards them as they leave the shop, grabbing her arm as the Kit Kat man nimbly melts away, to demand: 'Who is that man you were just talking to?'

'I don't know,' replies Sunny, taken aback by the accusation in her mother's tone of voice and gazing around for him as though searching for an ally.

'Now, you listen carefully to what I am going to say to you,' commands Dorothy in a grave, serious voice, roughly hauling Sunny out of the Kit Kat Man's range and bending down to position herself eye-to-eye with her. 'I can see that I can't trust you, so you will only play where I can see you from now on. And never, never, *ever* again talk to men you don't know.' Sunny senses that something has gone wrong, that there is perhaps something about men in general that is mysteriously not nice and could be disgusting, even. She returns the intensity of her mother's glare with glum acquiescence.

Later, long after she is tucked up in bed, Sunny re-lives the sharpness of their brief, earlier exchange and the serious upset her behaviour has apparently caused her mother. It leaves her feeling tainted, and sorry she can't explain to the Kit Kat man – forever banished – that she can never be his friend after this. It bothers her that he has paid for her chocolate, since – horrors – she might now be in some kind of debt to him. Much, much later, when the darkening evening has turned into night and she can't get to sleep, she hears whispering outside the cabin door and hopes and *prays* that it isn't him, because if it is she will be forced to be rude to him which will be mortally embarrassing and might hurt him, so that she – who craves harmony (oh, how she craves it, without knowing either that this feeling is a craving or what harmony is, quite) – may not be able to do it – and what then? Thoughts like this soon shape themselves into bat-wing shadows in her mind. *Oh dear* ... But it turns out to be only her mother, after all, saying goodnight to the couple in the next cabin to theirs. Sunny peers at Dorothy secretly through the camouflage of squinting eyes, pretending to be asleep, while Dorothy tries to muffle the rustling of her grey taffeta evening dress – a gown she bought with her mother in Montreal before she was married because, they decided, it brought out the brightness of her cider coloured eyes. In the event, that dress was worn for the very first time on this return voyage.

Dorothy sometimes forces herself to take a deck walk in the knife-edged freshness of January outside, fascinated to watch the heavy, sidling motion of forming and dissipating waves. The stiff frill and froth of the ship's wake splays tracks behind the ship that at first seem so very solid as they fan out. But markings like that are doomed to be temporary and soon enough turn into unstable hummocks, to be swallowed up and regurgitated by the liquid velocity out there separating the old and the new world. Strange thing, a wake, she reflects ... sometimes it *does* feel like a celebration – if a fleeting one – of the death, but also the life of a journey.

One calm day, she finds herself turning her head dangerously downwards, towards the point at which the icy sea appears to be breathing itself into a state of deep forgetfulness in a most hypnotic way, like an extinct animal. Oh, how easy it is to drift into this state herself these days. Glazing over, she makes an involuntary bend forward. During that brief movement she finds herself willing the surface of the ocean to rise up and meet her with the same desire drawing her towards an underworld obscured by all that water. Just in time, her dangerous reverie is stabilised, tempered by a random revelation that forces her to think that maybe there are two sorts of place governing her life. First comes the physical actuality of this ship she is on, whose re-mastered familiarity will soon enough welcome her back. But there is another place running alongside it, an imagined space, equally present, that forms a beguiling palimpsest in her imagination, and this is undoubtedly the darker of the two: a place out of time where the countless, dizzying flotsam of every passenger's narrative – from both then and now, her own included – is in the process of being plotted. How easy it is to give in to drowning, she decides, beguiled by the lazy bulk and sensuality of platinum coloured sea on a dark day that beckons so as it curls down the flank of the ship. She shudders at this thought, purposefully hauling herself back to the surface of her thoughts.

Before they even dock at St John, ready for the long train ride south to Montreal, too much staring at imponderables has begun to result in Dorothy experiencing old feelings of inauthenticity once more. Dr Strauss knew the cure for that and prescribed Valium. But her stock will soon run out. She will just have to ask her father to help with this small but vital necessity.

So – am I really coming home after all, she wonders, as the journey gradually approaches its destination? Incongruously, the nearer they come to land, the less she can persuade herself that this can really be the case. There is one big question forming now in her mind, bearing in mind the amount of catching up with her family that lies ahead: has "home" bothered to wait for her in any way since she abandoned it ten years ago? There is no easy answer to that, apart from a shiver of anxiety that strikes her as similar to the feeling brought on by a recurring dream in which she is pedalling a bicycle without being able to make it move forward.

She is lost in thought again, two days later, on the sleek, fast train transporting them to Montreal. Well, no, she is not physically lost, of course – but where, then, *is* Dorothy, exactly? The once familiar landscape rushes past in a series of blurred transparencies overlaying and overlapping each other in a state of flux that produces few co-ordinates. For short periods, it feels to her that she might be just one more object amongst a crazy miscellany of material flying past, and it is mildly distressing to acknowledge that all such objects in her line of vision have in common as they speed by is their lack of permanence.

A hundred miles or so on, she startles herself with uninvited prickings of nostalgia for that other home – the one back in England. She vows to put this down to cowardice in the face of the approaching reunion with her parents. Reluctantly, she allows the ebb and flow of her own uncertain bearings to merge with the palpable lilt of the train where they melt away, unresolved. It is confusing. Over time, maybe her memory of the old home in Canada has suffered a degree of distortion.

The family home in Montreal … it is relatively easy to bring to mind a rapid succession of partial sights, frozen into snapshots of the city and her old home. Yes, there is the greenhouse where gleeful games of hide-and-seek once took place among the tomatoes, and the gardener whooped and joined in the spirit of it, chasing the children this way and that … and oh, what a fuzzy welcome hovered around the soft hue of the blue-tinted night light in the porch … and what about that shelf of red and green books in her father's study which she was not allowed to take down because they were medical and might frighten her and anyway, he reminded her in his kindly way, curiosity killed the cat, didn't it? Relatively easy, yes, for her to make out that it is indeed an enchanted place.

Meanwhile, on the last lap of the trip she enjoys pointing out to Sunny (who grapples with an illusion of their train moving backwards each time another shrieks by in the opposite direction) an occasional landmark she *does* recall – a church tower here, a forest there, the mighty St Lawrence river – before anxiety crashes in, that most unwelcome of guests. This time, as the actuality of her return is very close, it produces a rash of pins and needles in her legs, spreading across her stomach. *Courage*, Dorothy tells herself, using the French pronunciation of the word. But it is as though some nameless, unidentifiable catastrophe has happened to her somewhere along the line, her only sure hold on herself right now being the lulling regularity of the rails and the repeating, mocking teasing of their *here and now, here and now, here and now*. She steels herself to make a strong show of being a grateful guest in her parents' house, even if this places her at an initial disadvantage.

A taxi is waiting to escort them back to the house and it all turns out to be awfully easy, this part of the transition. Then: exhilaration! The heart-warming novelty of her during the moments she is embraced and taken in by those she left behind! She has been perfectly right to come, then, despite being a failure. It will all turn out for the best, surely.

The girls have positioned themselves to greet her – those dear, sweet sisters. She runs towards Bets, now a young chorus line dancer, so slim and smart with her blonde cropped hair, who has been married and divorced already and doesn't come home that often any more, since her arty milieu has a different outlook from that of her parents. And how about solid Edith, now the mother of two children and living across town?

'Don't worry, D, she's the same with all of us – our men folk are never good enough for her,' launches Bets, the more direct of the two, when the three of them gather for a sisterly session in the day room after dinner, allowing Lilian to retire to her bedroom while Edward leaves the house for – who knows where? 'Uh-oh,' says Bets. 'I'd better tell you. We suspect he has a fancy lady.'

'Really?' says Dorothy, mildly scandalised by this bit of news. 'Do you know for sure? Does mother know?'

'Probably not, we think. But if she does she isn't saying.'

'It's not our business, though, don't you agree?' Edith chips in. 'It's between the two of them, isn't it?' Edith would rather not be included in any gossip, evidently. Dorothy wonders how this state of affairs might affect her visit.

The ghost of their diminutive mother, who is elsewhere in the house, descends during the short pause that follows this revelation and it becomes clear to Dorothy that each sister interprets their mother in a different way. To Edith, she is just "mom" whom she dutifully visits each week. To Bets, she has become a spikey sparring partner when they meet. To Dorothy herself, Lilian is someone she knows she mostly manages to disappoint.

'That cute little Sunny. You must bring her over to meet her cousins,' says Edith.

'How long are you planning to be here, D?' asks Bets, after she has described in detail her latest boyfriend and the studio bound routine of her days, sitting cross-legged on the sofa in a pair of cheerful Capri pants. 'It's so lovely to see you.'

'I don't know. I really don't know,' admits Dorothy. She is being entirely honest with them. She would like to open up further, wishing her sisters would just reach out and scoop out that hidden part of her which she finds so difficult to release. They have sensed something's up, after all, and Bets, who is experienced in such matters, obviously thinks she's left Robert. Yes, that's it: wouldn't it be good if these sisters could bear just a little of the burden of being Dorothy that she herself finds so hard at times? But she has her pride. She is the eldest, after all. She hunches her shoulders and makes do by letting the matter drop, for now.

'Well, look, good luck with your stay here, anyway' Bets throws in, sharing a knowing face with Edith that Dorothy fails to spot.

'How do you mean?' she asks, turning towards them.

'Oh, D, you can't have forgotten what she's like, can you? Anyway, you'll see.'

And see she does. Ten days later she has it all ironed out in her mind.

But before then, thank God for an unquestioning father, who is evidently used to doling out pills to women with the blues in a spirit of perfect acceptance that the blues are what happen to women when they get married, only glad he is able to accommodate such a condition with such a simple expedient. Dear papa, thinks Dorothy.

Lilian takes it upon herself to drive alongside Dorothy to Sunny's new school each morning for an eight o'clock start while Sunny is a novelty, which doesn't amount to many days, given her commitments. After that, it is not until the weather begins to relent that she attaches herself to Dorothy and Sunny periodically when a trip out of town seems desirable.

One day – when, to their relief, gloves and scarves can be left at home – the three of them can be seen sallying forth on a ride in a horse-drawn buggy winding its way up the mountain. Sunny sits facing the other two, and is quick to notice how her mother alters her demeanour when Lilian is out with them. Why is she putting on a show again, *impersonating* herself, wonders Sunny, sensing another of Dorothy's stilted efforts to please her mother? There's never a doubt in Sunny's mind which one of the pair of them is the dominant party here. Distracting herself by counting the red squirrels scurrying up the trees bordering the road, Sunny yearns for her mother to be more substantial or, at any rate, consistent. At the same time, it is fair to say that at this point in her short life Sunny thinks equally about how, at her new school, the *papier mache* totem pole she is making is shaping up, and how her new best friend Nancy likes to swap sandwiches with her during their break, and how triumphant she feels about being moved up to a higher group for her English classes.

'Oh, what's become of you, Dorothy,' asks Lilian at one point, with a superior sigh as their ascent continues. It is a question that instantly slices away the ground beneath Dorothy, leaving her wondering exactly that herself, but entirely unable to rise to a conversation about it. What *are* these barriers between people in one family about, she ponders instead. Is this what people mean when they say things like: *we don't get on in our family*? She keeps such thoughts to herself because she knows from experience how often she stumbles in her opinions and judgements – a guarantee of earning Lilian's scorn – and stupidity is surely a failing because, according to Lilian, well-bred girls are smart. So just as so often before, she retreats into silence for much of the rest of the journey, trying not to feel like a flawed piece of china that's not worth fixing as a draught of mutual incomprehension inserts itself between them at the approach of the summit.

Now it is time to disembark, making it possible for the three of them to separate for a short while: Lilian to establish a spot for their picnic, Sunny to dash from side to side of the railings of the viewing enclosure after sitting down for so long.

Dorothy takes the opportunity of inhaling deeply, gazing from a high vantage point at the splendour of the city spread out below in its unaccustomed wholeness.

Her city.

Just as she used to when she was young, she attempts vainly to identify their street. At this remove, buildings become somewhat flattened into an extensive mosaic of uneven shapes. Even their normal colours appear leeched of differentiation when their facades become obscured, robbed of residual individuality. Dorothy is struck by the sheer extent of Montreal's grandeur at this remove, raising a thin smile of satisfaction on her face. Moreover, although you might catch a twitch of movement hinting at traffic here and there, all evidence of *people* is removed – that's the other thing about such a vista. Above all, a city from this height is entirely devoid of humanity – it is simply a gigantic installation, a glorious hymn to human ingenuity. And yet, for sure, people *are* down there in their hundreds of thousands at this very moment, small creatures scurrying around. Her father is there, and so are her sisters. Even though they, too, are invisible, she understands their legitimacy in the labyrinth, as citizens. And her own? Could there be room for her here, too? All of a sudden, such a transition begins to look not just easy but perfectly right from way up here.

During this brief but significant pause – until her mother rallies her and calls out to Sunny to come and eat – Dorothy makes a pact with herself that there could be a real possibility of establishing tracks of her own over here once more. With all her heart, she realises this is what she wants to do, and it is a mighty relief to own up to it. Surely, ways could be found of overcoming her disgrace – after all, Bets had done it. Maybe her father would help out.

All too soon it is early June, not long before their return tickets tell them they are due to sail again. Dorothy has managed, so far, to put off dwelling on this event because she is still far from sure whether it is possible to take a stand and remain in Canada. Either way, there really is so much at stake. Consequently, she has managed to stall, several times, over taking actual steps in this direction. (*But what would I do here? How would I get along? How would I make ends meet?*).

School finishes at 1.00pm now the days are hot.

One day, they take a street car ride back home – just Dorothy and Sunny. Dorothy buys Sunny a pistachio popsicle, her favourite, from the drug store on the main street at the bottom of their road, and in the sunlight it quickly dribbles down her chin as they amble home.

On arrival, they discover Edward smoking his pipe in the garden and he calls out to Sunny to set up the croquet hoops, telling her grandpa will play a game with her if she would like that. Dorothy smiles at them both and plans to watch, keeping a proud distance by stepping back and leaning on the veranda. They can just about hear Lilian somewhere inside the house talking to the maid, so this brief interlude in the garden at the start of a sunny afternoon strikes Dorothy in all its aspects as something of a welcome respite. A boy from the other side of the road who is just a little older than Sunny and has become her occasional playmate sits down to follow the game from the shadows of his own veranda. How sweet the children seem, Dorothy notices: he claps each time Sunny scores.

At first, Sunny believes her grandfather is teasing her when he keels over. Nearby, Dorothy instinctively knows better and makes a sudden dash towards him, shouting at Sunny to get help by making pointing jabs towards the house from where she kneels by Edward. Obediently, Sunny runs indoors and finds Lilian with a list in one hand and a pen in the other, her silver-rimmed spectacles on the end of her nose. 'Come, quickly,' cries Sunny.

'Why? What's going on?'

'I don't know,' whimpers Sunny, thrown into a state of distress, and this is the truth. Outside, they discover Dorothy on her knees, rubbing her father's hand and tapping his sagging cheek. Sunny is suddenly afraid. She is also old enough to suspect she is surplus to requirements, and might be for some time to come.

She is proved right. No-one is the least bit interested in her as things begin to happen in quick succession out there where her grandfather lays, his head cradled in

Dorothy's arms. After a while, unnoticed, she decides to cross over the road and join the boy.

From the vantage point of the boy's verandah, the two children solemnly follow Edward being lifted onto a stretcher by men in uniform who carry him off to an ambulance parked on the driveway. The boy's mother is kind, so very kind, and Sunny warms to the way she puts her arm around her and leads her inside to have tea with the boy in their kitchen.

LANDLOCKED

19

Letchworth, England, 1956

She sits cross-legged in her neat cherry-print dress, picking absently at the grass.

All of a sudden, her back stiffens as pinpricks of laughter come pirouetting towards where she and her mother have laid down their rugs just beyond the white boundary line of the cricket pitch.

Malice is in the air today: this is what Dorothy's grim smile indicates, with a silent nod as if to confirm – even if only to herself – *I told you so*.

Sunny guesses the reason they are laughing at her mother – *if* that is what they are doing – has to be because she's foreign, therefore different. It's all she can think of and it's funny, because the word she would choose to describe the attitude of the row of ladies in deckchairs in front of the pavilion is just about the opposite of malice: it's more like *admiration*, in her experience, albeit from a studied distance. It is also infused with something else: cautious curiosity, maybe?

A familiar draught of unease wraps itself around her taut little shoulders. She knows she is too young to have proper opinions, let alone actual conversations with adults. Hers has been a subdued childhood so far, apart from lessons, especially during the solitary reaches of time between the end of one school day and the beginning of the next, even when they were in Canada. She is conscious that this is one result of being an only child. It doesn't stop her wondering from time to time about the many incongruities and the prevailing sadness of those perplexing and as yet unmappable limits of her conscious world. So far she has arrived at no certainty, either about this or about many other things.

When the distant cackle subsides, Sunny lies down flat on her back, her legs crossed at the ankles and her knees as red as the cherries on her dress after kneeling on the rug, then turns on her side to peer more closely at the far off gathering of cricket wives. This way, both their titters and her mother will surely slip pleasingly out of range and she will be able to re-enter the doldrums of the afternoon with nothing to consider beyond the sky itself, directly above. Soon, it feels like she is floating: the heat all round carries the weight of an invisible pillow very lightly bearing down on her as her body oh-so-gently resists it. Later in life – if she remembers this particular day at all – she will be aware that such a sensation is not uncommon here on the flatlands of East Anglia, where a person's head can be driven into a spin by the sucking sensation created by the concave dome of an overbearing sky. To steady herself, she squints at the leisurely mutations of a bulbous cloud continent traversing the blue sky, while through the gutters of her mind water begins to flow in a rocking motion ...

Ah, the sea. That must be what is making her giddy. It is barely a month since mother and daughter were in the middle of the Atlantic, heading back to Southampton on board the Queen Mary this time. Since their return, she has learned that this is not something to be dwelt upon, although she has been troubled lately by the lingering imprint of a dream riding on the fearful desolation of being left alone on a deserted quayside. This eventless scenario is always associated in Sunny's mind with her mother, even though she never appears in the dream, and it is perplexing because she is quite certain that Dorothy has never been alone upon arrival, anywhere. Well, then. Perhaps it is this that really causes the dizziness after all: it's like the kind of primeval panic characteristic of a *bad atmosphere* brought on by the sound of those women, which probably has no basis in reality.

Not that Sunny has been too bothered by her two recent Atlantic crossings (apart from being sick, of course). She recalls the sound of her shoes walking down wood panelled corridors and the shop where the Kit Kat Man hung around. She also remembers the receding highway of the ship's wake fanning out to create a fleeting signature of their journey. To Sunny at this time, big ships certainly are very grand places indeed, like palaces, though she has a fear of drowning (for certain, nothing good can come of it) and strives at all times to keep her head above water. Another fleeting memory is of a long train ride, represented by a series of sultry hooded lamps in the dining car suggestive of certain things adults were known to withhold from children. And how, for their supper, there was always thin and rather tasteless soup, shimmying in its dish to the rhythm of the train.

But for now, here they have established themselves, Sunny and Dorothy, by the farthest boundary. It is where they always sit.

Since her return, Dorothy has had the feeling that she's been forcibly grounded by a dead weight not of her own making. There is no alternative to being tethered to this spot by Robert's desire to play the damn cricket season out and it is her misfortune to arrive back in the middle of it. As the incomprehensible game drifts on, both Sunny and Dorothy sombrely register the delayed crack of ball on bat without comment as though it all might be a mirage, given the state of inertia it induces in both of them.

Who shall I be, over here for a second time? What *can* I be? It begins again, the old question. Attempting to weigh it up – and in search of an answer (how fugitive answers generally prove to be) – Dorothy reckons it might be good if she were able to perfect an attitude she defines as being "prim," by which she means something like happy to be frumpy and satisfied with her lot. She has studied the way those eagle-eyed, prim village women seem to share a secret which blesses them with the good fortune of being insulated against the perpetual doubting that plagues her. But to her their lives remain a kind of living death she cannot but reject, on balance. She has tried to maintain an outward show of equilibrium – oh, how she has tried – by crafting a studied smile in front of the mirror that causes her lips to turn down at the corners rather than up. But it isn't an easy fit, especially when your voice has a natural drawl to it, giving the impression of casualness rather than irony, an attitude she has registered but far from understood about these English people. If only she knew that this particular pose isn't achieving its object since it makes her out to be supercilious. Or *false*. It fascinates Sunny when she watches her mother putting on such airs, but not in a good way. It is unsettling.

There are only so many times you can take a stroll round the borders of a cricket pitch like this one, since it necessitates sneaking past the pavilion – that treacherous fortress – harbouring the enemy. Half an hour earlier, on her way back from accompanying Sunny to the outside toilet, Dorothy was rudely reminded of the perils of such perambulations when a slouching figure in deep field, dressed in heavy, yellowing whites, suddenly barked at her for obscuring the bowler's line of vision. *Huh?* 'What kind of dumb game is this?' she muttered to Sunny as she strode off, cross and humiliated.

'Why don't you go and find a four-leafed clover, hmm?' suggests Dorothy to Sunny (which, to her, is the equivalent of digging a hole only to fill it in, but Sunny – ever hopeful, ever willing at this stage – has yet to grasp the deception). She gives Sunny a friendly poke in the back. 'Go on. It might bring us luck.' Luck. Is that what she needs?

But Sunny has already found for herself another diversion, delving into Dorothy's bag for a small, leather bound photograph album with gold tassels which Dorothy brings with her in case anyone is one day *truly* interested in *her* and where she's come from, rather than *him* and his roots right here which sprout more and more stories she has little part in. Sunny always marvels at the squat black and white prints with their fashionably bevelled edges, and the various shots taken in a garden big enough for people to be grouped formally, as though for a celebration. Or they are arranging themselves by a lake crowded with yachts, or on ski slopes in winter where bantering youngsters tumble about in the snow. She loves to see how the features of all of them are sharpened by the contrasts created by monochrome black and white, endowing light and shade with an especially vivid quality that begs the observer to come closer in order to peer at the detail.

Dorothy leans over. 'There I am,' she says, hovering

by Sunny's shoulder. 'The deb, ha ha.' It's not a real laugh, and Sunny knows it: there's a self-accusatory sarcasm in her tone which Sunny instantly recognises. Dorothy's long, red fingernail emphasises the lines of a hip-skimming full-length evening dress in shiny satin. Sunny has heard about debs in England, but they seem to be aristocratic girls in stiff ball gowns, depicted curtseying to the Queen. Her English grandmother pointed out the dignified remoteness of such creatures one day when they appeared in her Daily Express.

'What are debs in Montreal?' Sunny ventures to enquire.

'What you need to remember, Sunny,' comes the weary reply from above her, 'is that only the best girls got into the papers out there. From the very best families.'

A few more pages are thoughtfully flipped over by Sunny while a little way off a sudden round of applause crackles stereophonically around the pitch and the iron clack of the score board in the process of being manually changed signals a new development in the funereal progress of the game, whose strategic narrative is entirely lost on Dorothy and Sunny. But pay attention! Take a closer look! Now *he* – Sunny's father – is offering them an exclusive wave of his bat as he wades with apparent insouciance towards the wicket in his pads. His stance, squaring up to the bowler, reminds them (if they need reminding) that he has temporarily migrated to another place altogether, an exclusive world of heroes in the making. Nevertheless, Sunny herself appreciates how he has singled them out and responds with a small, kindly wave of her own. She has no axe to grind. Not yet, anyway.

Once, when the match of the day was on their home pitch, she helped her English grandmother and a gaggle of elderly friends prepare scones and home made buns for a special cricket tea inside their own pavilion. Sometimes, she can't help feeling, it can be disconcerting to be stuck out on the edge with her mother at these away matches, to all intents and purposes nailed there by their own volition.

'Who is this boy?' Sunny asks, pausing and pointing at a figure with a large square head.

'What?'

'Him.'

Dorothy scrutinizes the photograph for a second or two. 'Ah, yes,' she says, finally. 'I remember. His name was Thomas. He would have been a bit younger than you are, then.'

'But who *is* he?'

Dorothy realises that it is a while since this boy has crossed her mind.

'Well, as far as I can remember he was a little boy who lived with us for a while when I was very, very young – too young to remember much. I think he must have come from Nova Scotia. Must have been one of the cousins.' Sunny points out that he looks like a big boy for his age, half bent over and laughing somewhat moronically at the camera. Suddenly, Sunny feels as though he's looking directly at *her*, as though he's laying down a challenge for her to appreciate his bygone, half told joke, whatever that joke might have been. In this picture he is positioned directly in front of Dorothy's father, whose hidden right hand might have been tickling him from behind, or maybe pinching him into some kind of submission. What strikes Sunny is that he seems so exuberant – so strange, flinging himself about like that, with his hair wild and his mouth open so wide. At the same time she – who often feels a touch peculiar about herself (though nobody, strictly nobody, knows about this) experiences a surge of sympathy for such a daring pose.

'What happened to him?'

'Oh, goodness me, Sunny, I don't know,' Dorothy answers. 'It's all so long ago. He was there. Then he went away. He stayed for a bit then one day he went back home, I guess. That's all I can remember. People do come and go, you know.' She takes the album from Sunny and snaps shut both it and their little dialogue.

Time loses its elasticity on match days. It feels to both of them like it is strung out like a piece of spent chewing gum, on the whole.

Then, as though a switch has been turned on, Dorothy announces: 'Hey, you know what? I have an idea.' Sunny sits up properly, as taught, with renewed hope in her eyes.

'What is it?'

'Why don't we go exploring.'

'You *bet*!' responds Sunny instantly (she still has traces of a quickly absorbed Canadian accent), leaping up and sweeping the back of her dress for bits of grass before Dorothy can change her mind. After all, there are a few hours to go before stumps are pulled at the end of play.

Without more ado they set off, discovering a convenient side exit where the boundary hedge is thin. Maybe, thinks Dorothy, their disappearance will cause a stir this time. She rather warms to this idea.

Because at lunch, tea, and especially when it's time for drinks afterwards, Dorothy would *like* to cause a stir, but only if she is sought out and *taken in* – fetched from the perimeter, led by the arm, escorted, looked after – in accordance with what, in her opinion, is due to her as the captain's wife. That would show them. Lately, she has been attempting to "show" *him* most of all – Robert, that is. Maybe her way of showing – creating little acts of hostility to make a stand against the sense of creeping annihilation that's been returning in ominous waves –

has been too subtle to date. Or else he is too damn clever to show he's noticed. Of course, she will eventually give in, marching Sunny towards the group she fears, wearing an expression the child knows only too well: a blend of bravado and feigned nonchalance which totally fails to disguise the rawness of her vulnerability.

But before this ritual performance commences, to Sunny's delight they are off and – oh! What joy! After ten minutes of so they come across an open-air lido full of shouting, splashing kids. But – oh no! Sunny hasn't a swimming costume. 'Never mind,' says Dorothy, perking up, 'you can just strip down to your pants! Why not?' Sunny doesn't hesitate, leaping noisily into the cold turquoise pool. From underwater she delights in watching the bubbles she has just created as they race her to the surface. Oh, to be back at sea where, for a blissful while, there were no bad moods and rows and silences a-buzz with ominous significance.

They remain at the pool until nearly closing time. Then Dorothy summons Sunny out of the water and roughly rubs her down with the rug they were sitting on back at the cricket ground, for want of a towel. Her wet pants cling to her body, sending small rivulets of water down her legs towards the blue and white tiles of the poolside. But – oh, no – again! No spare pants! 'Don't worry,' says Dorothy. 'You can have mine.' With a deft movement she slips her hands under her dress and fishes out the neat garment with its panelled front which covers her girdle, from which four suspenders clamp her nylons in place.

'They're far too big. They won't stay up.'

'No they are *not*. Come here a second. There you are. I'll put a knot in the back. See?'

Back at the pitch a little later a sing-song female voice erupts from the front of the pavilion through cupped hands acting as a megaphone: 'Dorothy? Oh, *Dorothy?* 'Where *are* you?' Sunny can't help noticing the figure of her father in the group, grumpily gesturing his wife and daughter to *come forward*, for heaven's sake. To save face, Dorothy pretends not to see him. It isn't until he turns back to his friends with a shrug that she grabs Sunny's hand and pushes her ahead.

During the long journey home in the black Ford Prefect, Sunny sits alone, as she always does, on the chilly brown leather runnels of the back seat, pinched into wakefulness by the sense of mutual resentment radiating from both parties in front, though as the energy of the day begins to slowly ebb away it takes with it some of the sting of Dorothy's earlier pique. Night time, Sunny observes – and she is observant beyond her years by this time – often seals the potency of her parents' feelings inside a welcome crust of resignation. Anyhow, few of the terse remarks coming from the front of the car make much sense to her, permeated as they are with innuendo. Besides, from the solitude of the back seat she has learned how to deflect them, being much more alert to the mood being created at the front than the words themselves. In case things turn nasty.

She leans back, nodding to the rhythm of passing street lights. She allows herself a private smile at the fact that she is wearing her mother's pants and that her mother, so coy and so stern by nature, is wearing *none at all.*

And yet ... anyone can see that the couple's relationship has taken a turn since Dorothy's return, entering another of its unchartable seasons. Overall, this amounts to efforts being made on both their parts, not necessarily whole-heartedly but in exploratory spurts. Hence Dorothy's attendance at these late-season cricket matches. On her part, she figures that maybe if disappointment becomes drier it can be managed more systematically. Having outstripped her welcome in Canada after Edward's disabling stroke and all the changes to the house that would have to be made to accommodate his much reduced state – something tells her that the best she can hope for now, as things stand, is to be able to call "home" the location she is presently in – over here, that is – and attempt to make it stick this time, instead of being a perpetual vagrant, a piece of surface seaweed driven back and forth across a maddeningly changeable sea. *Stop the world ... I want to get on* ...was the mental appeal she would have made once, on her own strictly limited terms. Not any more. It has to be enough for now to hover in this latest place, resigned to making a go of it for Sunny's sake, if little else.

So, yes, efforts are being made. For example, there is a holiday planned after his cricket is done with. It's to be a late summer weekend just for the three of them in a hotel in Eastbourne where Dorothy will be able to play at being a person of consequence, waited upon and a little curious to absorb the atmosphere of the place of her birth.

Once that summer Robert even laid aside time for a day trip, an attempt at a family day out. This featured a picnic, followed by a punt up river. That it ended in disaster Dorothy was just about able to take in her stride, conceding afterwards that at least he'd tried.

Of course, he knows perfectly well how to punt from his

own time as a student, but as soon as he casts off – standing barefoot in rolled up trousers on the platform at the rear of the vessel while Sunny and Dorothy recline on over-sized, dusty cushions further down, facing him – it soon becomes clear that he is rusty. Not that they find their somewhat circular progress of initial concern, although one or two other punts sharing a narrow stretch of the river are forced to take evasive action from the off. But things come to a head when he digs the pole in with one final frantic attempt to level things out – only to find, as the awkward, flat-bottomed boat slithers on, that the pole has become fixed to the muddy bottom of the river. Perhaps unwisely at this point he fails to gauge that he has only seconds to attempt to regain control, with the result that he clings on just long enough for it to be impossible for him to relinquish the pole without the boat becoming free-floating. This means that he is left clinging it to it (mercifully, it remains upright and embedded in the deep mud of the river), while the punt itself begins to slide away from under his feet. A group of students sitting on the bank set up a cheer. Children throwing bread at some ducks begin to laugh and point. Throughout, Dorothy attempts to hold onto her dignity in graceful silence, holding herself aloof from the unwanted audience. 'Get the bloody paddle,' Robert yells at last, which she does, snapping into action and managing to steer the vessel back to him. Ignoring spurious advice coming from another punt which has paused to enjoy the sight of a man with his legs curled round a wooden pole in the middle of the river, with one desperate heave Robert manages to twist the pole free and they continue on their way, enveloped by a deep sense of failure.

In one way, there was something that husband and wife might have found to share in this incident – if they were speaking to each other on an even playing field. By this time, each was grappling with the same question: why on earth was it that *other people* always seemed to be doing normal things together while mistakes like theirs and a vague sense of misadventure seemed to plague *their* lives, miring them in the "bad luck" of a series of unpredictable obstacles? It made both of them prone to being on their guard against the next embarrassment, surmising that other people's lives contained none of the awkward pitfalls they seemed doomed to experience. It was as though each was in a state of permanent revolt against the choppiness of their own marriage while at the same time harbouring a submerged longing for an idealised order each knew, deep down, that the other could not supply. And still Dorothy disguised the guts of her disappointment with that familiar upward tilt of the chin, and Sunny sometimes scrutinized her through half closed eyes and compared her mother to a ship with a faulty rudder.

For her own part, Dorothy tried not to remember her most recent debacle – that costly trip to Canada – just as she forced herself not to dwell on the hopelessness of her sick father's dependence on his greatly encumbered wife. Bets sent a picture of Edward with a stick in his hand and a nurse by his wheelchair in which he appeared much reduced. 'I have to tell you, D,' she wrote, 'they say he will never speak again, let alone walk.'

20

Apart from being a begrudging spectator at cricket matches, how *does* Dorothy occupy her time, once back in England, now that her friend Ruth has moved on? For one thing in particular she is deeply grateful: Dr Strauss resumes his visits without delay, bringing those familiar pills in their white circular boxes made of the softest cardboard with fluted edges which can be clutched so reassuringly in the palm of the hand, conveniently out of sight of prying eyes.

There is housework every day, of course – although this boils down mainly to ironing and cooking after the return from Canada, since concessions have at last been made on the domestic front, this time with the whole-hearted support of Sunny's grandmother who is determined not to risk losing her granddaughter again. The result is that the first of a succession of village women, "charladies," as Dorothy refers to them, now comes in twice a week to take care of the rougher work.

Also, Dorothy develops an interest of her own and discovers, almost by default, that she has a talent.

In the newsagent's shop she spots the first edition of a weekly cookery magazine and starts collecting.

Soon, that which her mother-in-law calls Dorothy's new "hobby" gives some definition to what she only glimpses vaguely about herself and the purpose of her life. As if to celebrate the receding memory of wartime food rationing, the recipes demand rich, succulent ingredients – double cream, sugar, butter, prime cuts of meat and fish – only the best. Flavours must be delicately and most precisely blended. The completed plate itself then becomes a backdrop for the satisfaction of creating a fresh order, all by herself. It is all such a contrast to the heavy country stews and pies Maud persists in dishing up, let alone the seasonal jugged hare left hanging outside the back door until the bud on its nose turns brown before being brought in to be skinned, its bloody entrails left in the kitchen sink – e*uggh!* Somehow, the art of a rich kind of cooking – which Dorothy adopts in a zealously literal way, measuring out the very last prescribed ounce of rice or flour or breadcrumbs each time she tries a new recipe – speaks to her in a most refreshing way of a time when money was not a worry, where people cared about delicate things. And then, wouldn't you know it, into her mind pops one of those fleeting flickers of what was once "home", that other place, back in Montreal. Nevertheless, the recipes are rich, logical and easy to follow and sometimes she wonders if they mayn't be recipes for life itself, or small portions of it.

She goes into town now and then to have her hair and nails done and browse through the elegant rails of a pompous ladies' dress shop calling itself Mademoiselle, quite capable of matching the archness of its doyenne with her own. Only a few cherished items from her original travelling trunk packed with personal items from Canada remain, including two tailored suits and the black vanity case lined with turquoise silk, topped up from time to time with fresh Elizabeth Arden bottles and horn-handled manicure items. A jeweller in his dark little workshop maintains the few decent pieces she owned that might yield a good price. Like the art nouveau necklace given to her by her mother when she was 18, with the instruction: 'This could be some insurance for you, if you ever need it.'

Other essentials sent on request from Canada by her sisters prove a double-edged benefit, since they serve to affirm once more how justified is her apartness from the women of the village (who are prepared to admire these "modern" items respectfully although they don't find much cause to covet them). But the downside of such treasures – packages containing soft, padded toilet paper, a coffee pot, Laura Secord chocolates – is that they call back into existence some of the old restlessness.

Is there to be no hope of real change? Is there never to be a miracle rescue for this woman of limited personal resources, groomed for marriage and dependence and very little else? No win on the football pools (which she subscribes to each week in great expectation)? No swoop of unexpected fortune from a premium bond? Like many of her era, she suspects she is about to be leap-frogged by a generation of young women waiting in the wings who are all too ready to raise their own voices, who will declare amongst themselves and to anyone who cares to listen: *get a job, take your life in your own hands, make your own fortune.* It is not a pleasant feeling, but Dorothy is standing by what she knows, which is the advantage of at least being a Married Woman, having been brought up to believe this is a legitimate and respectable end in itself, rather than a beginning. And on this subject, here is *her* confident wisdom: they don't know it, but those working women will be obliged to give it all up when they, too, get married and children start coming along. How will they feel about *that*? Since marriage is both her lot and her refuge she will resist to the end listening to anything that will complicate her views. It's too late for her to change her mind about that, anyway. Far too late.

Then, without warning, one sliver of light beams down upon the routine of her days on the eve of her fortieth birthday.

It happens that between eight and eleven o'clock in the morning – after everyone else has left the house and she has washed up and made the beds and done sundry other chores – she is apt to sit down and indulge in a cup of real coffee in celebration of a silken hour or two of privacy, now the car has spluttered off with Robert and Sunny has been dispatched to the bus stop for school.

Dorothy has lately acquired an item of clothing known as a housecoat to be worn specifically during these same hours. It is a full length garment with a high zip up the front forming a roll neck and made of soft, royal blue chenille, whose purpose – unlike that of a plain dressing gown – is to usher in those cosy transitional morning hours when *her* time prevails, to accompany them on their way, as it were. This housecoat enfolding her slim body feels to her like a silent friend which, like the tin of Players cigarettes she keeps beside her, her tranquilisers and her whisky, can be relied upon not to plague her with too many inner pinches.

It is around this time that Dorothy falls in love.

Wrapped in this very housecoat is the way Dr Mason (plain Mr Mason, then) greets her one fine spring morning. Mr Mason teaches geography in the same department as her husband and they have met before at college plays – always Shakespeare, always with men playing the girls parts, always a cause for Dorothy's eyes to glaze over as she battles the series of yawns challenging her facial muscles, unnoticed (she trusts) by the more enthusiastic elements in the auditorium.

'Oh, Dorothy, I'm so sorry to bother you,' insists Mr

Mason, registering her bewilderment at seeing a man on her doorstep at barely past breakfast time. 'I just thought I might catch Robert before he left and cadge a lift with him. My car's playing up and I've had to abandon it on your drive, I'm afraid.' (The unreliability of cars was a given in those days.)

'Oh, dear,' offers Dorothy. 'I'm sorry, he got off on time this morning. No, not sorry, I mean ...'

'Ah, that's a shame. Well, not a shame, I didn't mean ...'

Oh, these academic people, she thinks, watching in amused sympathy as he tries to extricate himself by attempting to reclaim words which seem to explode in several directions all at once, just like hers. She isn't entirely sure how to respond to mutual embarrassment, especially to a lean young man with kindly eyes which draw her towards him and make her feel instantly safe, just as Dr Strauss had done in the beginning, and before that, her father. She also notices for the first time how he stands at an angle, slightly stooped towards her, in the manner of one who is accustomed to explaining things with much patience to other people. His hair is pleasingly wavy and fair, she notices, though darkened by hair oil. He reminds her – standing there so youthfully, so optimistically – of her first beau, the one who died, leaving her in such a deep pit of longing all those years ago.

After a brief hesitation, she offers: 'Won't you come in? Have a cup of coffee with me?'

21

From time to time in people's lives a stretch of time can pass – it may last two, five, even ten years – when such a state of latency seems to govern lives jointly lived as to suggest that the duration in question must have been captured and held within a solidifying mist – the mist of time, no less – when diaries must be consulted retrospectively to recall exactly *what* took place *when* – if, indeed, anything worthy of retention did.

Let's say, then, that nothing has happened for a while in the Robinson household.

Hasn't it?

How do you measure ossified attitudes? How long does it take for a stone, once upon a time a molten object, to set and assume an immoveable shape? How do you point a finger at the stony point of no return and say: *here*: it started here, or there, or at a time too long ago to properly recall?

How does Dorothy begin to be certain about the most important change of all that was taking place during this particular span of oh, it must have been eight years or so – despite any apparent volition of her own? Was there ever a single second in the unfolding of this period when one era finally died and another surreptitiously established a foothold? Maybe not – maybe this is why she was sometimes thrown off balance by an injured sense of being left behind. Put another way: when was it that the tide truly turned during those interim years – because turn it certainly did. When did the relentless rolling stock of "now" turn into the ghostly remnant of all she had lived by up until then? When did she ever manage to establish that "*my* time, the time of my life" showed itself for the wilted testament it had become?

As her once proud body begins to stiffen just a little in her forties, and her features gradually acknowledge small signs of the passing of the years, she feels a dart of shame at the realisation that she might soon be referred to as "getting on".

Notwithstanding this, the three individuals contributing both to the idea and the physicality of the family – this *particular* family – are each, in their own way (and by embedded custom) used to holding close to their chests any probing of such an apparent lacuna in their lives. Granted, for each of them time's steady heartbeat plays out its impermanent record in a trail of blips regular and irregular, but at what point the habit of deliberate concealment becomes the keeping of secrets during this time would be a little difficult for either one of them to pinpoint.

However, the adult Robinsons are in no difficulty when it comes to the ghostly business of finding either a repository or an explanation for time seeming to ebb away into lostness during this period. *He* works. He plays cricket. *She* expands into their home when Maud moves to a sheltered housing bungalow half a mile away. She cooks Sunday lunch with dexterity and concentration and he duly channels a portion of it to his mother.

Each time Dorothy cooks now, the artistry of her culinary endorsement of the week just completed is arranged with defiant precision on the table, though nobody particularly lauds it any more. Dorothy herself derives satisfaction from the food she creates, although it strikes her sometimes that she might be overdressing it. Maybe it is her way of holding her own. Or, indeed, of *showing him*, without recourse to words every time, which are such dangerous things in both their hands. Often on a Sunday Michael Mason joins them, and the three adults take a stroll across the fields during the latter part of the afternoon while Sunny experiments with a cigarette in her bedroom and gets on with her reading.

As for those efforts that started to be made after she returned from Canada – they turned out to be shallow and short lived, after all. It didn't take long for them to peter out, starved of the will to persevere.

Dorothy's thoughts often begin these days with 'if only'. They come in two versions. *If only* the other person were to literally freeze, say, locked inside a single frame so he would not be able to touch her anymore. *If only* he would disappear mysteriously, become a puff of smoke without trace or history as though he had never been. It never seems too dreadful or heretical to her to think like this because such outcomes are, naturally, preposterous and futile. It is *all* preposterous. Quite absurd, really. By now she accepts that her long marriage has been a grand folly, the likes of which isn't seen much any more in these new times when people do as they please rather than what is right.

As for Michael Mason … he quickly discovered in her something no-one else over here had perceived: a softness she possessed, though she was ashamed to reveal it to anyone else but him in case it exposed her as weak. The very smell of him marked him out as different from Robert, whose maleness always had a whiff of iron about it, whether it came from the sweat of the playing field or something implacable in his nature. She began to believe that the two most significant people in her life until then – her mother and her husband – had much in common with each other – and indeed, she had to admit it: with herself, too – especially the way they each regarded everyone as a potential enemy, the taking on of whom was sometimes a relish and always a necessity. Michael's smell, on the other hand, reminded her of porcelain, which was cool and strokeable and soft to the touch. In his company, it was as though a rock holding her in place had slipped to one side, temporarily releasing her from its trap and permitting her to peak out gingerly from beneath it.

And Sunny?

Some nine years after her return from Canada, Sunny can be spotted in the garden one fine day in May during the mid-1960s, her back resting against the rhinoceros hide of an elderly laburnum tree whose leaves purr gentle shadows across her jeans. From time to time a squeal of sunlight runs through the yellow flowers of the tree, turning it into a kind of chandelier illuminating the two girls sitting beneath it within a halo of hopefulness.

Facing Sunny, cross-legged and squinting against the spotlight of the late spring sun, is her friend Sylvia.

Two teenage girls on one sun dappled afternoon. Ridiculously, neither is the least bit aware that the other is presently bearing on her back a weighty but invisible burden.

During the last five minutes or so Sylvia's visit has become *hideously* embarrassing to Sunny, but not through any direct fault of either of them. It's just that the two friends' conversation is rendered almost impossible, thanks to a piercing enfilade of harsh words coming from somewhere deep within the belly of the house. Sunny knows these episodes only too well. It used to be that the bitter words of her parents felt like blows raining down on *her*, but it is the angry interludes of taut silence that worry her most, infused with apparent scheming when each party stands off and prepares to re-group, because you can't defend yourself against those fraught, angry impasses in a straightforward way. If only she were able to share anything of this with Sylvia, Sylvia might have amazed her with a secret of her own in return: *oh, yes, I bet I know exactly what it's like for you. With my father, he gets drunk, you see. He seems to work up to it, then it all explodes, then there is a period of calm, then it all begins between them again.* Instead, unbeknown to each of them, the pair of them will remain equally harnessed by the weight of a chronic personal discomfort so ingrained and impacted within her treacherous backpack that it feels like normality. Best keep it private, then.

What load can be heavier than this? It contains Sunny's ongoing feud between a deluge of shame and the energy she needs to keep it from seeping out and revealing itself – poisonous substance that it is. That can't be allowed to happen. Sunny's burden forms a rolling accompaniment to her consciousness. All she can know for certain is that she's somehow *implicated* in what goes on in that house, day after day. The consequence of sharing such a concern with either of her parents is just too frightening to contemplate: it might result in chaos, she suspects; there would be repercussions, and the opening up of a war between three instead of two parties, probably. No wonder it is a wearying thing, this leaden sense of her own insecurity within the household. No wonder she has a tendency to day-dream, for relief. 'Sunny, will you please BUCK UP,' yells Dorothy from time to time. 'Just look at the state of your room. All that mess of books.' (Dorothy is not friendly towards books.) 'Can't you DO SOMETHING ABOUT IT? You should be ashamed of yourself.' But she is, oh, she is.

It follows that one unfortunate side effect of having unhappy parents is to make Sunny feel uncomfortable about herself. She has friends – Sylvia is one. But they tend to come and go, and this isn't solely due to the unpredictability of the environment. Dorothy has a way of refusing to acknowledge, let alone offer much of a welcome to Sunny's friends, the older she gets. The few girls who visit Sunny's house are rarely referred to by name by Dorothy, who is in the habit of referring to such young people as 'what's-her-name' or just ' – er …?' or 'that girl', which Sunny finds destabilising because it suggests that people she likes must be of no account. So she has learned to be on her guard when friends call and doesn't encourage them, because her mother can be guaranteed to react in ways that confirm that Sunny's generation is another species altogether, to be treated as more than a little bit suspect when it forces itself into her orbit.

Not surprisingly, Dorothy's suspicion of teenage girls also makes her critical towards them. 'What are you going to be doing, then – lounging around, I suppose?' she muttered earlier that day, alerted by the click made when Sylvia opened the garden gate. To Dorothy, *lounging about* is what teenage girls seem to do, and it unnerves her. Also, they have a way of bursting into shrieks of sudden laughter without apparent cause, which never fail to startle her and put her on the defensive. *Must be laughing at me.*

Today, the primitive verbal thrusts gaining momentum from inside the house seem particularly ferocious and random. Her father's bellowing has become a hoarse, wild bull sound. *La, la, la, la,* Sunny mentally chants, glancing at her watch, wondering when it will be time for Sylvia's bus. The female responses are even more alarming and equally primeval: skinned, ugly yelps and a dreadful shrill wail that sounds as though it is being scraped across a blackboard. *La, la, la, la, LA* .. It is impossible to make out either what exactly is being said, or who is the predator and who the prey. Maybe there is something of both in each of those dreadful, uncontrolled voices. An invisible rope tightens around Sunny and the garden air always puts out claws when she is assaulted by such sounds. Whatever is going on inside is out of sight and overshadowed. It smacks to Sunny of ancient myths she has read about, and the menace that lives in the forest.

A door is slammed in due course, rattling the guttering outside the kitchen, and Sylvia raises her eyes in alarm when the porch offers its own shudder in response. What happens next is that a slim, middle-aged female figure appears to be leaving the house in a hurry – escaping, perhaps – and heading for the common on the other side of the road. Shortly after this, the back door is opened and Sunny's father steps out more serenely than seems feasible with that gross, fake smile on his face.

He nods awkwardly at the girls and proceeds to cycle off fast in the opposite direction.

'Right, then,' decides Sunny, clapping her hands together once and rising up. 'Would you like me to walk you to the bus stop?'

Sylvia stirs, stretches her arms. 'If you want to,' she sighs. 'Would you mind if I had a drink before I go? Would that be alright?' *Now that they've gone, she means*, thinks Sunny, *so it's safe to go in.*

'Yeah, I'll get it,' she shoots back, casual as can be. Lemonade or orange juice?'

'Well, mmm ... orange, please.'

So much for their revision. James Joyce will have to

wait for another time. They are reading *A Portrait of the Artist as a Young Man*. 'What do you think he *really* means by "silence, exile and cunning"?' Sunny had begun to ask Sylvia before they were interrupted. Belatedly, Sylvia began to suggest: 'He means getting away, I should think. Without fighting'. Jumping ship, then, thinks Sunny, gathering her pile of notes. Sylvia, she is aware, operates on the fringe of making her own bid to get away from home, in ways that Sunny admires but considers might be a little too dangerous for her. For example, Sylvia often hitch-hikes home from school – there's a craze for it amongst some of the more daring girls – and she has an older boyfriend who wants to be an actor, which sounds mysterious and attractive (as opposed to becoming an accountant or working in a bank, ha ha: who would be square enough to do something like that?). There's a certain dozy-eyed sense of guarding her own privacy that Sunny has noticed lately about Sylvia, which signals to her that the couple are probably having sex in his bedsit.

'Yes. I can do you orange if you like – or how about a whisky and soda?' Sunny throws in as an afterthought in an attempt to lighten the mood and make Sylvia feel as though she isn't being shunted off (which she is). This is only half in jest, since Sunny herself has been taking sips out of the whisky bottle and topping it up with water until it looks as pale as a dry sherry, instead of mellow brown. She'll deny it, of course, if confronted. Let them take the bottle back to the off-license and complain.

Feigning nonchalance, Sunny nimbly heads for the kitchen. She has just started the cold tap running in preparation for Sylvia's orange squash when there is a vigorous knocking on the front door.

What now?

A large man with a map in his hand, wearing an

open-necked shirt with its brand-new creases still intact, takes a pace back when she opens it.

'Well, hallo there,' he says, with an optimistic grin. Sunny registers what sounds like an Australian accent. 'How are you today, little lady?'

Another salesman? He'll not be the first to call that week. This one appears to be emitting a false bonhomie that strikes her as horribly out of keeping with the mood of the afternoon. It jars on her. He has a cheesy smile, she notices, like all of his kind who come calling, and to compound her distaste his shirt is so obviously on its first outing, exuding a just manufactured smell.

She tilts her head as her mother would do, in a manner she suspects might be construed as mildly insolent though this is not her intention.

'I'm here on a special trip,' he says, with a broad grin. (Yep, thinks Sunny, heard it all before, that's what they always say.) 'Does a Dorothy Robinson live here by chance?'

Sunny spots Dorothy from the corner of her eye, far off under the shade of a tree at the edge of the green. She is crouched on her haunches, her head resting on her knees. Big sobs at intervals appear to dance across the patterned cotton of her dress. Sunny imagines a "nice Sunny" – not herself, obviously – who would be able to escape from the rigidity of her own body (encumbered by the backpack) and go over there bearing comfort at a time like this when it is obviously needed. Nice Sunny, she believes, would be a person so lavish with empathy she would be big enough not to recoil when she was not shown what she regarded was the respect she was owed by her mother. Instead, she seems to suffer from a condition that involves dammed up compassion. Many times, she has tried to reach inside herself and make a connection with it – to find out whether compassion is just a word, or whether there is something there. But her familiar self always finds a reason not to pursue this line of self-examination, though it mostly leaves her feeling she has fallen short in relation to her mother – failed her, in effect. Often fearful, sometimes bored, ever on the alert for the next outburst, or the even grimmer uncertainty of the battlefield of her parents' stalking of each other, Sunny shrinks from the mayhem of it in the same way she cowers in the dentist's chair, in the sure knowledge that at this stage neither of the people on whom she is obliged to depend will back down until either *he* walks out or *she* bursts into a frustrated wave of weeping that marks the beginning of a defeat. Just like today.

With all these things in mind, she slips past the man on the doorstep.

'Mum, there's a man. He wants to see you.'

'Who? What?' Dorothy seems confused, shifting her head slightly to reveal eyes bloodshot from crying, glinting glassily.

'I don't know. He didn't say.'

Dorothy groans and replaces her head onto her knees.

'Has your friend gone?'

'She will, soon.'

'Here – can you just fix this for me?' She passes Sunny a necklace with a small gold clasp she has been gripping, leaving a line of tiny red circles on the skin of her palm.

Sunny loves skin. She especially loves the soft pliability of the skin of babies, and the innocent nakedness of the unlined skin at the back of people's necks where there are no eyes to confuse you. But she recoils from the skin her mother is holding out to her, lifting her hair so Sunny can see where to fix the clasp. For some obscure reason that skin, today, becomes a sign of her mother's betrayal. It is undoubtedly hostile, and the downy little bristles there seem to stand on guard as the clasp is duly fastened.

Another sigh signals Dorothy's return to the foetal position and her inaccessibility. 'Tell this – man, who ever he is – to go away,' instructs Dorothy out of the side of her mouth. 'You know what to do. We don't want anything he's selling. Get rid of him. And it's about time so-and-so went too, don't you think?'

'Sylvia.'

Sunny skips back and relays to the man that Dorothy is not prepared to take callers. 'Ah, that's a real shame,' he says. 'Who are you, then, pretty girl?'

She grimaces openly at 'pretty girl'. 'I'm Sunny,' she replies in a measured way.

'OK. Sunny. Well, Sunny, it's been a pleasure meeting you. A real pleasure. Please tell Mrs Robinson that I called.' He offers her a business card which she accepts absently because she remembers her waiting friend at that moment and runs back to join her. On her way, she tosses the card in the rubbish bin along with the empty orange squash bottle, where it melds with lunch time's leftovers and is taken away later that day by the refuse truck. Too many travelling salesmen had a habit of coming a-knocking lately: men selling dusters and face creams or wanting you to sign up for magazine subscriptions or take on more insurance.

After walking Sylvia to the bus stop, Sunny buys a bar of Fry's peppermint cream chocolate and a packet of five Embassy cigarettes to smoke in the privacy of her bedroom during the course of the following week. Nothing has been mentioned about this new endeavour. Like the siphoned-off whisky, it is one of a number of things no-one has noticed Sunny doing lately, now she is seventeen.

Back at home, Sunny must sort out her notes because

in less than an hour she has her weekly appointment with Dr Mason, who is acting as her geography tutor. When he was plain Mr Mason he used to teach with her father but now he has another, more important job at the university. Lately, he has invited her to call him "Michael", which she is trying to make herself do without blushing.

Being impatient to quit the wasteland which calls itself her home, for some time now it has been Sunny's ambition to establish a place at the university for herself. She fantasizes daily about having a room of her own, where she would cook simple meals and people would drop in casually, bringing bottles of wine and cigarettes. For several years she has been incubating her own vague plan for freedom, deciding that it all depends on getting good 'A' level results. Anything else can wait. She has trained herself to be very focussed about this.

Next, she draws an outline of heavy eyeliner around each of her eyes. She bestows only a passing thought on her mother, now in self-imposed isolation in another part of the house after dragging herself in from the common. It's not personal, but the incident has made her wonder in an abstract way about the state of being different from others, which seems to have been her mother's lot all along. In a way – this is Sunny's current wisdom – it doesn't matter whether or not you try to align yourself with conventional values because the attribute of "being different" has become a modish parody of itself just lately, as far as people of her own age group are concerned, since most of her contemporaries are at pains to copy each other in conformity with the main tribe. To these girls, difference signifies the grand canyon of a gap between themselves and their out-of-date parents. It is how Sunny feels, too. It occurs to Sunny that all the hollow anguish and fear harboured by people like her mother – weighed down by a sense of a difference about themselves instead of being elevated by it – is an unhealthy aberration. This gives her even more cause to behave as though her own estrangement from Dorothy could turn out to be quite normal, in a way.

Dr Mason – Michael – knocks at the door at half past seven sharp, as arranged. It's a tentative, quizzical sort of knock which Sunny recognizes immediately. Dorothy, her face washed and in that state of sleep-walking that often follows in the wake of a major row, picks up her magazine from the sitting room after nodding to him, then retires to her bedroom. Sunny's father has phoned to say he will eat his supper with his mother. This means they have the house practically to themselves. Good, thinks Sunny, ushering him forward with a bright smile.

'Hi Sunny,' he greets her, brisk and tentative at the same time, and a little bit amusing: like an adult who is still learning, thinks Sunny, which is a rare enough state to warrant admiration. She delights in hearing him call her by her own name, as though he were presenting her with the gift of it. As though she *is* a gift. He settles down to read what she has written for him, the tips of his fingers pushing against each other and half hiding his mouth in a manner she assumes is properly academic. He listens patiently and without interruption to her sometimes probing, sometimes scattered reflections on the part landscape plays in the development of dispersed communities, and his way of listening makes her wonder whether she could be a person whose thoughts counted. Often, on his way to the university in the morning, he drops a book or pamphlet or journal off for her to read in advance, which her mother keeps for her on her return. To Sunny's unfailing delight, these special loans left out on the kitchen table come freighted with intellectual promise.

('Do you fancy him? I bet he fancies you,' teases Sylvia. 'Oh, shut up,' says Sunny.)

Even unhappy people seem to stumble upon a cause for celebration every so often. A few months later, when Sunny gets her results, which are good, and it is confirmed that she will be going to the college of her choice that autumn, Dorothy begins to stir herself. She is mildly surprised to discover that her daughter's achievement gives her something to talk about when she is having her hair done or collecting the groceries, as though it has rubbed off a little on herself. She even discovers a reason to linger while the Austrian lady gathers an audience in the post office with her tales of how her own boys, all apprentices now, are earning good money. It ends up giving her an idea: why shouldn't they throw a swanky party in a hotel in town to celebrate, in the way of Montreal parties for debs in the old days? It would be a way of marking Sunny's 18th birthday as well as her academic success. There would be proper, printed invitations. She would invite Robert's friends. Ha – they would see what she could pull off. Why hadn't she thought of something like that before? She would show them. She certainly would. Just as she had been instructed by her mother, all those petty-seeming and bothersome lessons in etiquette would finally be made to come into their own.

And so it transpires that on a warm early evening in late September there is flurry of activity in the house, with people dropping in to leave presents and cards and Sunny and Dorothy zipping each other into their long evening dresses while Robert fiddles with his cuffs and straightens himself into his dinner jacket. Even the old relations who won't be able to come to the hotel where the party is to take place begin to pop in, to view them in their finery. They have to give it to her: Dorothy has masterminded the whole thing and is even now on the phone negotiating the taxi that will be picking them up.

Eventually, Michael Mason makes his familiar, tentative knock on the back door and Sunny herself dashes to answer it. How important he has been in helping her towards that room of her own. It is now so close to being taken up that she can almost walk up to it and put her very own key in its door at last, she realises, in a sudden rush of affection for him. He is dressed informally, she notices, in an open necked shirt and corduroy trousers, but never mind that. He has an envelope in his hand. 'Oh,' says Sunny, 'is that for me? For my birthday? Thank you! *Thank* you!'

'Well, actually no,' he replies, running a hand through his hair and peering beyond her into the sitting room before striding forward. Taken aback somewhat, Sunny has no choice but to make way for him before she is called to the doorstep in anticipation of the taxi. She is all ready now. She is wearing a deep blue silk dress, low on the shoulders, and her thick red curls are tied back loosely as a concession to Dorothy's wishes, just like they used to be when she was young.

But here's the thing: one of the most challenging memories Sunny will retain of her party is the sight of Michael Mason's back as he pushes roughly past her to slip his envelope into her mother's hand, after which she spied him only once more, striding directly back to his car, parked outside. She supposed he was rushing home to get changed.

But she was wrong.

He failed to meet them later at the hotel, though from

time to time during the evening she looked out for him, disappointed by his absence.

Just before taking up her university place, she learned that he had been made a Reader at a university in the west of England, and that his little cottage in the next village was up for sale.

MOORINGS

22

East Anglia, 2002

A travel agent's office lies towards the west side of town in an area Dorothy is familiar with, since here also resides her hairdresser and manicurist, both still indispensable to her. Long widowed and in her mid-eighties now, through sheer determination she is still identifiable by her stately posture and facial features which have developed from the fraught incandescence of her youth into a more sedate attractiveness. This, and the neat, close-fitting clothes she wears so well, mark her out as a person who merits a second look, despite her age, and maybe she is on the brink of being able to respond to … what? A man in her life again? Ridiculous nonsense! Michael Mason's morning visits all those years ago could never be equalled, she has long figured this out in her heart. How could they?

Nearly forty years on, she still reminisces about those visits, and with the distance of time they are remembered benignly, the preciousness of memory at this late stage of her life cancelling out any bitterness or sense of loss. The simple delight of being in each other's company created by two shy people in their own hesitant way out of initial awkwardness during a few precious years of gilded mornings – it had been a fertile acquaintance, but could lead to nothing more radical for a person like Dorothy. It was a delicate and beautiful thing, as she fondly remembered it from time to time: one of the few things in her life she could say belonged to herself alone and nobody else. It had made the anticipation of his visits almost as cherishable as the reality of them. It made her feel oddly proud of herself, serene and at ease. Who would understand that? Who could comprehend how precious it had been? Especially since it all ended in enforced guilt and humiliation when Robert unexpectedly turned back one morning shortly before Sunny's party in order to retrieve a forgotten book. What struck him was the sight of the blue housecoat on the living room floor and he sat down in a chair for a moment and began to wonder.

Oh, you fool, she is in the habit of telling herself each time Michael Mason comes to mind nowadays, inwardly cringing at the way Robert had trampled on the whole thing so unnecessarily, utterly despoiling it. *You fool* – to have entertained such a gentle and harmless sort of love, only for it to be cut down, rudely interfered with and turned into something tawdry by Robert. He really shouldn't have sent Michael Mason away like that, there was no excuse for it. There was no cause to ban him from the house. After all, what did it amount to? Only her acquisition of a passing grace and stature beyond anything she had ever dreamed of possessing, something she would never have suspected she was capable of sustaining: it was a blessing bestowed upon her by knowing she was admired by a younger man, a *kind* man who would never take advantage of her or force her hand. Or make her so *angry*, as Robert had done.

But it would be fair to say that Dorothy is almost at ease with her life at this point, as long as she avoids the more painful aspects of looking back. She has being playing around with a vague desire to give herself a holiday, lately – hence this visit to a travel agent. Why not? She is free to do so, there is no-one left to stop her. To embark on a cruise, maybe? Such ideas ferment slowly out of a mild sense of goal-lessness these days, and they either tend to peter out naturally or begin to throw up a few auspicious images in passing – in this case, the uplifting, biting saltiness of the sea, experienced in younger times during four Atlantic crossings. There is something greatly promising to her in such images – but wouldn't such a plan be just another foolishness? *Do people like me do things like this?* Is it really possible to go on such an adventure, to raise herself out of what she is beginning to regard as the rather empty sanctuary of her present life, even though it is pretty much acceptable, on the whole?

The fact is, Dorothy has arrived at that point when anything that happens is so incrementally small, so full of an accretion of old repetitions, that her life often takes on the shape of a small coracle bobbing without apparent purpose in the middle of a lagoon. And yet, there *is* unfinished business about the very state of being alive, she has come to believe – there has to be, surely, as long as life itself prevails. For example, when she set out earlier that morning she was undoubtedly in an enterprising mood, game enough to find out what that something could turn out to be.

Only to be assailed by these niggling misgivings about her own capabilities.

For the past few months she has been putting things in order at home, sorting out once and for all the small cache of mementoes and photographs from long ago in Canada, some in a leather-bound album, others a slippery pile of loose prints in an old cardboard box. This is more like it, surely, at her age – better than dreaming of the sea? Oh, come on – *courage, Dorothy*, she reminds herself, nudging open the travel agent's door with her shapely left thigh.

It started as a morning out, anyway. She wants very much to hold on to its buoyancy if she can.

Most mornings she likes to sit with a cup of tea and the Telegraph crossword (at which she has become rather adept) in a comfy chair by a window where she can keep an eye on the corner of the open field stretching out beyond the back garden. Now that her bad feelings are so much diminished, it pleases her to keep track of the changing face of that field from time to time, prepared to be mildly surprised as the ground slowly but surely transforms itself from a fuzz of indeterminate green shoots into the studded tips of yellowing wheat, or the hissing whiskers of sinuous barley. She notices, too, the mild sadness that descends on the village as it looks towards winter following the harvest, and the tousled margin of the field's aftermath left behind by the combine harvester. It is connected to a sense she has that anything that moves forward – time, the weather, traffic, the growing of crops, her life – tends to leave behind a jumbled repository of displaced evidence. So it is that on country roads nearby, cars send dust and gravel into untidy heaps in the middle of junctions, depositing the anonymous, temporary footprints of those busy passers-by who are more concerned with rushing off to make inroads elsewhere. *Well, I belong in that aftermath now,* she thinks, visualising herself dribbling around in the dust on a road without a name.

At the other end of the day, when there is nothing much to watch on the television, another project has been taking shape alongside the audacity of venturing out to sea once more. Certain notions have bubbled up, revolving around her family, or what might be left of it, prompted by a desire to explore where she might be able to place herself comfortably on this earth, once and for all. A major limitation of her album of black-and-white people is that they can only provide her with airless shapes, reduced to the bare bones of the humanity they originally set out with in days gone by. But the marvel of them, to Dorothy, is that each time she scrutinizes the individuals in her old photographs they tantalise her with their continuing existence in a time not their own but subsequent time – *her* time (what's left of it), right here and now. Could she not answer them, then, by paying some sort of homage to those people there who had done "death", that experience she has yet to know, though sometimes these days she thinks she feels it coming? Under her scrutiny they become *only* their own death, thanks to the limitations of their fixed, old-fashioned poses. It is clear to her that very soon, bereft of her own living memory bestowing upon them one last spark of recognition, these people will be knowable only as emblems of a passing era, as antique as – oh, her mother's art nouveau necklace that she still keeps in its box in a drawer, such an out-dated piece, and quite beyond ever wearing – not even valuable, thanks to its clunky appearance.

On thoughtful evenings like this, she takes note of the arrow of dying light that travels across the lawn faster than normal at this time of year, scooping up another day. Year upon year she has watched as the earth draws in its breath at the onset of darkness, and at day break begins to release it once more in a soundless sigh that runs below the turning of the hours, as if to demonstrate to her that nothing changes more predictably than the natural process of degradation taking place everywhere.

But especially here, in and around her home.

Of course, her memory isn't what it used to be. Nowadays it seems layered in wavy lines that can't always be relied upon to intersect. When a lapse occurs she reproaches herself out loud. This morning, for instance: *'idiot!'* she chided, when she took out a dinner plate instead of her usual cereal bowl ... and: *'oh, you fool!'*, when that plate slipped through her stiffening fingers and smashed on the kitchen floor. And a scathing: 'oh, *for heaven's sake!'* when she realised that she had been looking at an out of date TV guide for some minutes in order to find out what was on that night. With such utterances replacing opportunities for conversation, it is as though she is creating a sporadic sound track for her life in a quest to *earth* it at last – just like the radio must be earthed, in order for it to function properly.

It is during less muddled moments that, if she has one of her photos close to hand, a significant moment might erupt out of the mysteries of forgetting with astonishing clarity. Look at that funny, faded face, for instance. Did he ever stop smiling, that boy in the photograph? Wait a minute – he could still be *alive*, couldn't he? After all, *she* was, and he wasn't that much older than her when she had known him. She avoids his eyes at first, though they seem to be pleading for a simple sign of reciprocity. He is a complex composition, straining towards her as though making a bid to escape the frame of the snapshot, though it cannot but condemn him to hover forever on the very precipice of his becoming, his forever unknowable next movement doomed never to be seen or understood. She notices the creases in a jacket which, with a little concentration, seem almost to shush and crackle with hardened mud stains as she stares deeply at his flattened form. Surely, that is an overlooked breakfast deposit on a lapel which she has never noticed there before, hastily and ineffectively rubbed just prior to the flash of the camera? Squinting, she picks out the axis of his left wrist, forming an angle with his arm in the way only this particular wrist can, and a facial expression generated by what she senses a deep yearning to be acknowledged. More: there are what must be teeth marks made only seconds earlier on a rough piece of bread he clutches in his hand. And look: he wears gaitered trousers in the way of the old times, this boy, lately passed down, maybe, sagging at the waist with buttons missing. Taken as a whole, it adds up to one lost second of a boy's life. And yet, she reminds herself – he *could* be still alive.

It is in widowhood that Dorothy has gradually discovered the spark of a desire to connect. Small wonder she felt especially drawn to the past in this respect – it was what she knew best, after all. To rescue it – or *him* – that boy – from the curse of being forgotten, lost without trace, to give him – to give *her*, as a result – a place, however humble, in the scheme of things: this is what she wants now, most of all. The more she scrutinizes him, the more he becomes like a phantom ship bobbing all alone on a swell, which strikes her with melancholy. She would do her best to reclaim him: that much she felt she owed him.

Something turned in her heart when that boy went and she's never been entirely sure what it was. Where is he? Why, why will he not present himself now – a one-time boy, perhaps a one-time man, at the very least a one-time spark of life which must have run through its seasons pretty much in parallel with her own. The photo in its entirety breaks in upon her again, even as she takes a first glance around the travel agent's interior with its shelves lined with glossy brochures in harsh primary colours. He was kind to her. He bought her candy out of his meagre pocket money. He was the one who always reached out for her hand when they crossed the tram lines of a busy urban street. And yet, no-one had bothered much with him. Except her. That was mean, wasn't it? As if he were of no account to anyone. Why would her mother never talk about that boy? Why did they never visit Nova Scotia and see him?

Sunny would know what to do about it. But Sunny isn't available any more. Sunny is long gone. Dorothy had watched, powerless, while Sunny was borne away from her on the strength of what at the time felt like the force of a rip tide. Sunny didn't once look back, after university. All that's left of Sunny is a meagre bundle of postcards, each scrawled with a single platitude, delivering next to nothing – insults, almost, masquerading as duty. 'Mountains in Nepal beautiful.' 'Hope your back is better.' 'Have a great Easter.' 'Too many people here in Manila.' No, Sunny never looked back, rarely visiting, although they never did, to her reckoning, actually fall out. But her absence has left Dorothy confused, hurt and rueful. So much so that she has prettified these treacherous postcards by tying them with purple ribbon, as you would a bunch of bereavement letters.

At long intervals, intermittent phone calls come from Sunny, always at inconvenient times, revealing hardly anything, as though Dorothy is deemed unworthy of entertaining a proper dialogue. Sunny has taken herself off to that place called the future, a place in which Dorothy herself can claim no foothold because it is a new world, made up of people who smoke in the street and wear inelegant clothes and swear and *want, want, want*, in such a shameless way, particularly the girls. She had been invited – but only once – to the flat in Chiswick that Sunny has shared for a number of years with a man who calls himself a poet, which always sat uncomfortably with her. She has a lingering suspicion that maybe she showed it on that occasion. Could it be that she caused offence? Maybe this has something to do with why Sunny stays away. If only she could mend ... Is it only she who feels scratched and pained by this? It irks her that there is no way of finding out, that she hasn't the words or the courage to initiate a conversation with her accomplished daughter (Sunny is a lawyer, something Dorothy feels both proud of and at the same time crushed by). It is all so unsatisfactory, this uneasy blend of envy, nervousness, resentment and incomprehension on her part – and just when she might have expected a mellowing on Sunny's part, a second chance for the two of them. If, say, a grandchild were to turn up and she could be on hand to help and advise ... But it was too late now for anything like that.

Instead, Dorothy will find herself standing all alone at the newly built French windows leading to the garden during October evenings as the light starts to fade more quickly. At times like this, with a whisky and ginger ale in her hand, Sunny flashes through her mind in a tumbling pack of cards that provide passing glimpses of what she chooses to call "incidents," each one a flake bearing a single, static image rather than the narrative unwinding of a time in their lives. Eventually, thank the lord, the mature trees can be relied upon to absorb all thoughts of Sunny, their darkening green underbellies sagging whist their thinning canopies still retain a rash of colour thanks to the annual striptease going on out there in the natural world. Voluptuous trees, thinks Dorothy. If past their prime. The approaching night tends, these days, to contain healing properties, granting her the power to seal regret, disappointment, fear, and her old friend anxiety, inside a welcome crust of resignation, on the whole. And so – with the fortification of alcohol warming her from within – by the time an hour or two has ticked away, all that remains is to sign off: *day, I give you up; I render you done.* The relief of it. Welcome the void. Until morning comes around again.

'Hallo, can I help?' The girl in the travel agent's seems unoccupied, glad of a customer.

'No thank you,' she replies with a start, as though the question is absurd, causing the girl to back off.

She is determined to take her time browsing, her mind pleasantly full of blousy waves, the throb of a big liner's engines, meals like exotic feasts and compactly furnished cabins. Those Atlantic trips made when she was a young woman – they have become leeched of colour during the long interim, rather like ageing hand-tinted photographic prints which have faded over time, their tinny pink and sugary blue tones bestowing upon them a fairytale aspect. It is early days in the incubation of this current plan to make one last journey. There must be no rush.

Might not even happen.

Doesn't matter.

'Are you alright there?' the persistent girl asks, a little later.

'Let me tell you something,' she shoots back. 'I've sailed before, and I know quite a bit about the sea. Both my grandfathers were sailors.'

'Really?'

'It's true.'

She brings to mind the colourful career of one grandfather – Captain Adam Pengarth, merchant adventurer – who dared to take on unknown waters, who exultantly wrote about the dangers he lived through for anyone who cared to know. Should it be the

Mediterranean, then, she half addresses this ancestor? Or the Pacific this time, maybe? She dispatches one fleeting afterthought towards that other one, the grandfather on her mother's side whom she never met, who might even have been (admittedly on sketchy speculative evidence) an admiral.

'I think I'll just take away some of these leaflets away with me, if I may,' Dorothy brings herself to say in due course.

'Of course, love. Just give us a ring when you are ready, then.' *Love? Whatever next?* "Love" anyway: it is a dumb fancy she has long outgrown, relieved to be rid of the bothersome futility of yearning for another.

Darn it! Where am I?

It's happened again, just as she settles into driving along with her handbag and a pile of brochures perching on the passenger seat next to her. This sporadic inability to recognise where she is always turns familiar terrain into the menacing experience of being on a way never travelled before, a *tabula rasa* on which to project suppositions which have nothing to do with her past experience of the place. These episodes remind her of how the television behaves when a poor signal fragments the picture and the splintered image takes a while to re-adjust. Thankfully, it tends to take only one landmark to trigger a re-alignment. Today, this happens to be a flashy burger bar, built on the remains of a pub where once she had sung war time songs with others – how odd, how far away, how melancholy such an activity strikes her now, as recognition floods in.

Yes, and here comes the graduate centre where Sunny used to go secretly with Michael Mason sometimes to learn geography, with Dorothy's connivance, after

Robert had turned him away. And he would drop her off at home later. Poised out of sight behind a curtain, Dorothy would listen for the sound of his car – and in the pause before Sunny opened the passenger door she would be on tenterhooks, wondering if Sunny, just being polite, would ask if he would like to come in. But this never happened, thank the lord, because he would have had to refuse, and what would Sunny have made of *that*? How could she have explained to Sunny what it really meant? She remembers keenly the grotesque discipline of bearing herself with all the poise she could muster as she reigned over Sunny's very special party that she had put so much effort into, refusing yet to believe that Michael Mason would not be coming calling on her any more, not ever. And having to bear herself regally, flashing smiles here and there although her heart was beginning to break, after reading the letter he had thrust into her hand before vanishing.

Driving along, restored to herself once more, she mechanically folds such thoughts away.

If all contact with Canada is at an end, then at least a trip could put paid to that, even though her parents and sisters have pre-deceased her and their children are – who knows where? Lost, all lost. Families have a tendency to ebb and flow, thinks Dorothy as she drives on, wondering whether she inhabits the flat end of an inward flow, floating aboard the peak of a tide at the fleeting moment it briefly stops before turning back. That places Sunny already way out at sea, then, heading ever further away on the current. Living with that man in London and travelling all over the world in the course of her work – Alan is it? Alec?

They never knew who I was, none of them.

Alright – it isn't who I am, it's who I might have been that I always wanted them to see. Was this foolishness, too?

Never mind, there are some rewards: her own car, for example, and her own home at last to do with as she pleases. "Bumping along": that's the phrase they use in the village for the state she's reached: she's heard it uttered more than once in response to a greeting. ('Oh, just bumping along, dear. What about you?')

There have been late capitulations on her part, made quite naturally in the end. Like her habit of taking a short walk most afternoons through the village, during which she is comfortable to pause for a few minutes to reciprocate people's courteous nods instead of hurrying by, aware that her looks have not failed her even now but rather – along with her solitude – feel as though they are coming into their own.

She notices, also, the gentle perambulations of elderly people in the village, as if in slow motion, their greying heads like overblown dandelions. One day, when she was passing a wide shop window, she followed their progress in reverse and they revealed themselves to her as if in a darkened mirror, those dandelion heads on their promenade. Amongst them, there was one who seemed to stand out in a rather striking way. She failed at first to recognize who it was, until it dawned on her that it was *herself* she was staring at, her own grey hair but a version of theirs. I am one of them, after all, it struck her – one of the crowd. This was not a wistful thought. In fact, it surprised her with a sense of mild relief.

Occasionally, she wonders – very tentatively – whether it could possibly have been herself, then, not them, that caused her to feel like a stranger.

I was a stranger to myself, in those days.

But I am no longer quite so strange.

I don't know why this is so, but it is.

The Austrian lady was divorced some years ago. For some reason, it has become the easiest thing in the world for Dorothy to chat to her now – it just happened one day – and ever since the pair have greeted each other as though they were long time acquaintances. Nothing overly personal, of course, but perhaps she is learning what the Austrian lady had been familiar with all along: the parched art of endurance, sustained through patience and dogged, unquenchable effort, which has the power to drown disappointment under the weight of its own determined cheerfulness.

Oh, what the heck?

It's too late, now.

Gone, gone, gone were most of her chances and she knew it, but never mind. *No matter,* she mouths to herself, with a vertiginous sense of having squandered something so vast and important that should really have been treated with more care.

To hell with it. It's almost done now.

Whenever she watches a weepy film on the television it makes her suspect that the *idea* of love might have always been there, within her, waiting to be ignited, albeit without much input on her part. But maybe that was her mother's wisdom in the end, not her own.

Her mother … that time she came to England – the only time – when Sunny was – what? Around seventeen, eighteen? She shudders at the thought of how they fell out when Lilian assumed, during her brief stay as a guest in the cottage by the green, a scarcely suppressed and maddeningly patronizing pretence of manners as soon as she had figured out what was going on there, what with Robert's frequent absence and strange old ladies dropping in all the time. Well, Dorothy had seen through that alright – and made bold to let her mother know that it was just *not on*. She had her pride, even if she privately agreed with her mother.

And what did Lilian do? Off she took herself to a place called Ealing in some part of London on one of the last days before she was due to sail back to Montreal – one of London's *decent* parts, she called it, as though the village at the edge of the fens was inferior in all respects. Why, at the time, hadn't she insisted on accompanying her mother, and maybe that way getting to meet some relatives she never knew she had? Didn't Lilian once say she had sisters? Might the admiral have lived there? Why had such questions never been pursued at the time? How life rushes past when you are young and details are squandered – meaningful, important signs that might help make sense of a bigger whole.

Living alone, as Dorothy does, is pretty much like being on the front line of existence, she sometimes feels, especially on Sundays when Sunny's call might arrive, once in a blue moon, catching her off guard and at a loss what to say, turning it into yet another missed opportunity. After each of these calls, a kind of hood wraps itself around her – something associated with Sunny but also with her own earliest childhood, ever since she began to study the old photos again, especially of the boy who disappeared without saying goodbye. What could it be? Loneliness, is it? Is this what it is to be lonely?

Nearing home, she turns a corner sharply, throwing out her left arm to stop the cruise brochures and her bag toppling into the passenger foot well. Oh, enough of the darned brochures. Suddenly, accelerating hard, she feels absolutely sure that what she most of all wants is to make progress with one last project, though it may defeat her and she doesn't know if she has the necessary apparatus to see it through. But she will have a go at it. Why not?

To get herself a passage on a big ship and try to discover any relative who might still, like her, be alive, in order to offer to share this privileged state with them. That boy – a cousin, wasn't he, from Nova Scotia? That's all she has to go on, but wouldn't it be something, to meet up with him again?

This strikes her as such a profound thought, such a thrilling idea, such an unaccustomed, downright bold and unusual plan that a rash of goose bumps fires up in her fingers and trembles all the way up her arms.

Coming up to a junction crossed by a busy carriageway, and quite taken with the thought of it, she fails to look to the right and her car carries on with bold disregard towards the mainstream of traffic thundering directly across her path, where a lorry hits it side on with great force.

23

Ealing, 1964

Now here's something that doesn't happen very often on Oak Street, or what's left of it after the war: a gleaming black London cab gliding to a halt in front of a terraced house with a deep green door dulled and chipped by the depredations of time and weather and in urgent need of a re-paint. A group of girls put on hold their game of hopscotch to watch this spectacle.

During the last hour of her journey to this very spot, Lilian has been mentally cataloguing the multiple changes imposed upon the suburban landscape along the well worn route from Liverpool Street Station due west. Underlying her curiosity were pockets of resentment regarding her "treatment" by Dorothy, as it came back to her, begging some mental redaction to make it palatable. After going to *all that effort* to cross the Atlantic to visit Dorothy and reacquaint herself with her now teenage grandchild it had turned sour on her, spoiled by her daughter's poor hospitality and even worse manners, in her opinion. Why on earth did Dorothy have to marry that sporty red-haired man (and bequeath such dreadful hair on their child)? Lilian just could not be expected to settle in the flint and brick house by the village green, there being no proper bathroom, at least by her standards. The result was that on her journey towards Ealing, her indignation was well-fermented, and she claimed for herself the satisfaction of being entirely justified.

But enough of that for now. It is time to put on a good face for the meeting to come, one that is characterized, today, by a rare trace of nervousness on her part.

I will send Sunny some chocolates, she resolves, and feels instantly better about her somewhat ungraceful exit from Dorothy's marital home.

With the taxi stationary but its engine still ticking over, she deftly applies a dark line of lipstick, finishing her face off with a few pats of face powder to stop her cheeks glowing, lowering carefully over her face the thin black lace veil attached to a close fitting felt hat of the same colour she wears when out. One net curtain in the window of the house of her destination – a dingy pebble-dashed terraced building – moves fractionally then snaps back to join its partner, she is quick to spot, tossing the tail of her fox wrap over her left shoulder and pointing a short, nyloned leg towards the pavement. Stepping out in shiny, medium-heeled court shoes, she makes her way with almost coquettish deliberation along a mean concrete path infiltrated by weeds.

The door mysteriously opens before she reaches it.

'Mrs Dalton says to come in,' offers a woman in nurse's uniform. 'She's been waiting in the front room. Follow me, please.' Proceeding as bidden, Lilian finds herself barely managing to disguise a sniff in the vicinity of the dark green hall carpet, fraying at the edges – a refuge, surely, for years and years of steam from old gravy and boiled vegetables.

'Here, let me help you,' says the nurse when they reach the hall stand, a multi-purpose piece of furniture with a mirror and open nook in which to place umbrellas. Lilian automatically hands over her fox wrap together with her shapely, high-collared velvet coat as though this nurse is the maid, which causes the nurse to bristle. 'Go in, won't you?' says the nurse, with exaggerated formality, briefly glaring at the guest's rear view before popping her head round the door to call out: 'I'll come in later, Mrs Dalton. You just leave them tea things where they are when you've finished with them. Are you comfortable now?'

'Yes dear,' comes a wheezy response from the cracked voice of Jemima Dalton. 'Lil, here Lil, come in, do.'

A two bar electric fire glows a demonic orange in the grate and the room is unnaturally warm. Lilian fans her face with her hand and prepares to position herself near enough to her one-time benefactor that they will be able to hear each other. Lilian is not far off seventy, but she takes care of herself. Lord, she does. Always has done. Jemima, she quickly works out, must be eighty-eight, the same age her mother would have been if she hadn't died so young. 'Sit there, dear,' indicates Jemima, pointing towards an easy chair which has been positioned in advance to face her own cushioned podium on the sofa, where she presides over a sturdy occasional table pre-set with teapot and cosy, cups and saucers, milk jug, sugar bowl and matching plate of dry biscuits.

Lilian plucks a cigarette from the silver case in her clutch bag before drawing out a matching lighter. It is only then that "Lil" sits down, as bidden, ready to confront Jemima Dalton eye to eye.

'I'm getting old, dear,' opens Jemima in response to Lilian's surveillance. 'Yes, I am. Aren't we all?' And indeed, what Lilian sees before her is a body much shrunken into itself, reminding her of the way that milk, boiled up to a state of froth in a saucepan then recedes, forming on its surface a mothy residue of yellow skin. The hair, entirely white, is cut in the style of the 1920s in a sharp bob and severely hair-gripped to one side. But the eyes, of indeterminate colour, gaze equally sharply into Lilian's own, until both of them feel obliged to look away.

'Do I understand you've come up from the country this morning?' inquires Jemima Dalton.

'Yes. Indeed I have,' issues forth Lilian's mannered Canadian accent.

'You'll have come here from right across London, then,' says Jemima. 'Goodness me, you'll have come along the *laundry* route, won't you? Queensway. Shepherd's Bush. Acton. Up the Uxbridge Road. The old laundry route.'

Don't taunt me, lady, thinks Lilian, put on the defensive. I am no Lil.

For some seconds they observe each other, and for each of them watchfulness is like a moat around a watery bag of contrary emotions and questions which it may or may not be permissible to air, given the passing of time. *Let's see how it goes, first, where it might lead and how it might flow*, thinks Lilian. From the other direction, Jemima seems keen to glean a scrap or two for later tittle-tattle, eyeing her closely. Lilian has been bracing herself for a trace of resentment on the part of her mother's old friend, that the ageing daughter should simply turn up like this out of the blue after all these years of – well, of nothing whatsoever: never any gratitude for being taken in all that time ago, no thanks, nor even the courtesy of a note from time to time.

'Would you be mother, Lil?' Jemima invites silkily. 'My poor old stiff fingers don't do the trick any more.' Is there the slightest emphasis on the word "mother" or does Lilian imagine it?

As requested, she pours two cups of tea with a deftness born of practice.

'Tell me about your family, dear,' invites Jemima after

her guest declines a biscuit. Which Lilian is happy to do, in well-practised, off-handedly glowing terms.

The conversation moves on to Ealing, her one time home, and the grassy craters left long ago by the old German bombs, some of them still remaining in the form of shallow, weedy pits. 'They're going to knock this street down eventually, you know,' says Jemima. 'Demolish what's left of it. Going to put up new flats. I shall be in one of them, God willing. Nothing stays the same, does it, girl?' And from here she proceeds to talk of various things: of how the street had celebrated with a party at the end of the rationing, how difficult it was to buy decent wallpaper even now, and how people have had to settle into humdrum post war lives without there being much money about these days. 'I don't suppose it's like that where you come from, Lil' she concludes.

'Well, no, I don't suppose it is,' replies Lilian with careful patience, forbearing to introduce this woman to her lunch club at one of Montreal's best hotels, her bridge evenings, her big house and her comfortable widowhood.

'My poor old Vic, you remember him?' asks Jemima. 'He died – oh, it was not too long after this last war.' But the odour of the car man's stinking tobacco will never leave this room, thinks Lilian, and the room itself has certainly shrivelled, despite its hefty, original Edwardian trimmings: the top-heavy fringed standing lamp with its yellowing shade, the cramped mantelpiece, the cumbersome sideboard with its fat, scuffed legs. No, she has not forgotten one iota of it.

'I was sad to hear of poor little Violet,' offers Jemima. 'She never complained. Always worked hard. Just her luck to get consumption like her poor mother. But to pass away on a train taking her up north … I never did understand how that came about. What a do.'

Lilian stiffens at this scrap of information, which she has not expected at all and does not know how to reply.

After a pause, Jemima continues: 'What about Mary Ellen, though? Setting up a little school in Croydon with the money Violet left – though goodness knows where she got that from … '

A feeling of deep unease grips Lilian, followed by the most uncanny sense of dread which threatens to destabilise her as she tries to establish a connection between these two slivers of news.

A train up north? Could it be possible that this uncharacteristic and ultimately tragic journey of Violet's was to Liverpool? Could it be – no, surely not – that Violet never arrived to meet that poor boy? Whatever might have happened to him, in the circumstances? Hold on – Mary Ellen's "new wealth" – was it feasible that it came originally from the coffers of Edward Pengarth?

It's really only a matter of time before this old woman will light upon Bill Smithyes, she guesses, dizzy with shock. Does she need that? She only came on a whim, after all, having left herself with an awkward day to spare before her ship sailed, following the falling out with Dorothy. Though maybe there was also a sneaking desire to investigate the possibility of making peace with the old woman facing her, who had been so loyal to her mother, after all, and had given Lilian herself a home when she had nothing. Nothing at all.

Then – like a footballer who has been idly flipping a ball up and down on the top of his boot and suddenly decides to aim a shot at the goal – Jemima makes her play, and the direction it takes it is so unexpected that Lilian reels from a second wave of shock, quite as catastrophic as the one just delivered, when Jemima changes tack once again.

'Shall you be visiting your boy now you're here?'

A hot flush of the variety she thought she had been rid of for many years streams through Lilian's body.

'My boy?'

'Yes, dear, who else do you think I'm talking about? He's got a shop on Cumberland Street. You know, the garage. Funny how he became a car man too. I expect you'll be visiting him. Top man there, he is now.'

'Yes, indeed.' She manages one single peel of icy mirth to which Jemima makes her own contribution, for slightly longer, perhaps, than this snippet of information warrants.

'Lovely chap, Tom Smithyes. More tea, dear?'

I think not, decides Lilian.

Already, it is the heel of the afternoon.

A siren not far away announces the completion of a factory's afternoon shift while a pair of passing schoolboys outside on the street set up a howl of glee to celebrate their freedom, one of them tumbling into the hedge. A large wasp bumps its nose repeatedly against the window pane.

'Had a lot of those this year,' murmurs Jemima, eyeing Lilian closely.

It is getting late.

Yes, how late it is, thinks Lilian, relieved that such ordinary observations have forced a turn in the direction of their conversation.

It is certainly all too late.

She glances discreetly at the yellowed face of the old clock on the mantelpiece with its dogged, grinding tick, but it is not the clip-clipping away of another day which grips her: it's far worse than that. The sound of her son's name on Jemima's lips has torn through her understanding, leaving her perilously undefended. Lilian almost buckles, taking each successive blow as she knows she must and quickly internalising it. As seconds tick by, it is difficult – impossible, really – to deal with so many missing links, all at once. Especially when keeping face, somehow, is paramount to her.

Is this what the old woman has been after all along, she wonders? To turn that old guilt into a living thing once more so that she can take vicarious pleasure in watching its effect?

Hardly. If she could bring herself to rise above her scepticism, Lilian might have spotted Jemima losing any superficial interest she may have had in an exercise designed to cause pointless humiliation. But she doesn't. Determined to maintain her equilibrium, she misses what Jemima's eyes are really signalling: *You were a naughty girl, Lil, but I can't wish you harm. I never did.* For Jemima can see for herself the infinitely more fundamental pain of Lilian's remorse, even if she never knew the extent of it. Now, *that* is a burden she would not wish on anyone.

'Perhaps you'd better be on your way, dear,' she relents, her words marking time with the clock. 'Wouldn't want to keep you.' It is not for Jemima to suggest reunions. He might not wish it, for one thing. But for the first time in many years she feels pity for the small figure on the chair in front of her, whose stiff bearing tells her that there can be no resolution, no respite, only the necessity of bearing her loss of her son to the end. 'Yes, home you go, Lil. Back over there. And I wish you a safe journey, dear. You know I do.'

'Is that really the time?' replies Lilian as soon as she dares. 'Oh, my, yes, I must be getting along. What a pleasure it has been to see you again.' And then, as though she is indeed finished, with surprising agility she rises, bending down to place a cold kiss on Jemima's forehead because she, too, has at last sniffed the air of a truce, for which she discovers she is rather grateful. After that, she loses little time in picking up her coat, wrap and hat from the hall. 'Thank you for tea,' she calls out towards the little front room in an afterthought. 'I'll see myself out.'

And what does it matter if she makes such a bluff exit, for she knows she will never pass this way again.

With wild speculation firing her mind, she walks briskly towards the main thoroughfare, and from here past the fishmonger, grocer, bread shop, tailor, barber, the paraffin shop, dairy, haberdashery store; then on a little further, past a pub with a purple tiled front, a green grocer's cart, Woolworths, with its wooden floor, registering none of them, particularly, because it feels as though her pace is motored by a force from beyond her own volition.

Finally, she turns the corner leading into another familiar street.

Indeed, there is the garage on the right, just as Jemima Dalton had suggested, with cars parked on its forecourt: two Austin A40s, chunky and harmless, and three brand new Austin Cambridges in sparkling blue. Two stubby manual petrol pumps are being minded by a young attendant in overalls who dreamily draws a wet mop back and forth across the forecourt while he waits for the next car to pull up. There is a name painted on a wooden board above a small showroom and her gaze is caught by what comes next: '... and Daughters'. *Daughters?* Did daughters – did, for heaven's sake, what might even be more *grandchildren* of her own – what a thought – partake in retailing of this nature these days? How on earth had that clumsy boy arrived back here in this very spot, anyway? It doesn't add up. It is beyond belief.

She worries she might sag, might even disgrace herself in some way in front of such a place.

What next?

Automatically, she takes refuge in re-applying her lipstick, using one of the garage's glass windows as a mirror, then tugs her veil into place. Taking measured steps, she moves towards the door of this showroom – an incongruously smart, elderly female in this part of the world – and receives a respectful stare from a couple in drab overcoats with their noses near the glass. Though Lilian is undeniably small and – if not yet frail, then built like a starling – she elbows her way to a point a little way behind the pair to where she can just peer between them into a prism of the interior. Here, another young man in a cheap but dapper grey suit stands by, hopeful of custom, eager to serve. In fact, with no less than three interested parties hovering, it behoves him to come outside and usher them in. 'No obligation,' he assures them.

Feeling like a stray cat the couple have let in with them inadvertently, Lilian perfunctorily surveys the new stock before making bold to enquire where the man in charge might be. 'I can help you myself, madam,' the salesman insists. But when she merely nods politely and makes as if to move away, he calls out: 'He's at home helping put the scaffold up. His chimney fell down the other night in the wind. He shan't be long, if you wish to wait. He's only round the corner.'

Before he has finished his little speech, Lilian has folded herself round the door and is off once more.

A few deep breaths of fresh air later and she feels partially restored – enough to carry on, anyway.

There is no harm, she tells herself, in taking a peek. In fact, she feels overwhelmingly, irrationally drawn towards the location indicated by the salesman, although this is an endeavour which is undoubtedly fraught with danger.

Sure enough, a house bearing a skeleton of scaffold comes into view, some fifty yards off. The tips of her high heels make a clicking sound on uneven slabs of the York stone pavement, a sound that is so stylish where she comes from but seems blunted, here, with no-one to appreciate it.

The house is not hard to identify because it is the only one with a figure in silhouette on the roof. It turns out to be a 1930s suburban villa, with a merry, glassy sun radiating from the small window built into its porch. The round ends of its one, overly-large front window remind her of the bulkiness of those old-fashioned, free-standing baths people once had. But it is a friendly façade, with an undeniable family feel to it. On the front lawn she spots a child's rocking horse, and towards the rear – a glimpse of its hinterland appears through a wooden gate at the side, languishing on a single hinge – she spies an abundance of clothes drying on a line: men's shirts, lady's blouses, children's dresses, all pegged in order and ranked pleasingly, according to size. And there is a clothes horse further back, modestly hung with various items of underwear, similarly grouped. Small people live here, she concludes, people who know how to save, to look forward, to cherish their home. *So he is not alone*, she thinks, *if it is indeed he, and he is looked after*. This gives her cause for both relief and sorrow.

She stands for a moment facing the house, then braces herself to gaze up towards the roof. While the man up there dips into a tool bag balanced on one of his knees, she searches her mind for clues to verify recognition, tracing the outline of his features and mentally reaching out to touch by proxy a head that she had surely once, so very long ago, stroked and combed. She does not expect the tears forming like acid in her eyes, blurring her vision and making her wince against their bitterness. How she resists such weakness, even now; the sentimentality of it doesn't sit easily with her – it never did. And yet, during the next few moments, she wills herself to stand there in front of him and follow his movements with care as he takes out a hammer and tests its strength in the air before applying it to the nail he holds in place by the depleted chimney. She is less surprised by the dying fall of a wave of pure sorrow so all-consuming that it anchors her to the ground while at the same time pulling her, against its force, towards that house, his refuge.

'Hallo down there,' comes a cheery voice from up high. 'I've just got a little bit more fastening to do then I'll be down.' It appears to belong to the man in a peaked cap who is straddling the roof. 'Did you want something? Can I help?'

Gazing back at him without words to offer in reply, there is no doubt in her mind that it would be a cruelty to reveal herself after all the time that has passed.

Turning abruptly to face the road, as though caught red-handed, she will not linger, therefore, not at all curious to know whether he has spotted any small aspect of her that might strike a chord with him. She will not intrude on this environment of peace and contentment he has somehow managed to create. In denying him for a second time, she is quite sure she is doing her best for him at this late stage. She has no hesitation in indicating with a small, flapping hand motion that she does not require anything at all, and starts to stride purposefully in the direction of the underground station nearby.

Sitting on a half empty train to Victoria Station, thence to the docks at Southampton, it strikes her as just as well that she cannot bring to mind in too much detail what his face looked like, that man way up there on the roof.

24

Liverpool, England, 1921

Run, then …

And run he did, and in time he noticed not fractured pavements, weakened verges or dusty roads but only what felt like a never ending, featureless canyon, with himself – an ant like figure on its floor – straining to move forwards whilst pushing his elbows sideways against the narrowing walls squeezing the life out of him. But run on he would, and it was as though he was powered by a bolt of lightning piercing the small of his back, ignited by his own primeval fear.

Eventually, the spark ran out.

He awoke before sunrise on the third day, roused by something sniffling at his face, a small night creature. He sensed its curiosity must be benign because what grudge could such a creature possibly bear him? He meant no harm to anything or anyone. He scratched his hair, then his face and arms, and a plume of hunger knotting at the base of his empty stomach caused him to sit bolt upright in discomfort. His eyes made out the outline of the town or city he had found his way out of by a broad scattering of dim lights in the middle distance, over which a grey rim of milky light was beginning to create a contrast with the receding night sky. There was no sign of the sea any more. Moreover, time itself had lost its bearings, as far as he was concerned: whether it was night or day was no longer as important as it once was. Whether such time was named by a month or day of the week was even less so on this chilly December morning. He began to hum a nonsensical tune, made up on the spot, to keep himself company.

He found it hard to think.

In the end, his stomach prompted him.

It made him take a few fundamental bearings from the hedge where he had ended up the night before, instinctively rounding his back against its lower branches so there would be a small protective overhang in case of rain.

It prompted him to stand up and make a quick survey of the land thereabouts – such of it that he could make out – and a moving lantern a little way off revealed a row of drowsy cows shifting themselves into a line behind a man holding a wooden staff.

It drew him towards this man and gave him the energy to take his cap off and offer a smile.

It emboldened him to ask whether there was a chance of some milk and bread. And this time he was in luck.

By the time the day had begun to bloom and he had been sent on his way by the herdsman with a full stomach and more for later in his bag, life – living – began to take on a different perspective. He would make for the nearest main road and see what happened from there. His spirits felt lighter because, above all, he knew he would not be looking back: in that direction lay only pain and confusion and uncertain danger. These things might be ahead, too, for all he knew, but he was all for taking his chances now.

He was picked up before midday.

A conscientious citizen shivering at a bus stop caught a whiff of him as he limped by. This thoughtful man went out of his way to grip the boy kindly but firmly by the arm while waving down a policeman to aid him in the civil act of taking another stray to the orphanage. He didn't resist. Neither did he complain. To be able to abandon the necessity of making any more fugitive decisions was something of a welcome relief, he found.

At the orphanage he was briskly interrogated, and not for one moment was he believed. Boys didn't cross the Atlantic on their own: he was therefore a runaway, or he had been abandoned. They decided, on balance, that he didn't look like a gypsy. But he had caused offence with his tale.

'You're lying, boy,' announced his interrogator. 'We don't have any of that here. You'd better start learning, quick.'

He received a series of perfunctory blows which left white raised tracks on the back of his legs that stung for the following twenty-four hours. Before these unfortunate tide marks disappeared, he had not only questioned the veracity of his own memory but had seen the sense of treating its fractured last traces as so much unnecessary flotsam.

They fed him in that place. They gave him a spare set of roughly textured clothes and allocated him a hard bunk in a dormitory full of boys far more cunning than himself. He was minded to act as though he was grateful for this, too, and so he was – getting something for nothing felt like a real privilege, to his way of thinking, even when that something came with a nagging emptiness that remained after basic needs had been met, and when he was periodically hit about the body for no earthly reason he could fathom. At least there was a bed, rather than an uncertain roadside on which to lay his head each night.

One day, not long after that, they removed his tonsils – he took his turn in a long line with other boys – and in no time he was on the move again with fifty other strays like himself, freshly scrubbed and with heads shaven for what was promising to be another journey. With the rest of the orphans, he travelled on a creaking bus to a place by the sea called Tilbury, a long way off, then sailed for Melbourne in Australia via Capetown on the RMS Naldera, a three funnelled ship painted black and white.

On board the big ship, they gave him a new name. 'Whatever kind of a name is "Smithyes?"' demanded the man whose job it was to tick names of those present on the ship's manifest and deal with their papers. It seemed to peeve him. 'Someone must have got it wrong. There – Smith – that's better.' So he became Thomas Smith, the third surname he had possessed during his short life, and this was the one which stuck.

On arrival in Australia some six weeks later, along with each of the other boys – to their bemusement – he was given a small leather bible whose pages were so thin they whispered at him when he thumbed them in order to read the peppercorn lettering inside. A label on the front instructed him: 'Be strong and of good courage; be not afraid, neither be thou dismayed; for the Lord thy God is with thee withersoever thou goest.' This struck him as probably sensible, as well as rather comforting, and he resolved to trust the advice conveyed to him here. He was also presented with a number by which he would be identified – 68 – and asked whether he was Protestant or Catholic. When he told them he didn't know, he was placed with the larger group of Protestant boys.

Six years passed.

He was only able to appreciate the scale of the distance he'd travelled when he was in his last year at school, coming up for fourteen. It pleased him to trace lines with his finger on a map of the world hanging up in the schoolroom, following its webs of rivers, roads and national boundaries with his index finger. So this is what they meant when they told him he had been half way around the world. It turned out to be true: from England, the eastern Atlantic followed the coast of Africa right to its tip before it changed into the Southern Sea. At the other end was Australia, his present home. Of Canada he remembered barely a thing.

Later, they put him to work in a factory, but he longed to find something a bit more rewarding than a continuation of the strict, institutional ways to which he had become accustomed. He remembered how he liked the look of jaunty little England on the map in his old schoolroom – on balance, it seemed to him the place least likely to subsume and subdue all that his stifled spirit leaned towards. He also liked the look of two pretty young princesses in that country he'd seen in a newspaper.

After a few more years, he picked his moment and ran away and no-one came looking for him to take him back. He made his way slowly towards the coast, hitching rides from itinerant sheep shearers and travelling adventurers and receiving sustenance from Christian shelters, and missions along the way. He learned to trust such people, who neither questioned his existence nor made demands on him other than asking him to lend a hand with the clearing up or to peel a few potatoes. The good will he encountered he never forgot. It spoke to his own.

Eventually, after living in a city by the sea for a time, he got himself a job as a cabin boy on a P and O "electric ship" called the SS Strathnaver, all white this time with yellow funnels – a floating town, to be sure, and the first of a family of five new "Strath" ships with a distinctly Scottish flavour to their names. From Sydney, this vessel made its way north-westwards. He was an assistant steward, sharing a cabin with another whom he rarely saw because their shifts were different. Sometimes he was put to work cleaning passageways and cabins, sometimes setting and clearing dining tables and preparing the "night lunches" required by those on watch. On such nights, after his work was done, he would make his way to the smoking room, long emptied of passengers, and rest his legs on one of the easy chairs in front of the dying embers of an open fire.

It was a different route to that of his arrival, this time heading right up the eastern side of Africa towards the Gulf of Aqaba and the Suez Canal. When it reached first Alexandria, then Marseilles, this ship began to take on fresh groups of passengers, rich refugees fleeing what, rumour had it, was becoming an uncertain state of affairs in Germany once again. The presence of such people added both tension and an air of contrived celebration to the atmosphere on board, and he was glad of their tips.

The Strathnavar docked, finally, at Southampton, and some of the passengers lingered there in hope of a forward passage to Canada or New York while there was yet time.

Not Thomas Smith.

It was in his mind to settle, now he'd earned his freedom.

Inside a strange red kiosk, he managed to make a telephone call to the number someone had stitched into the sleeve of his old jacket in case the person called Auntie Violet was delayed. He had not come across it until England was lowering itself below the horizon and he was hot and cramped beside half a dozen others on their way to Australia, and in his haste he'd turned that jacket – one of the few original possessions he was allowed to keep – inside out in order to make a pillow for himself. The scrap of paper he treasured, because it reassured him that he had come from *somewhere*, at some time, and it was a comfort to know that.

'Wait a minute,' said a voice at the other end of the line, sparking into life. 'Violet Fitch, you mean? She's been dead – oooh – 13 years or more now, by I should guess, poor soul. Sorry, love.'

He thanked her – he was not at all grateful for such news but he was always gracious with his thanks – and was about to put the receiver back on its hook and retrieve the residue of his money from the button marked "B" when he heard her almost shout: 'Oi, don't go away. I can tell you where her family lives, or used to at any rate.'

Family? Here was an auspicious word to Thomas Smith, who associated it with all the things he had not managed to attract to himself: qualities like love, and comfort and support, and being tickled and teased in affectionate safety, as he'd observed walking the streets in Australia. Maybe he idealised it. Maybe, in ignorance and blind hope, he wondered if there could possibly be a place for the likes of himself inside a family, somewhere. But what family would it turn out to be?

He was directed to a place called Ealing, on the west side of London. He stood on a doorstep with all he owned in one kitbag slung over his shoulder. He was grinning with anticipation even before Vic Dalton, the car man, opened the door. 'No, I'm not a Mr Fitch,' he said to Thomas, surveying him closely. 'But don't stand there, boy, come in. You may not know who I am but I have an idea I might know who you might be. Come here, Jemima, do … look what's turned up.'

He was ushered into a cloud of heat and pipe smoke and the door closed behind him.

And this is where the adult life of the boy begins: with a small act of spontaneous tenderness and ready hospitality which, with luck, will send out its lone signal to meet with others and multiply. This is his new world.

He doesn't know what to say when they ask where he's come from on account of his funny mixture of accents and he gives the only answer he has arrived at: 'Me? I'm a man of the world!' They laugh readily along with him. Because they laugh, so does he. It turns out that the Daltons are about to give this surprise visitor a proper welcome. Just like the one they once gave his mother.

The important thing is to move forward, not backwards, the couple tell him when he tries to make sense of the fact that these people are not, in fact, his blood family. A mutual glance between the pair turns out to be an automatic pact to be circumspect if questions about his parents arise. It seems to be for the best.

Anyway, he must look forward now. He wants very much to look forward.

The car man has just retired but the pair of them often amble down to a local garage where he used to work in order to chat with the men working there. One day, Thomas Smith asks if he can take a look under the bonnet of one of the cars, only to be mesmerised by the labyrinth of pipes and tight chambers he discovers there. He proves to have an aptitude for tinkering with cars and is easily encouraged to enter this business by the car man himself.

Thomas Smith was deemed unfit to enlist when war is declared in 1939. He learned that what had always been mistaken for crass clumsiness while he was a boy, earning him both scorn and repeated punishment, turned out to be weak eyesight, after all.

But he managed to do his bit.

While on duty as an air raid warden in the war that eventually catches up with him in Ealing from across the Continent, Thomas shows exemplary fortitude, faced with fire bombs that bring with them the widespread desolation that always follows a night of destruction.

Over the course of several years he carries many injured souls to safety in his own powerful arms. He finds himself often in the company of a nurse called Doreen, a kind, sensible and modest sort of girl, and it is she who he comes to marry. They discover, as the peace once more gradually establishes itself, that they cannot have children, so they adopt a little girl and in due course another as well, to keep her company. Aware every day of the fruitfulness beyond dreaming that has by inexplicable good fortune come his way, Thomas Smith's contentment increases, and the years roll on.

With real sadness, not long after that war, he mourns the death of his dearest friend, the old car man, but it is no trouble to him to drop in on Jemima, his widow, every day and without fail. Doreen cooks more than they need and he takes Jemima a sturdy meal each evening and sits with her until her chatter has run its course.

On a late summer day in 1964, she lets slip that his mother had lately been to England visiting her daughter. Thomas finds this hard to take in and it leads him to wonder about Canada for the first time in many years. He remembers little more than certain feelings engendered by the place. Of *her*: nothing whatsoever. But the protective affection he once bore towards one little girl in particular lights him up for a moment. Could this be her? Could it be his sister Dorothy? He decides to follow this up.

With Doreen's encouragement and the name of a certain village to set him on his way – thanks to enquiries made at the library by Jemima – he takes a train from Liverpool Street on his day off in search of Dorothy, wanting nothing from her but anxious to present himself and perhaps be of service to her. He asks a question or two in several village shops after his journey and it doesn't take him long to arrive at the flint and brick house by the green. When he is turned away by a teenager with the most gloriously unruly red hair he readily accepts it – there have been all too many occasions when the smile has been wiped off his face, and, 'oh, well' has been the most prudent way of dealing with an awkward situation. On the train back to London he decides, on balance, that it must be for the best that a meeting is not to be. Best not interfere where he is not wanted – that is, if it had even been her, which seems a bit unlikely to him in his weighing up of the day. Back in Ealing after the children are in bed, he relates his tale to Doreen over a toad-in-the-hole she has prepared because it is one of his favourites – just in case (she has thought ahead about his excursion) he is disappointed.

In time, neither of his girls show an interest in being car women themselves, but although they move away it is never long before they return, finding it no chore to maintain a day-by-day relationship with beloved parents via the telephone, and eventually by email. He leaves the words ' … and Daughters' on the garage sign as a tribute to them, and glances up with pride at the words each morning when he arrives for work. 'Thomas Smith and Daughters': the inscription makes him feel he is keeping them close, in spirit. At other times, he turns his energy to the soup kitchen he has set up with a few others in his church, the church where, unbeknown to him, his parents were married.

A few years on, with his pension from the garage and what they have saved up, and after providing generously for their children and a number of grandchildren, Thomas and Doreen book themselves a little treat: a holiday in Spain. Dressed to the nines, they embark upon a plane journey – a maiden voyage and their only one, because soon after their return Thomas begins to lose weight and becomes ill.

In an Ealing churchyard now, names on many of the older gravestones are weathered by rain, sprouting scabs of lichen that resemble age spots on elderly hands, or barnacles on the flank of a sturdy liner. Some of them pitch sideways, as though tugged by a slow-moving subterranean tide, until they settle in a drunken list to port. It is a place where every blousy cloud hovering over the graves, bubbling with promise, seems to harbour the significance of stored memory in a more enduring way than do the minds of many of the long dispersed families whose members are buried here, alongside he who was first known as Thomas Smithyes.

Maybe one day Sunny will find herself summoned to this place by a clue here, a more determined search there, nagged by unanswered questions about a lost child in a faded photograph once cherished by her mother and since inherited by herself. If so, then over here, in a quiet spot near the keeper's lodge, she may come across a memorial stone which, on careful scrutiny, still bears the modest inscription: RIP T Smith. But because history has already changed his name and turned it into a kind of fiction – as it mostly does to those whose lot is to be unre-encountered – it's almost certain that she will pass on by.

More Books From ThunderPoint Publishing Ltd.

Mule Train
by Huw Francis
ISBN: 978-0-9575689-0-7 (kindle)
ISBN: 978-0-9575689-1-4 (Paperback)

Four lives come together in the remote and spectacular mountains bordering Afghanistan and explode in a deadly cocktail of treachery, betrayal and violence.

Written with a deep love of Pakistan and the Pakistani people, Mule Train will sweep you from Karachi in the south to the Shandur Pass in the north, through the dangerous borderland alongside Afghanistan, in an adventure that will keep you gripped throughout.

The Birds That Never Flew
by Margot McCuaig

Shortlisted for the
Dundee International Book Prize 2012
Longlisted for the Polari First Book Prize 2014

ISBN: 978-0-9575689-3-8 (Kindle)
ISBN: 978-0-9575689-2-1 (Paperback)

Battered and bruised, Elizabeth has taken her daughter and left her abusive husband Patrick. Again. In the bleak and impersonal Glasgow housing office Elizabeth meets the provocatively intriguing drug addict Sadie, who is desperate to get her own life back on track.

The two women forge a fierce and interdependent relationship as they try to rebuild their shattered lives, but despite their bold, and sometimes illegal attempts it seems impossible to escape from the abuse they have always known, and tragedy strikes.

More than a decade later Elizabeth has started to implement her perfect revenge - until a surreal Glaswegian Virgin Mary steps in with imperfect timing and a less than divine attitude to stick a spoke in the wheel of retribution.

Tragic, darkly funny and irreverent, The Birds That Never Flew ushers in a new and vibrant voice in Scottish literature.

A Good Death
by Helen Davis

ISBN: 978-0-9575689-7-6 (eBook)
ISBN: 978-0-9575689-6-9 (Paperback)

'A good death is better than a bad conscience,' said Sophie.

1983 - Georgie, Theo, Sophie and Helena, four disparate young Cambridge undergraduates, set out to scale Ausangate, one of the highest and most sacred peaks in the Andes.

Seduced into employing the handsome and enigmatic Wamani as a guide, the four women are initiated into the mystically dangerous side of Peru, Wamani and themselves as they travel from Cuzco to the mountain, a journey that will shape their lives forever.

2013 - though the women are still close, the secrets and betrayals of Ausangate chafe at the friendship.

A girls' weekend at a lonely Fenland farmhouse descends into conflict with the insensitive inclusion of an overbearing young academic toyboy brought along by Theo. Sparked by his unexpected presence, pent up petty jealousies, recriminations and bitterness finally explode the truth of Ausangate, setting the women on a new and dangerous path.

Sharply observant and darkly comic, Helen Davis's début novel is an elegant tale of murder, seduction, vengeance, and the value of a good friendship.

Toxic
by Jackie McLean
Shortlisted for the Yeovil Book Prize 2011
ISBN: 978-0-9575689-8-3 (eBook)
ISBN: 978-0-9575689-9-0 (Paperback)

The recklessly brilliant DI Donna Davenport, struggling to hide a secret from police colleagues and get over the break-up with her partner, has been suspended from duty for a fiery and inappropriate outburst to the press.

DI Evanton, an old-fashioned, hard-living misogynistic copper has been newly demoted for thumping a suspect, and transferred to Dundee with a final warning ringing in his ears and a reputation that precedes him.

And in the peaceful, rolling Tayside farmland a deadly store of MIC, the toxin that devastated Bhopal, is being illegally stored by a criminal gang smuggling the valuable substance necessary for making cheap pesticides.

An anonymous tip-off starts a desperate search for the MIC that is complicated by the uneasy partnership between Davenport and Evanton and their growing mistrust of each others actions.

Compelling and authentic, Toxic is a tense and fast paced crime thriller.

In The Shadow Of The Hill
by Helen Forbes

ISBN: 978-0-9929768-1-1 (eBook)
ISBN: 978-0-9929768-0-4 (Paperback)

An elderly woman is found battered to death in the common stairwell of an Inverness block of flats.

Detective Sergeant Joe Galbraith starts what seems like one more depressing investigation of the untimely death of a poor unfortunate who was in the wrong place, at the wrong time.

As the investigation spreads across Scotland it reaches into a past that Joe has tried to forget, and takes him back to the Hebridean island of Harris, where he spent his childhood.

Among the mountains and the stunning landscape of religiously conservative Harris, in the shadow of Ceapabhal, long buried events and a tragic story are slowly uncovered, and the investigation takes on an altogether more sinister aspect.

In The Shadow Of The Hill skilfully captures the intricacies and malevolence of the underbelly of Highland and Island life, bringing tragedy and vengeance to the magical beauty of the Outer Hebrides.

Lightning Source UK Ltd.
Milton Keynes UK
UKOW07f0852150215

246288UK00005B/92/P